LITTLE BOOK of MURDER

NICKI THORNTON

CHIMNEYS
PUBLISHING

CHIMNEYS PUBLISHING

www.chimneyspublishing.co.uk

First edition by Chimneys Publishing 2025
Copyright © Nicki Thornton 2025
The moral right of the author has been asserted.

Paperback 978-1-068-27000-0

Printed and bound by
CPI Group (UK) Ltd, Croydon, CR0 4YY

Cover design by Holly Astle

ACKNOWLEDGMENTS

Welcome to the world of the Little Bookshop of Murders.

I've written six books for children with the amazing publisher, Chicken House. My first book with Chimney's Publishing has been hugely exciting, and a learning curve and there have been a team of supportive people without whom this book would not exist, and you would not be here reading.

First, my husband, Mark, who not only supports me in my sometimes off-the-wall decisions, but always tries to learn with me as I go along, which I really appreciate. This journey has only been possible with him by my side.

I've been totally in love with my cover design since the amazing Holly Astle got involved. I couldn't have worked with a better designer. Check out her work here www.hollyastle.co.uk.

Alex Thornton redesigned my website and offered design support. And Tim Thornton gets a shout-out for support too as we are nothing if not a family business.

We followed Barry Hutchinson's Page to Published (pagetopublished.com) for much of the 'how to' blueprint for indie authors and through him discovered my editor, Hanna Elizabeth, who was a joy to work with.

My friend Chris Towndrow was generous with invaluable advice www.chrissieharrison.co.uk

All my writing friends, particularly The Furies, were super helpful in giving feedback on everything from titles to text. Particularly Tracy Darnton, Tania Tay and Kate West.

And thank you for reading. Without readers there would be no role for authors.

Tell me what you think via my website, or drop a review in the usual places if you'd like to, it's the best thing you can do to support any author if you enjoy their books.

This one is to celebrate the new family business
and everyone in Team Thornton who has helped launch
Chimneys Publishing.
Thank you for being on this journey with me.
You are all the absolute best x

1.

'So the book you want has a red cover. You saw it in here a few months ago?' I look across the bookshop counter hopefully at the customer, who is looking back hopefully at me. 'Those are my only clues? Anything else? At all?'

As well as her near-impossible request, this customer has brought in a disappointed expression and a definite Arctic chill. And not just on her puffa jacket.

Behind her, the world outside is covered by a thick layer of frost, making Crossways' historic high street look like a nostalgic Christmas card or an advertisement for warm mittens or fur-lined undies. Icicles dangle attractively – if potentially lethally – from gutters.

That view is one of the things I love about my new life. I also like finding the perfect book for people. Sometimes I am even quite good at it, which is lucky as it's about the only bit of bookselling I seem to be any good at. Selling enough books to pay the bills? Could be going better.

'My mother wanted it for Christmas and was upset no one bought it for her,' says my customer.

Funnily enough, one thing I can claim to be an expert in is disappointed mothers, I don't say.

I do say, 'What does your mum like to read? That might narrow it down.'

'Murders. It would have been about a murder. Mum loves a good murder.'

'Murder *mystery*,' I can't help but correct her.

Actual murders are absolutely no part of my lovely new bookshop life and are firmly in my past.

'Murder mystery covers this season have all been red,' I tell her. 'But it does help narrow it down. There are—'

'It was in *your* window,' my customer says accusingly. 'And why is this bookshop called Between the Lines? I don't get that as a name for a bookshop.'

'You are not the first to say that,' I tell her politely. 'Like many of my decisions, it was probably a mistake.'

She buys two (out of a possible four) books. Great sales for me in bitter January. Even though I have a feeling I'll be refunding that money in a day or so.

January's been a battle of the evils – too little money through the till, too little sunshine, too much time to think.

Right now, even an awkward customer is a welcome distraction from my new favourite pastime – challenging myself to answer my own near-impossible question: *Why did I ever imagine I could run a bookshop?*

'I'm sure she'll love them both!' I call cheerily as my customer leaves. 'I did!'

Plus, this wintry day was always going to be hard. It's an anniversary I'd love to be able to stop thinking about.

The door opens again to let in a gust of piercing wind and the welcome sight of Liv Trent shaking off the arctic chill from her fabulously expensive coat that elegantly matches her light-coloured boots.

Liv properly intimidates me by always managing to look awesome. She's older than me by a couple of decades, so has more practice, I guess, but I still doubt I will ever get my hair to be that well-behaved even in a sharp January wind. Being awesome is her most annoying habit (along with being bossy and being right – *usually*).

Today I mostly envy her coat because it looks warm.

'There is one easy step you could take that would really improve things in here,' says Liv, straight into her exhausting bottomless well of good ideas as she strides to where I'm huddled behind the counter.

One of the unexpected, positive benefits of this new life is the customers who have become friends. Even if I have to put up with Liv telling me she's full of good advice and is always right. Actually, I really don't like those bits.

'Let me think now… What would make things better… Oh, yes! A paying customer? Too much to hope you're here to buy a book?'

'No wonder it's quiet as the grave in here, it feels as cold as the bloody grave!' Liv scolds me and rubs her arms (very theatrically). 'Keera what are you thinking? Any customer you entice in will rush back outside to warm up! If I hadn't come in, you might have been found frozen and unable to move, let alone able to sell a book.' She glances around. 'Or keep the place tidy.'

I don't object when Liv reaches behind the counter and cranks up the heating, because Liv is quite possibly right. I do try not to instantly worry about bills.

But then I'm getting better at dealing with my worries.

I'm getting really practised at just not thinking about them the moment they arrive.

'I'm unable to move because I've discovered three jumpers are not enough to stop me freezing, but do actually restrict the movement of my arms,' I say.

'Is that seriously your excuse for this shop being such a state? What are all these boxes?' Liv asks, prodding one with the toe of an expensive boot.

When Liv drops in I know she's on her way somewhere better – a lunch with arty friends, the latest fad exercise class, volunteering for one of many activities and charities I cannot keep up with. She drops in frequently to give me a break as I can only dream of paying staff or having the luxury of taking time away to eat. Or pee.

'It looks like you're packing up and closing… You aren't, are you?'

Liv looks horrified enough at this thought that I laugh, even if it's a laugh tinged with desperation.

'January is not exactly prime time for bookshops,' I say.

'Keera, January is the perfect time to cosy up with a book. What's happened to your warm, welcoming browsing ambience?'

'I think it vanished, along with my ability to pay for heating. Tea?'

I'm careful to shuffle this morning's bad-news letter away from Liv's very sharp eyes and go to squeeze myself into what I laughingly call my back office, where there is a kettle and a sink and rather too much unsold stock.

'Sadly, it doesn't take a genius with spreadsheets to see that packing up and closing is exactly what I should be doing,' I call as the kettle goes on. 'Lucky, perhaps, I'm not great with spreadsheets. I am very busy doing returns... and other... professional bookshoppy things. One thing I've discovered—anything to do with books involves a remarkable amount of cardboard.'

'Nope. Keera, what you are doing is making a mess. What's this chalkboard doing cluttering up behind the counter? Now, if it's Earl Grey, only if you have almond milk, or oat, as I'm doing Veganuary. Otherwise green. And just to warn you as well as warm you—I'm here with bad news.'

'Great! I don't think I have enough of that. Can't you announce you're here with a foolproof strategy to make Crossways folk buy books with the same enthusiasm they eat up gossip?' I happen on a clean mug. 'Or failing that, magic to get them to spend their millions here?'

There's no oat, just iffy dairy. I think the fridge is on its way out. Maybe I'm in a race with the fridge to see who will be turfed out first. I fish out green tea bags.

I thought after a year it'd feel like I've been selling books at Between the Lines forever. Instead, I feel I'll never belong, will never rise to the challenge of selling enough books to pay the bills. Or solve the many mysteries of Crossways. To a city girl like me, this villagey, gossipy place is as unknowable as stepping into an alien world.

Liv helps me navigate the minefields – who on the parish council to be nice to, who in the golf club I should avoid. It's tricky to stay on the right side in a small community when I cannot yet fathom what the right side even is.

I call over the kettle reluctantly considering doing its one job. 'This bookselling lark is more complicated than I ever imagined. But yes, I should put up that chalkboard. It's advertising my book of the month. I should also choose a book of the month.'

The cosy reading chair would be comfortable if it wasn't smothered with the unsold celebrity biographies of people who weren't quite celebrities. I should start tackling Christmas returns. And my adopted bookshop cat will be in soon to complain with his overly loud miaow that I've run out of cat snacks.

'I get that January must be flat after all the Christmas glitter. I mostly called in to check you're all right,' Liv says kindly. 'I know what day it is.'

'Thanks for remembering.'

'And I'm afraid I do have sad news about one of your customers.'

I go through with hot mugs and stop. Liv must have clocked me hiding my bad-news letter as she's waving it, with its demands and aggressive signature at the bottom.

'So—I was glad you popped in, until the invasion of privacy.' I slam her tea on the counter as I go to snatch the letter from her.

She twists it out of my reach, frowning at the contents. 'People can't go about sending threatening letters and extracting money by extortion.'

'I think that is the definition of a landlord.'

'Exactly! That's why there are laws against it… There are laws against it? You should know?'

Liv is fishing (not for the first time). One of the things I don't like about this new life is how Crossways people think that keeping your life private is not an option. I might be as nosy as the next person, but I have no intention of letting anyone into the secrets of my earlier existence and what led me to give up on my old life and craving wholesome village bookselling.

'I'll handle it,' I snap, more firmly than I mean to.

'Fine.' Liv's look hints she knows my way of dealing with it is to ignore it. Liv sips the tea and plants her butt on the gently warming heater. 'It's Mrs McFlintock—'

'The bad news is about small, aggressive, rude, and most definitely not my favourite customer, Mrs McFlintock? I swear she comes in here to practise a new way of being rude. She never buys anything, just delights in taunting me that she only ever buys online. What's the bad news—she's given up reading?'

'She was seen disappearing off in an ambulance.'

'Ah. Ok. Yeah, sorry, I didn't mean any of that, obviously. Is she all right?'

'She was in an ambulance, so my guess is not great. And everyone knows about that unfortunate thing that happened between you two. So I'm here to ask: what are you going to do about it?'

2.

'What am I going to...? Do I need to...? How do you even...?' I'm shocked Liv even knows about my slightly heated exchange with Mrs McFlintock. Actually, I shouldn't be as one feature of Crossways that I could live without is how quickly gossip spreads. 'What happened to Mrs M?'

'Apart from you kicking her out of bookgroup? Had a fall down the stairs, I think,' says Liv. 'I suppose she's quite old.'

'Not that old. Seventies? And robust,' I murmur, thinking about how she faced up to me. 'Old enough so that rather than saying she fell over, people say she *had a fall*. Which makes it sound much more serious. Is it serious?'

'All I know is you had that unfortunate run-in with her.' Liv regards me over the rim of her mug and gives me a pitying look that tells me *everyone* already knows.

'Run in? Yes... well... *run in*—really?' I've been involved with run-ins, I've seen the knife wounds and the stitches. 'Our argument was about bookgroup.'

Before Liv can offer advice, the door opens again. Another non-customer rushes in on a blast of that fierce

January wind. Another customer who has blurred into a friend. Another of the well-heeled of Crossways, who I wish would read a lot faster.

Cady Bushell shuts the door firmly.

I'm pleased to see her, and the bag of pastries from my would-be favourite bakery just along Crossways high street. It would be my favourite if I could get near to affording the prices of their fancy, delicious baked goods. That letter from the landlord is going to push more than delicious pastries even further out of my reach.

'Hi Cady, huge guess: you haven't come rushing in to buy a book either?'

'Something terrible has happened. Mrs M fell down her stairs and...' Cady spies Liv and guesses Liv's here, playing rumour-machine, and that she's lost this round. 'She was very old.'

'Not that old,' Liv and I manage to say together.

'Tragic. And *so awkward* for you,' Cady adds. 'That run-in. I mean—*seriously* bad timing.'

'Run-in! Honestly!'

'You banned Mrs M from bookgroup?' Cady quizzes me. 'You didn't really!'

'Ban! Of course not.' But I squirm as I remember that slightly heated conversation. I should have handled things better. I suppose I do have a tendency to be rude if I get stressed.

But Mrs M said she wasn't going to finish the bookgroup's current book (because my choice was so terrible), therefore bookgroup wasn't allowed to discuss the end. I gently pointed out she couldn't really be afraid of spoilers for a book she had no intention of finishing. How I'd misjudged Mrs M's reaction.

I might have let things escalate. I might have got a little stressed. No, I definitely got stressed. She didn't back down. Instead, she threw a foul accusation at me. I might have felt threatened if she hadn't been a foot shorter than me and wearing flowery trousers.

Of course, in the essence of terrible timing, that was the moment a rare customer arrived wanting a copy of the latest Sally Rooney, but only if it was out in paperback.

'Tea?'

'Sounds great, and oh! I've got a poster advertising for new members for bookgroup,' says Cady, in that way that she has where she can suddenly be talking about quite a different subject.

Cady is a fizzing ball of energy, say-what-you-think, apologise afterwards kind of person. I love her because she wins the dubious accolade of making me feel almost organised. But Cady tries to make up for it by volunteering to run things, which works out as badly as anyone might imagine.

Cady likes a strongly romantic story. Or one of those Lisa Jewell types, where the story is told from the point of view of a really dark character.

Liv has a cool intellect and tends towards literary fiction, but never wants to stand out as one of the smartest people in any room. She likes to stand out for her addiction to fun and parties.

'Cady, thank you so much for volunteering to take over organising bookgroup,' I say, as I reluctantly leave my place near the heater. 'But do you really think we can handle more members?' (We definitely can't.)

'Well, we can't possibly get more people meeting in here,' says Cady, frowning at my multiplying boxes. 'I thought—Bookgroup at my house?' She makes the suggestion uncertainly.

'That's a generous offer. You have such a lovely home.'

Cady's face breaks into a huge grin.

Cady supports me so well. I wish I could do more for her, because she has more than her fair share of trouble, which you really cannot avoid knowing in Crossways.

Cady goes to put the poster in the window, partly dislodging her untidy bun of dirty blonde hair that's already coming loose from that awful gusty wind outside.

'I'll order more of the next book we're discussing.' None of This is True by Lisa Jewell. 'Good choice, it'll get people talking.'

Cady turns and beams, and dislodges part of my window display, sending books tumbling. She apologises profusely. I go to help, but Liv waves me in the direction of the kettle and takes over setting things to rights.

As I squeeze myself back into my minuscule back office, I don't miss another disappointed gaze as Cady looks around my less-than-tidy shop.

'What are all these boxes?' she asks Liv in a low voice. 'She's not packing up and leaving is she?'

'This is all an essential part of running a bookshop, so Keera claims,' I hear Liv reply as the ancient kettle thinks about boiling again. 'I say she's making a mess and is in danger of losing her cosy browsing ambience.'

'I can hear you both talking about me as if you could do a better job of running things than me. I'd rather hear your plan of what to do now everyone will give me the cold shoulder as I rowed with Crossways' longest-standing citizen the day before she had an unfortunate accident.'

Cady's proper builder's tea, so it'll be the milk that's a bit iffy. No sugar. She usually has sugar, but she's on Diet January.

'I thought people referred to Mrs M as a local "personality" because no one likes her very much. Honestly, that whole sweet appearance… She totally had me fooled. Where does she get such nasty ideas from?'

I do also worry that the horrible thing Mrs M said about me might get around. That won't do me any favours.

'Keera!' calls Cady warningly.

'I know, I let my mouth run away with me. But Mrs M would win an award as my most unpleasant customer. If you'd both come here with the news someone had *shoved* her down the stairs, I wouldn't have been surprised.'

'Keera, please!' Cady says again.

'Sorry. I don't know why my instinct is to make jokes in awful situations. I do feel terrible that I might not have been in the best mood to deal with Mrs M yesterday. Some people get sweary when they get stressed. I very occasionally forget to be polite.'

'Keera, you cannot go around saying any of that about Mrs M!' pleads Cady. 'Think of the optics.'

'Optics! I wasn't planning to *go around* saying it! Luckily she's nothing if not tough, and I'm sure she'll be back here soon enough, finding a new way to ruin my day. It's almost as if that's her hobby.'

I go through with tea and see two horrified faces. 'No, sorry, my bad. All that about Mrs M came out really wrong. I'm always blurting out the wrong thing. I mean, of course, I do hope Mrs M is all right. And I will try to make amends and mend my ways. What are the right sort of apology flowers to take to the most vindictive woman in Crossways?'

Cady shakes her head so her already untidy bun falls out completely.

'Didn't Liv say?' Cady shoots Liv a worried look. 'Of course Mrs McFlintock isn't going to be all right. She was dead when her daughter found her.'

3.

Dead? I feel as winded as if someone punched me under the ribs. 'Mrs McFlintock is dead? Cady are you sure? Crossways gossip isn't fully reliable.'

Cady nods.

I hand her the iffy tea. We swap. She hands me a bag from the wildly expensive artisanal bakery I pass every day, drooling like a kid walking past a forbidden sweet shop. The bag will contain a vegan blueberry croissant, and it takes immense willpower not to start shovelling it in. In fact, I don't resist.

'Thanks, I think I need a sugar rush. But Mrs M… She was so… And now she's gone? It feels unbelievable. It also feels like I carry bad luck like some kind of cursed charm.'

'It is very unfortunate that one of your customers died just a day after you rowed with her,' says Liv.

'Yes, it can't hurt to squish any idea there was bad feeling,' advises Cady.

'There wasn't any bad feeling,' I say.

But there was. A lot of bad feeling.

'Maybe you do need to smooth things over,' says Cady.

'Isn't it a bit late for that?' I murmur through my pastry.

'It's never too late,' says Liv.

'Well, no, but sometimes it really—'

'I meant, maybe with her daughter, Stacey?' Cady responds. 'She's one of your customers too, isn't she? You don't want to lose her support. Or anyone's.'

'Yes, I know Stacey. She loves sex and gore dressed up in period costume.'

'Keera means Stacey loves historical fiction,' Liv explains to Cady, then turns to me with one raised eyebrow (something else I aspire to be able to do). 'It wouldn't hurt to call in. As long as you can remember this is a charm offensive. That means don't lose your temper or be rude.'

'You say that as if I lose my temper and am rude often.'

'Just do your best,' says Liv after a pause. 'And remember what happened when I introduced you to the chair of the parish council. We'll look after things here.'

'You mean now? But I'm busy with planning my events schedule. And things.'

'Events? That's great!' Liv picks up on this too enthusiastically. 'So glad you're getting your passion back for this bookshop. I feared all these boxes meant... Anyway, you can give me a sneak peek at who's on the guest list. Maybe I can help with that while you're gone.'

It only takes a moment's hesitation.

'There isn't anyone on the guest list is there?' Liv guesses correctly.

'All the big authors go to the well-established bookshops,' I say, which is mostly true. 'It takes a while to build up your cred.' Also true.

But also, I opened a bookshop because I wanted a quiet life and Liv's idea of the way to bookshop success is to make a party of it – evening events, with me as the hostess, offering wine and possibly crisps, making small talk. Interviewing authors. In my bookshop dream I was hiding behind the counter, popping out to chat books occasionally and ringing sales endlessly through the till.

Cady moves aside the pile of unwanted celebrity biographies to slump into the reading chair. 'There's always so much you suddenly realise you need to do… I expect Stacey'll be at her mum's house.'

Sadly, Cady's no stranger to the aftermath of a sudden death. 'I bet the ambulance had a helluva time getting there,' she says. 'Mrs M was in one of those cottages right down by Harcourt Pools. No proper road.'

And there it is.

I should stop being astonished by this side of village life. It's such a small place that coincidence happens with ridiculous regularity. It's all connected in a way it really isn't in a city.

'Crossways is kind of like living in a spider web, don't you think?' I say. 'You can get a feeling of disturbance from very far away.'

I can tell by the two pairs of beady eyes looking at me that Liv and Cady aren't entirely on my wavelength.

But Liv called in to give me the chance to get out and do one important mission today. It's one I don't want to mention in front of Cady. I keep a few secrets. Who doesn't? But Harcourt Pools was where I was headed anyway. It feels like a sign that seeking out Mrs M's daughter, Stacey, is the right move, even though ruffling feathers comes so much easier to me than smoothing them.

'You go patch things up,' Liv instructs me with her usual brooking-no-arguments decisiveness. 'No customers to deal with, Cady, it's Dry-sales January and a grim time for bookshops. We carry on with what Keera was doing.'

Cady turns to me helplessly, retying her hair as she does when she's anxious. 'What were you doing? I'm sure whatever it was, I'll be useless at it!'

'It was making the place untidy with boxes and calling it returns and event planning,' says Liv. 'I think we'll cope.'

'Cady, you aren't bad at anything,' I say. 'You are my guiding light. Proof that all you need in life is determination to carry on. All you need do while I'm out is two things you're both better at than me— Make sure I don't actively lose either sales or customers.'

Or that another one dies.

I get my coat.

I also grab a packet of biscuits and a slab of Cadbury's Dairy Milk I had ready. I have a lot to learn in this new life I've chosen, almost none of it has been the kind of things I thought. But one thing stays the same – there are not many situations where chocolate and/or biscuits don't help. I step outside and return to stick my head back in. 'You're right about one thing, Liv.'

She crooks a single eyebrow at me. 'Only one?'

'It is *much* warmer outside.'

4.

I hate this place, particularly in winter when everything is just grey. Even my headlights barely penetrate the mist rising from the river as it roars over the weir.

But I hate it even in summer when a series of twisting river loops creates inlets with beaches of dirty shingle. It's considered a local beauty spot.

Along the towpath, one of the colourful houseboats runs a pop-up cafe offering homemade vegan brownies and flapjacks. Even that can't make me love this place.

On this freezing day I can't even imagine there are ever children in wetsuits or shivering in swimsuits, or bare feet leaving footprints in the thick, grey mud. This time of year even the hardened dog walkers hardly make it out here. It's just me, parking the car and sitting a moment, listening to the engine ticking, bracing myself for stepping into a heavy grey mist in an inadequate coat.

A year ago, this is where Helena Craven died.

Helena was my first customer who became a friend, soon after I opened the shop. All I'd wanted was to achieve my two simple aims: to leave the troubles of my past life behind me and start a new chapter. And sell enough books to pay the bills. Simple.

But I was alone, out of my depth. It was all done on a shoestring. I took Helena's friendship to be a sign that I might, for once, have made the right decision in moving to the alien Crossways, even though it felt like journeying out of the solar system rather than simply swapping the city for a village. Then, in a tragic accident, Helena died.

She left behind two grieving teenage children, a grieving husband, and me.

Cady, as Helena's cousin, was the one who stepped in to try to help the distraught family. She's still doing it now, and she ended up helping me.

The second I open the car door I hear it – the torrent of water churning through the sluices, roaring its dark and dangerous threat like a monster.

To a city dweller like me, it's a reminder of the raw power of nature. I'm not used to nature being so up close, or facing that nature can be more deadly than a knife in any alley. I hate coming here because I cannot stop imagining Helena's terrifying last moments.

I force myself to get out, and put my foot straight into a pothole filled with icy water. The wind cuts me like tiny shards of glass.

Somewhere to my right will be the River Rise Cottages where Mrs McFlintock lived. But I head away from there, walking towards the warning sound, forcing myself to go closer to the water, reminding myself to go careful. So easy to lose your footing when it's so slippery underfoot and the fog blurs everything, makes it difficult to see how close you are to the edge.

Nowhere could be more freezing or murkier than this desolate place. Nothing but gloom and the ever-present threat of roaring, raging water. This is the last place I want to be, but I have to start walking, asking myself, *What am I doing here?* Shivering in this bleak grey. Not just Harcourt Pools, but here in Crossways. Barely clinging to my dream.

An inner voice whispers that maybe my mum was right. She said it's not so much that trouble follows me around as... *Do I really attract it? Can I never have a simpler life?*

The worst thing Supportive Mum could imagine was me getting into debt. So far, I've kept the promise that I would do the sensible thing and give up this mad dive into the risky world of bookselling before I lose serious money. But that aggressive letter from my landlord's agent, the jolly-sounding Key Keepers, means my chance of keeping out of serious debt looks precarious.

I thought that was my bad news of the day. Then this terrible news about Mrs M arrived along with the consequences of my own runaway mouth, my expertise at poor timing and even worse decision-making. Now if I cannot find a way to sweet-talk both Stacey and the landlord... Will that be it?

My bookshop is a tiny (if messy) space, but it's mine. I have customers, very few like Mrs McFlintock, who was truly awful. I've started a bookgroup. Wholesome. Everyone loves bookshops. So I need to quickly get better at sweet-talking. Because I'm not great at walking away either. I'm not giving up the bookshop without a fight. No one's taking it away from me. The only promise I made to myself was that in my new life I'd steer away from trouble. I haven't even been able to do that, have I? Look at where I am now.

Looking around, I don't want to see him. I hope I'm alone. It would be great if he hadn't felt the need to come. But I force myself to walk further along the path that runs right by the edge of the water, carefully squelching the edges of the riverbank, wishing I'd taken the time to change into wellies, pulling my too-thin coat around me, hoping this will be a wasted trip.

'*And you can't resist a sob-story,*' Mum had said, in her incredibly long and possibly too accurate list of why I'm uniquely unsuited to running a small village business.

'Even in your lectures covering everything that could go wrong,' I say, in the conversation I'm frequently having with her in my head, 'you didn't warn me about having to smooth things over following an unfortunate death of a customer and a badly timed row. Or the unexpected legacy of another death. Or a responsibility I never wanted. Or driving in a heavy mist to a grim place.'

'But I did,' Mum answers in my head. 'I warned you – you don't just attract trouble, you go after it. You'll end up trying to clean up Crossways.'

'Ah, but that's the whole point. Crossways doesn't need cleaning up.'

And then I see him, and I feel a rush of gratitude that I've found him and that I knew he'd be here. Finally, one decision I've got right. Because who can ever turn away troubled kids?

5.

'Hello, Pip,' I say gently.

I walk right up to him, but carefully, because he's a hunched figure standing right at the edge, looking down at the foamy scum forming on the surface of the raging water. I don't want to startle him. I want him to step back.

'Hey! It's such a glorious day I couldn't resist hoping I could join you out here enjoying this gorgeous weather.'

I touch him gently, wish I could go in for a hug. One, light touch tells me he's freezing. I wonder how long he's been here and how quickly I can get him away.

When he turns, his face is mostly obscured by a hood and a long, dark fringe. He's so small, thin, and pale you'd never figure him for seventeen.

'I know you are great at locations, but rubbish at food for picnics.' I hand over the purple-wrapped bar of Cadbury's Dairy Milk.

Pip doesn't speak, but he takes the chocolate (original, he's told me he doesn't like the 'weird, wtf flavours'). He lets me just stand there next to him, doesn't break into the bar yet. He doesn't walk away. But he doesn't step back either. He's soaking from standing this close, absorbing the mist rising from the raging water.

I don't ask how things are, or how he's doing. It's the anniversary of his mum's death. I guess we'd both see that as a stupid question.

So we stand there, watching the water. Even the smell of it is ugly today.

It was here, a year ago, I learned bookselling is far from a simple balance of how to sell enough books to pay rent and eat. It can be about life and death. I never predicted how much I'd get involved. In my idyllic image, I was just selling books. I'd spent too long in murky waters. I longed to step into a world that was a little bit sunnier. I needed to boost my belief that there are good things about humanity. I thought when I stumbled on Crossways, it was the perfect place to look.

I never dreamed how quickly I'd become part of the tangle of lives in my new community. But I think I can recognise someone wanting to run away.

I want so much for Pip – to be on a better path, have a fresh start, find a route that will lead, eventually, to him putting this trauma behind him. Not looping back to here.

Right now I want Pip to move, come away from the edge, but I let him do it in his own time.

He never speaks much, but he can be relied upon to take the chocolate, and as far as I'm concerned, that's a result. I know he trusts me, and that means so much. Who am I to say that even after a year, he should be coping better with his mum's death?

I watch him as he stuffs four bites into his mouth, folds the packet, and saves the rest.

'I'm here cos I need to talk to someone who lost their mum today,' I say tentatively, and explain, as we stand in the soaking mist, that someone died. An accident. 'Thought you could come with me. Expect we could all do with a cup of tea and some biscuits.' I step away, hoping he'll follow. 'Because I did a stupid thing.'

That forces a grin from him. 'Doesn't sound like you.'

'Nah, I can't believe it either. Must be a one-off, right?'

I'm relieved when he steps back from being so very close to the edge. I let out an audible sigh, but hopefully it gets caught up with the torrential roar.

I don't want him to know my deepest worries – that I can never be certain why he comes here.

I hope it's just to blot it all out. This place is such an intensity of nature, it's almost hypnotic, like standing on the top of a tall building. There's a pull to make you want to jump that's so strong, you don't get much of a chance to focus on anything else other than your will to fight it. I know he's still trying to make sense of everything. But I cannot help my fear that it's because he's contemplating whether he wants to join his mother.

Sometimes there is no making sense. Is it worse if it's an accident? I know Pip has wanted answers he's never going to get. Sometimes there is no certainty. No closure.

'What stupid thing did you do?' he asks.

'Well, you know me. I might blurt things out when I get stressed, and regret them later. I should get help, see that person the school made you see— You still doing that?'

Pip shakes his head. 'She got me writing things down. Suppose I still do that.'

'Does it help?'

There's a pause. 'Not how I think she thought it would. So what did you say? I thought you said you were going to see someone who lost their mum.'

'Yeah well, it's complicated. Things are always complicated.'

I explain a bit more. 'So I want to make things right if I can, with Mrs McFlintock's daughter, Stacey. You'll be good for her. I bet she's just like you, trying to make some kind of sense of something awful that makes you feel marked out for bad luck.' That definitely did not come out right, but luckily Pip falls in step with me.

'Mrs McFlintock? Yeah, I know her,' he says, surprising me.

'She was a customer— Is that how you knew her?'

Pip ended up helping me out in the shop for part of last year.

I count it as a series of lucky coincidences. Liv coming into the shop, insisting I go out and take a break on one of those first really hot days last spring. Me, splashing out on a rare takeaway from Halfway and deciding to sit outside on the bench by the controversial bus stop (moved about a hundred metres to huge, wronged outcry).

Pip, heading up from the road that leads to Harcourt Pools.

I called out a hello to him, and when he came over, the thing that struck me first was how he looked at my sandwich and coffee. How quickly he demolished them when I handed them over.

I've met a lot of troubled teenagers, so I guess I clocked pretty quickly that he should have been at school. I guessed where he'd been, but it was a long way from home – home being the nearest town, Harcourt, a few miles from Crossways.

Took me longer and a lot of building up trust later to work out he was skipping school every day. He took different routes, sometimes across muddy fields. Just walking? Or working out how far he could walk? His footsteps invariably led to Harcourt Pools.

But what if one day he just kept walking, became another missing child, another statistic? What if he jumped?

So I stepped in. I gently made arrangements. Gradually, with Pip's consent, I talked to the right people. He skipped doing his GCSEs. He helped me out some days instead.

Here we are a year on. I haven't seen him so much since he went back to school in September, dropping down a year. This year will be the GCSEs, I guess.

I'm about to ask, when Pip amazes me by turning to me with a grin.

'Not surprised you two had a row.'

'Why would you possibly think that?'

'Stubborn. Not one to back down, either of you. Her neighbours are just tourists and people connected to the university, holiday lets that go for a fortune in the summer, so they want her house too. Think she quite enjoyed getting in their way.'

Despite my own claim that everyone is connected to everything around here, I'm surprised he knows so much. I guess Pip and Mrs M crossed in the shop? Unless Mrs M saw him down here and spoke to him. That was kindly. It makes me adjust my view of her.

Maybe a grieving teenage son reached a kind streak in that malevolent old bat. I like to feel better about her. Never really like to think ill of the dead. But also... does that mean he's back spending time here?

I feel guilty for not having checked in on him in a while. Too wrapped up in my own troubles.

I take a sideways glance, wishing I could see behind Pip's curtain of hair and tell what he is thinking. It is so difficult to ever know you are doing the right thing by other people, teenagers doubly so.

Three of the four remote riverside cottages we approach do look unoccupied. Doesn't surprise me if they've been turned into lucrative Airbnbs. Happens around here a lot.

We're near a university city, so we get visiting academics, we get tourists, and there are too few hotels and plenty of people wanting to cash in if they've got a spare room. I'm sure Pip's right and that someone would have been after Mrs M's house too.

But who would book to stay here in freezing, grey January? Then add in the potholed road to get here, and it's a schlep to a shop or reach other human beings, chips, or a pub. Even though she was a tough old bird, how did Mrs M cope living all the way out here on her own with no neighbours?

I don't like to think of her being so isolated. Or dying on her own.

Is taking him to meet Stacey utterly wrong? Everyone wants Pip to get past it, move on. Reminding him about unlucky accidents is so far from smart. I have such a track record of poor decisions. But before I can say this is a terrible idea, I think Pip's keen to get inside, get somewhere warm, because he's gone ahead and is knocking on the door.

6.

Two cars, a powerful BMW and a tiny Fiat 500, are outside the fourth and farthest cottage, closest to the evil water. Odds are Stacey will be here.

No doorbell. Single windows ground and first floor, no front garden, just a half-hearted cluster of a dozen stacked clay and two big plastic plant pots, empty if you don't count the weeds.

'If I try hard, I can just about imagine this could be nice in the summer,' I say.

But it's not true. I'm too aware of the roar of the water and I find it impossible to stop myself imagining Helen being pulled under. Too, too horrible. If anyone went in, they wouldn't stand a chance of changing their mind.

Did she go in deliberately? Did she change her mind?

'And when the weather's good, it's a magnet for day-trippers. So, it's either isolated or packed. I couldn't live here, and I live in a crummy flat above a fragrant takeaway on the sad side of Harcourt. Obviously just a stepping stone on my path towards my successful, idyllic rural life.'

'Why do you live in a horrible flat?' Pip asks.

'Because a vegan blueberry croissant is out of my budget, let alone the housing market in Crossways.'

Waiting makes me feel increasingly nervous about my ability to do this right.

Despite all Liv and Cady's encouragement, this feels intrusive, probably because the sort of death-knocks I'm used to are ones where police are involved. But Pip could do with a hot drink and being somewhere warm and I still need to do the making amends bit, so I knock again, wondering how to ask Pip – is it just the anniversary that's brought him here? I hope he's not coming here regularly like he used to.

'I used to take things in my stride like cells, police interviews, bloody crime scenes. Why am I so nervous about this?'

'Because this is different? ' says Pip. 'This is a daughter who's just lost her mum, who you were rude to and rowed with the day before she died.'

'It was hardly a— Well, yes, I guess you could put it like that. It's possible my mouth ran away from me and I might have said things I shouldn't.'

I think Pip has grown. Which means I haven't seen him in a while, which is good, I think. He's been back at school since September.

I was pleased and proud as any real parent when he agreed to go back, swallow the humiliation of dropping down, redoing the year, knuckling down at a second chance at his GCSEs. It was a huge step. Sometimes normality and a routine are what you need when you feel you've been marked out for something extraordinarily cruel, unlucky, and painful.

This place is not healthy for Pip. I don't think Stacey's going to answer, even if she's in. I should get him away.

'I can see why Mrs M found it hard to maintain a cheery disposition, toughing it out here, although she was astonishingly awful to me. I knew she was the most malicious gossip in Crossways, but I'd never been on the receiving end of the full Mrs M before. But she was one of the most unpleasant women I had the misfortune to meet since moving to Crossways.'

The door opens, taking me completely by surprise. Stacey's bundled in a thick grey cardigan. Her short, light-coloured hair looks flat and dull. Behind thick-framed glasses, I see she's been crying. I really, really hope she is also hard of hearing and didn't catch what I just said. So much for smoothing things over. I really need to learn not to let my mouth run away with me.

I try for a big smile, then realise that is completely the wrong face for this situation and pick serious-yet-concerned-pained-sympathy, but I have a feeling I probably look like I'm knocking because I have a desperate need for the loo.

'Hi, Stacey! I hope we're not bothering you. I'm so incredibly sorry to hear about your mum. I was here and just wanted to check if you were all right. Thought there might be something I could do to help. This is Pip Craven, he lost his mum here a year ago, you probably remember it. He could do with some company. I thought we could all do with some biscuits.' I wave my apology-offer of bourbons. 'And tea?'

I'm not sure if it's the shared tragedy or the offer of half-decent biscuits, but she eyes me and Pip suspiciously for a second from behind her heavy glasses, then it gets us in the door. Hopefully that means I actively dodged making things seriously worse by her overhearing me bad-mouthing her mum. *Must do better.*

We step into a narrow hallway decorated with authentic, hard, Victorian quarry tiles at the foot of very steep stairs designed to take up as little space as possible, rather than be easy to use. I shiver and cannot avoid looking at where Stacey must have found her mum.

I imagine Stacey letting herself in the front door. The realisation. The shock. Was there blood? Very possibly as the entrance smells of a fresh lavender polish and recent cleaning.

I glance at Pip, doubting even more if this was such a great idea, bringing him somewhere with such a recent connection to death. But we are in. No turning back.

'I really am so sorry to hear the news about your mother's accident. Shall I put the kettle on? What would we do without tea?'

Straight from awkward subject to tea; how very provincial.

Stacey has clearly been crying, and tears spring again, but she manages a nod.

Front room immediately to the left, kitchen at the rear. It's exactly the sort of time-warp house, just the setup I could imagine Mrs McFlintock living in. The tea things are easy to find. There's a teapot, even though she lived alone, alongside a very fancy coffee machine that doesn't look like it gets much use, even though Mrs M must have shelled out hundreds for it. I guess she must have liked coffee. A lot.

'There's hot chocolate, Pip?' I call. Cady often makes him hot chocolate. 'I don't trust myself to work out the coffee machine. There's instant.'

'Tea for me!' calls back Stacey. She and Pip have gone into the front room.

I wanted to get Pip somewhere warm, but it's cold enough in here that I don't remove my coat. I find lots of clean mugs.

'Mum said she used that coffee machine when she had visitors, but I was never sure she worked it out really. It was me who always wanted one of those coffee makers, but I could never have afforded it. Waste of money. It just sits there.'

I'm pleased Stacey said Mrs M had visitors. Because the story this house is telling is of an isolated life.

Of course, I feel guilty all over again for the fracas over bookgroup. She probably just wanted the company.

But did she really have to sit there every meeting and find things to say to deliberately make it so awkward for everyone else?

That gleam she'd get, her little gimlet eyes glittering.

And what she accused me of rocked me.

You wouldn't want that getting about.

No. I wouldn't. And the way she said it sounded like she'd enjoy putting that horrible story around about me.

Apart from the coffeemaker, the rest of the kitchen is ancient, although there's also a fancy food mixer.

'Did your mother like baking too?' I call.

Maybe Mrs M was more nurturing than I gave her credit for.

'Not really, but there should be some sugar,' Stacey calls back. 'I don't normally, but for the shock, you know.'

Out back there's not much of a garden. It's an expensively paved yard for somewhere that's little more than a place to store bins. But the small space is edged with raised beds and, even in winter, someone's been imaginative enough, so there's a bit of colour.

So she was a gardener too.

I'm trained to be a seeker of truth, to look for the flaws and the gaps in the arguments. I examine signs. It's hard-wired. I call it being interested in people, and I can take it if people say I'm just plain nosy. But I cannot help but be surprised Mrs M had such comforting, nurturing hobbies. It's taken me by surprise, but people will always do that.

I come into contact with so many people in the bookshop, some I barely exchange a good morning with, others will chat away and I hear their life story almost as soon as they are inside. Very few chat only about books. Some people you get to know very well. Others I see all the time, but do not know at all.

I try to imagine Mrs M having visitors, making them expensive coffee and using her fancy mixer to bake them little cakes. I fail. But it is amazing how you can see someone differently from stepping inside their house.

I find milk. I try not to be bothered by the poignancy of a single piece of salmon on a plate in the fridge that will never be enjoyed.

Being here in the aftermath of a sudden death... why did I think it might help Pip? It's bringing to the surface everything I've been squashing down this last year. Like wishing I'd done more for Helena Craven. The not knowing. *Did she deliberately do what she did?*

She had a few troubles. I blame myself for not spotting how bad things were, even though we were friends for only a short time. I sense Cady comes to help me partly because of that shared feeling that we should have seen it coming, done more, done something.

Sugar's tricky to find. In the cupboard below the kettle are plates and a white ceramic container with a lid. I think I've struck lucky, but where I thought there might be sugar, instead there's a fat book bound in brown faux leather. Crammed into the sugar caddy?

Is this another thing I've learned since stepping inside Mrs M's home – it looks like Mrs M was possibly getting a little mixed up and forgetful? She seemed so sharp. Maybe I didn't figure out Mrs M too well at all.

I locate an open bag of sugar. I put two spoonfuls into one of the mugs.

I think I'm ready. Here, in her home, I really do regret that argument with her. I regret even more that it happened the day before she died. I remind myself I'm here for one reason. *Right, time to make amends. I can do this. I am not going to screw it up.*

7.

I've found a tray and even enjoyed feeling rather old-fashioned as I put the biscuits I brought on a flowery plate. I take it all into the living room, where Stacey is talking kindly to Pip about his mum. I'm not the least bit surprised she knew Helena. Everyone here is connected.

Stacey and Pip are perched on a sofa against a window, leaving me with the chair that looks outwards. In summer, it'll be a wonderful view no doubt. I have an uncomfortable sense this was Mrs McFlintock's chair, as I have to move a newspaper from the seat. I don't miss the poignancy of a half-finished crossword.

'How old was your mother?' I ask, reminding myself not to be intrusive, no need to start asking impertinent questions. *Just make polite small talk, make amends and leave.*

'Early eighties, but everyone said she seemed much younger. I thought she'd have gone on for years.' Stacey removes her heavy glasses to dry her eyes as tears have sprung again.

Guess I'm not surprised Mrs M was older than I thought. I won't mention the notebook in the sugar caddy.

'She always struck me as being in her prime. And I'm really sorry, I don't know if you heard… but last time we spoke, we had a little disagreement about bookgroup.' I take a deep breath. 'I never had a chance to apologise for upsetting her, and now I feel so bad.'

'I'll be honest. Mum had little disagreements with a lot of people. Big disagreements sometimes!' Stacey waves away my apology as easily as she dunks a bourbon biscuit in her tea.

'Well, that's very kind and understanding of you.'

So that's done and was easier than I thought.

Pip sips his hot chocolate and reaches for another biscuit. Stacey munches her bourbon, ready to chatter. I'm busy wondering how little small talk is too little so we can exit without being rude.

'And I can see she liked gardening.'

'Oh, lord no! Loathed it! Hated it so much she paid for a gardener, and she only had a yard. Another waste of money—never knew where she got her money from! Mum didn't mention she fell out with you. But she was mad the day she died. It was that awful hairdresser.'

'One of her little disagreements was with Joely?'

I know Mrs M used the salon a few doors down from me, because you can't help but know a lot about people in such a small village.

'Oh yes, Mum was in a right tizzy when she called me, said her whole day had to be changed.'

'What happened?'

'I was supposed to drive her. She has a much better car than me, I've just got that old Fiat. I asked her enough times why I couldn't have her car.'

Stacey munches thoughtfully. 'Guess it's mine now. But she hates driving. Hated,' Stacey corrects herself, with another wipe of her eyes. 'Never understood why I drove her everywhere and she wouldn't let me have the decent car. Well. I guess it's all mine now.'

It's more than a decent car. I don't know a lot about cars, but that's proper fancy, and another assumption I made about Mrs M turns out to be wrong. I didn't have Mrs McFlintock as a BMW driver (although it sounds as if she didn't drive it – so why have it at all?). I'd guessed the cars were the other way around, the small Fiat being Mrs M's. I don't know why my brain insists on noticing discrepancies and logging them.

'Every month I drove her to the hairdresser's. We'd have lunch. But the day she died, it all went wrong. I would have been here earlier, but the whole day got changed, all because of that Joely.'

Stacey wipes her eyes again. 'I guess it was good, in a way, how they said she'd have died instantly and nothing could've been done. I think I'd always have wondered if she suffered, you know? Hate to think she might have been lying there.'

I glance nervously at Pip drinking his hot chocolate and dunking bourbons, but I know he's taking it all in. I bet he's picturing the shock of walking in and discovering her mother's body at the bottom of the stairs.

'That hairdresser messed her about before. "Not properly qualified," Mum said.'

'Joely is definitely qualified,' I say quickly.

38

I would have said something sharper, but Pip being here reminds me not to get angry. Having Pip around always makes me want to be a better person.

Even Supportive Mum, with her never-ending list of reasons why the bookshop was another of my terrible decisions, never dreamed I'd end up some unofficial, almost half-adoptive parent to some troubled teenage kid whose life has been turned upside down. I'm as clueless about that as I am about bookselling.

Even so, it feels like one thing I've not made a hash of.

'Oh, Mum knew a lot about people. I used to tell Mum, finding out gossip was her only hobby and that she should find a new one.' Stacey giggles, but removes her glasses at more tears. 'The things she could tell you!'

'Isn't it terrible how untrue stories get about?' I say with admirable calm, but a new worry.

I'm doing rather a good job of smoothing things over, but it sounds like Joely managed to fall out with the unpleasant Mrs M too. So Joely could be shunned for upsetting Mrs McFlintock just before she died. Joely, unlike me, is hardly the sort to upset anyone. She's a delightful person and doesn't deserve it.

'I'm sorry your mum had an all-round bad day, but are you sure it was Joely who upset her?' I say. 'I couldn't help but see she had bad news from Key Keepers & Co, the rental agency.'

Stacey gives me a quizzical look. But when I moved Mrs M's newspaper with the half-finished crossword, I saw the letter, signed with the familiar aggressive signature of the landlord's agent, Minty Carstairs. I only had to move the newspaper a little more to read it and discovered I'd made another wrong assumption.

Mrs McFlintock had clearly lived here for years. I assumed she owned her home. But Mrs M received the same letter as me, telling her that the rent was soaring.

That letter was a punch in the guts to me. Mrs M was over eighty, it must have been grim receiving that. No wonder she was cross and upset when Joely then, unfortunately, called to change her appointment.

A small voice inside me whispers that this was on top of the row I had with her the day before. That was a whole bad twenty-four hours for Mrs McFlintock.

Is it surprising she wasn't concentrating on what she should be doing – like keeping her footing on some pretty lethal-looking stairs?

I try to quieten the anger, but a fire of injustice flares. It's a familiar flame, the need to act, to do something, the inability to sit on the sidelines, a spark that took me into the legal profession in the first place. But it's in my past, I have moved on.

Pip told me someone wanted Mrs M's house to turn into an Airbnb like her neighbours. But it hardly matters now, even if there was an effort from Minty Carstairs to get an old lady out of her long-time home. It's none of my business. And my opinion of Mrs M hasn't changed. She was a piece of work. I am not getting involved.

Then my mouth just takes over. 'It's none of my business, but that's a strong letter for anyone to receive,

40

and I'd be tempted to go around and tell Minty Carstairs exactly what I think. She should think of the consequences of sending out letters like this, particularly to vulnerable old people living alone.'

Stacey takes the letter from me and frowns as she reads it.

I'm surprised yet again, this time at Stacey's reaction.

'Oh no, she wouldn't have been worried about this. It's just a mistake.'

'That sounds… fortunate.' And not at all likely. I bite my lip, try to say nothing. But I cannot help but be curious at the easy way she dismisses it. 'You sound very certain. Surely this would have only added to what already sounds like an upsetting day for your mum.'

'Oh no. Mum boasted she was the only person in Crossways whose rent went down rather than up this year! Mum might have been old, but she was losing none of her sharpness… Well, she was losing her memory a little—not that she was having any of it, of course. But I could see it in little ways. Like I know she started being careful to write down things she didn't want to forget. But she'd have known this can't be right. Knowing Mum, she would've enjoyed the fact that it was an opportunity to point out Minty Carstairs's mistake. Minty kept trying to get her out so this could be a holiday let like the other cottages.'

'Well, I'd love her secret of how to get your rent to go down in Crossways.'

'Wouldn't we all love all of Mum's little secrets! She had some deal going on with that Minty. Something about

Mum having no neighbours anymore, just people here one day, then gone. It's pretty grim in winter. No one around.'

I cannot see Minty and Key Keepers keeping the rent low because they felt sorry for Mrs McFlintock being alone on the edge of Harcourt Pools with no neighbours. Is this another of Mrs M's made-up stories?

I would be interested in the truth. But my work here is done. I've smoothed things over with Stacey. I need to return to worrying about begging publishers to take back unsold stock and magicking my events schedule into existence. I need to keep my business afloat. I do need to smooth over my own rental situation.

Maybe now is a good time to go talk to Minty Carstairs, she of the demanding letters and aggressive signature, while I'm on a roll with this unruffling of feathers. Yes, Key Keepers do deserve a call.

Of course, I absolutely must be sure I do not bring up how angry that letter to Mrs M made me.

Stacey dismissed it easily as a mistake, but I'm not so easy to convince that Mrs M wouldn't have got stressed by it. Add in my argument with her, and the mix-up with Joely. It's a shame it all led to Stacey not being here when she should have been.

Mrs M would have been here all alone, dealing with all of that. And then tumbling down the stairs in a fatal fall.

But none of it is any of my business.

8.

Key Keepers has a tiny upper office above the gun shop in Crossways. It's called Crossways Outdoor Clothing, and I was genuinely shocked when I saw it. The fact that its customers must all like clothing in a particular shade of drab green was bad enough, but you can walk into a shop and buy a gun. I mean, there are rules. It's just that where I'm from, things work differently.

I'm all fired up to dive straight in and have it out with Minty.

But there's a sign pinned to the door saying the office is temporarily closed – all staff out on business. The business of haranguing their clients and putting on the squeeze for more money, I guess.

Minty Carstairs and my chance to get her to care about my business will have to wait.

I should go back to my shop, although with a twinge of guilt mixed with self-doubt, with Liv and Cady there, I'm certain everything will be in better shape than when I left.

Then I almost cannon into someone. Every time I walk down Crossways high street I bump into people I know, but it would have to be Rick.

Pip's dad is the last person I want to bump into for several reasons. Not least that I've just dropped Pip at home and know he's ditched school again to visit Harcourt Pools like old times. But no way am I mentioning it. I do feel guilty that I'm not going to put his dad in the picture. But I feel Pip's trust is at stake here, and that's more important.

'Hey Keera, in a hurry?'

'Sorry Rick, I was lost in a world of my own.'

I almost tell Rick he's looking well, but of course it's the anniversary of his wife's death, so for once, I stop myself from blurting out the wrong thing.

But I'm sensing a change in the air, which is good.

A year has passed since Helena's death. Is it too much to hope the Craven family is finally moving on?

But I almost had to do a double-take as nothing changes a person's appearance as much as their hair (useful tip if ever you need to disappear). Rick's used to be long, wavy, and past his collar, making him look roguish and unserious.

'Tough day today. On your way to buy a book?' This has become my standard small-talk for every situation, even though Rick's not a reader.

He grins at me, a lopsided, easily charming grin, and his warm brown eyes twinkle at me. 'Last book I read was when I was at school.'

'Are you in Crossways for work?'

'Not much gardening work needs doing in January,' Rick confesses.

'Book sales aren't rolling in either! I've been to visit Stacey,' I say. 'Mrs McFlintock's daughter—her mother died. I expect you've heard.'

'Yes. Poor old Mrs McFlintock.'

I give a quick glance around, pleased it's freezing today and the high street is growing dark already and is nearly deserted.

I don't want to be seen chatting to Rick because of that awful accusation Mrs M flung at me. I refuse to let small-minded gossip stop me from being friendly to whoever I like. But that's another lie I'm telling myself.

Thanks to Mrs M and her malicious made-up stories, I feel awkward as we fall into step heading back to my shop in case someone sees us (who am I kidding – someone will definitely see). I cannot believe she made up something so awful over a row about bookgroup. I guess Mrs M will never have chance to spread that rumour now. Once gossip starts, it's almost impossible to get it to stop.

But I try to hurry past the impressive plate-glass fronted premises of Crossways Estates, run by estate agent Grant Michaels. It may as well be called Gossip Central because all that glass isn't so much a showcase for what properties are available, as a window onto everything happening in Crossways.

Grant loves Crossways, loves his job, but he also loves knowing everything. He supports anything that he feels makes Crossways 'more desirable' and he drops in frequently to show his support for having a bookshop in the village. He's even in bookgroup, even if I suspect his opinions are from skimming reviews on Goodreads, rather than actually reading.

'I went to offer my condolences as we had an unfortunate falling out the day before she died,' I say. 'I don't want everyone in Crossways gossiping about what a terrible person I am. They don't buy nearly enough books from me as it is.'

Rick grins. 'No one could think you were a bad person.'

'Let's hope! That's kind. I don't get how people in Crossways think, you know?'

Mrs M threw at me the idea that people are saying there's something off about my relationship with Pip, that I have hidden motivations for helping him. She hinted I want to get close to his dad. I would particularly hate it if Rick feels like that. What even put the sordid idea in Mrs M's mind?

'I doubt there's anyone who hadn't rowed with her,' says Rick. 'She… Well, I did her garden and she was…'

'Picky?'

Rick carries on grinning. 'I couldn't possibly comment.'

'I should have guessed it was you who created that lovely space out of almost nothing. You have such a talent.'

'Thank you, Keera. Have to say, I've never worked so hard since…'

Rick's response to Helena's death was to throw himself into work. I saw his van everywhere, but of course that meant he was never at home. Pip's sister, Alys, shut herself in her room and filled her mind with A-level studying. And Pip…

'Luckily none of my other clients come close to Mrs M for being ruthless. She'd try it all on to make me feel bad charging her at all, tried to pretend she'd paid because she knew I'm terrible at paperwork and it'd take me weeks to go back and check—if I remembered at all! Proper horror really.' Rick chuckles. 'Always pleaded poverty. Yet had that car! Never saw her drive it. I always wondered—what was her secret? Was she some secret millionaire? Maybe it'll all come out now.'

'That would be a twist—if she had a big secret of her own, as I think she was behind all the Crossways rumours, and most of those she just made up.'

Through the glass door of Between the Lines I can see actual customers. I wouldn't put it past Liv and Cady to have phoned round friends and insisted they needed something new to read. Liv's there on her own now.

'Do you know where Cady is?' Rick asks. 'I've got so little work on and I need a distraction today. And can you believe it, I've been asked to pass on an invitation for Cady to stand for the parish council! I don't think they know what they'd be letting themselves in for. Three times lately she's forgotten her own door keys and I've had to drive across town to let her in.'

'Someone probably knows Cady can't say no to anyone.'

Rick and Cady both deserve to move on. And I do have a little hope that their happy ending might even be together. Scatty Cady was there to scoop up the whole Craven family in the aftermath of Helena's death, and what she did is amazing. Helena was her cousin, so Cady might have thought she should be the one to step in. But how many people would have gone over every day, making sure they ate, had clean clothes, when none of them seemed capable of even putting food in the fridge?

She covered up just how terrible things were until she broke down one day.

'The house is just so... There's no dishwasher, the oven's on the blink, everything takes forever, and I've ended up sleeping over on the sofa so often it's not doing my back any good. I started driving the washing to and from my home—my washing machine works and I can get it dry—but I'm so... I forget half the things at theirs and leave things at mine. I get it so wrong. Alys hates me.'

'Alys is dealing with the fact her mum died,' I'd told her. 'Alys probably hates everyone.'

Most people would have seen easing herself away, leaving the Cravens to start to find a way to function without her, as the sensible thing to do. But Cady came up with her own very-Cady solution. She moved them all to her house.

She organised everything with as little disruption to them as possible. She moved Pip's entire bedroom, so he slept in the same bed and even looked at the familiar wardrobe. She moved every single poster from his walls and stuck them back in the exact same position on hers. Just in a bigger room.

My efforts of keeping Pip busy a few days a week in the shop and getting him back into the habit of reading paled in comparison.

'Cady slipped away to visit the January sale of that classy boutique at the other end of Crossways high street,' says Liv when we step inside the shop, which miraculously feels tidier. 'If I were you, Rick, I'd catch her before she spends too much.'

We both watch him go. I don't know if heading into the sunset together is something they want for themselves, or that's just my wishful thinking. But I share a glance with Liv.

'Do you think those two will ever see they are perfect for each other and just do the decent thing and get together?' Liv asks me.

'I'm glad it's not just me who thinks that. I have to resist nudging them along.' I sigh. 'But Liv, thank you for all of this! I'll thank Cady later. Just goes to show how well things go when I'm not around!'

It's warm, my reading chair is no longer storing unloved biographies by minor celebrities trying to recapture the glory days.

My chalkboard has found its way onto the wall behind the till (still awaiting the choice of my 'book of the month'). The boxes have slid away from the shop floor, stowed in a precarious tower in my tiny storeroom office.

'Everything go ok? Or at least as well as can be expected?' Liv asks tentatively.

'Actually, I didn't even mess up. It was good advice to go and talk to Stacey. I said pleasant things. And I found Pip, and it looks like everyone had a more successful afternoon with me not actually being here. I learned things too. Mrs M had a falling out with Joely. And Minty at Key Keepers was on her back too. I think she had an all-round horrendous time just before she died, which is awful to think about. But it means there's one last thing I should probably do. If you could hang on here a little longer?'

'That might give me time to fix that table with the dodgy leg that you fell in love with from the secondhand furniture place up the road.'

'The one that tips everything onto the floor? I'll be as quick as I can!'

Liv gets so much done. She has the ability not to allow her mind to wander to questions that she should absolutely not be bothering about. Like how Mrs McFlintock could splash an absolute fortune on a fancy car she didn't even drive? Or who has rights to her valuable riverside property now?

9.

Broken Pieces by Pip. Making sense of things that cannot possibly make sense, Day 183

Daily Challenge – try to get the police interested, failing that, avoid them

His mum hadn't left a note.

At least, not the sort of note people meant. A useful note that explained everything, or even anything, '*To my distraught family and friends*' and ending with the words '*I'm sorry. x*'

The lack of note was a detail the police used as an excuse to keep dropping by with more questions no one could answer. The police wanted things tidied away, but were clueless.

It became a stalemate.

Their visits became a bit like those from down-on-their-luck relatives. You put up with them taking up room on the sofa, but you didn't make the smallest attempt to make them feel the slightest bit welcome. Everyone resisted putting on the kettle in case it prolonged the visit.

It didn't stop the questions. Just dropped by as we have a couple more things. We just want to be sure, you know, that we've covered everything, and we know you want this cleared up as much as we do.'

Why would she have been there? Any further ideas now you've had a chance to think about it? That place, that time. Could she have been meeting someone? Sounds like she had things on her mind. Would be good to get to the bottom of it.

It didn't matter how often they asked, or how many different ways they put the same questions, there were no answers. It became almost a game. They pretended they hadn't given up. When they stopped coming – that was worse.

That was when Pip realised his mum's death was done with, the official investigation over. All that was left was to admit she was gone, never coming back, try to find a way to move on and face that there never would be any answers. That did not stop Pip from wanting answers.

Sometimes he imagined the ghost of his mother watching. 'Make them take an interest, Pip. There is an answer. You're just not seeing it.'

He often had a feeling of someone in his shadow. In the fragile peace he was trying to make with life, it was surprising how much it helped to feel that her ghost was there. Like she hadn't completely gone.

He never told anyone because they would think he should be creeped out, rather than actually wanting to be haunted by the ghost of your mother. But he liked it. So he never told anyone, particularly not the shrink, who came a little later.

Not grieving, mentally unstable.

He had advice all the time. *Put it all behind you.* Move on. Accept it. Get over it.

It was because people didn't know what to say. And silence is more uncomfortable than platitudes. It wasn't easy to keep on pretending that he was making progress. But if he just pretended he was moving on, he could get away with anything. Because that was all people wanted. People left him alone.

Little rituals helped. Putting on his uniform and heading off at the right time, returning at the right time. As if everything was normal. Just pretending. And getting away with it. He went to the place often. Stupid really. But he hadn't been there, in that moment when he could have saved her. He'd been at school, obliviously learning useless facts he'd never need and perfecting the skill he'd never need: *how to write essays.* What a waste of time.

When he closed his eyes, he imagined the final moments of his mother's life, her struggling to survive, trying not to go under, gasping for breath, clawing the water, calling for him.

'Pip!' Only he hadn't been there.

Inevitably, he'd spent so much time pretending to be at school that when he'd been caught, he'd been forced to accept the idea of taking the year again.

McAllister (self-appointed teacher who cares) was the one who told him if he retook, rather than changing schools, teachers would give him a long rope (as if he had forgotten the rest of that saying).

Then there had been Cady hovering uncomfortably in the doorway, not quite taking the risk of perching next to him on his bed. Too motherly? Too intrusive. *Too right.* Suggesting a change of school might be better. He'd sat at the computer, pretending to listen to her smiley voice, smelling her rose soap, his fingers twitching to get back into the game.

'Start at a different school; a way of reinventing yourself,' she'd offered. '*You could be anything you want,*' said in a whispery sort of voice.

Just by changing schools, he could miraculously become just some other boy? Could he?

The truth was that even at a new school, everyone would know. Because everyone always knows. That he was the boy whose mum had died in a stupid, pointless accident.

If he stayed where the teachers knew his story, it was his best chance to carry on; going to school, but not going. Or not being present. All he had to do to keep using his Get out of Jail Free card. All he had to do was agree to a humiliating return, slip down a year, sit with the younger kids. All his friends moving on. Agreeing he should be put on some hideous self-inflicted loop. Destined to relive the most awful year of his life for a second time.

Surely everyone could see the irony, that this was the opposite of moving on – this was moving backwards. If he carried on, he might end up back at the starting square, like that game. How many things relied on a roll of the dice, where the wrong move could result in your dying in a stupid, pointless accident?

If he could slip backwards, he'd find himself at their old home. It would seem so cramped now, and even that thought made him accept that a tiny part of him had moved on.

At some point, Cady would get fed up with them and send them all sliding backwards. He wasn't looking forward to that. Well. He wasn't looking forward to anything at all. That was an ability that had definitely been lost.

10.

'Hi, Keera. Lovely to see you, darling. How are things?' trills Joely.

Joely is so stylish, with long hair in complicated braids. Is it compulsory to have amazing hair if you're in the business?

I know Joely because she's a reader (romantasy, the spicier the better), not because she cuts my hair. I can't afford to get my hair cut, particularly in Crossways, so I pretend I've been wanting to grow my hair long for years.

I'm trying to do the same favour Liv and Cady did for me. They gave me good advice in dealing with the possible fallout of my row with Mrs M. We are all caught in the spiderweb that is Crossways. I want to warn Joely but there's a cloaked customer in a chair, dark hair clippings on the white-tiled floor, and the smell of hair product mixed with the chemical tang of colourant. It tells me the customer will be here a while.

'I just went to call in on Mrs McFlintock's daughter, offer my condolences…' I say awkwardly.

'I know, terrible news. I cannot believe she's gone.'

'I think she may have been a little cross with me,' I say carefully. 'How about you?'

'Cross was her default mode.' It's the customer who chimes in. I wish I could place her, but no chance with all that foil and bits in her hair like an alien extra. 'Sounds like she was up to her old tricks.' She looks at Joely in the mirror.

'Old tricks?' I ask.

'Astonishing what an awful lot of trouble one sweet-looking little old lady could manage to stir up,' the customer goes on with a wry chuckle.

'I don't think she was cross with me,' says Joely, her face wrinkling. 'I went out of my way to help her.'

'But she was due here the day she died? Only, you changed her appointment at the last minute?'

'No chance! I wouldn't do that! I was too scared of her.' Joely pulls a face.

'Everyone was a bit scared of her,' says the customer.

'But she was tiny,' I say. 'She wore flowery trousers.'

'Yeah, didn't she play that sweet little old lady card well?' chuckles Joely in a non-malicious way. 'But once she got in a state about how she didn't like how I'd done her hair and started telling everyone who'd listen I was no good at my job.'

'Why would she do that?' I ask.

'Well. I did give her a discount for about a year after to sweeten her up.' Joely deftly begins to unwrap the complicated hair system she's set up.

'Did you see that fancy top-of-the-range car she never drove?' says the customer. 'Maybe you weren't the only one giving her a little discount. That car made her daughter mad. She made everyone mad. She liked nothing better than to set a rumour flying and see where it landed. Once they take flight, it is difficult to prove they aren't true, isn't it?'

Joely sighs. 'In my case, the timing could not have been worse. I was after bigger premises. You know what competition's like for properties in Crossways. Unlucky for me she put out that story about my not being qualified. Made me look a bad risk. Yep, Mrs M really cost me. So, yes, I was scared of her! And no, I'd never have called and changed her appointment!'

'But her appointment was cancelled?' I cannot help but ask. Because Stacey did put off going to her mum's until the afternoon. A shame, when Mrs M must have been having a stressful time.

'Yes. But because *she* called *me* and cancelled. Said I had to sort it, get her another quick, cos her hair really needed doing. Totally inconvenient for me, but I rearranged a couple of other clients. Told her it was just fine when it was totally not fine.'

'Because you wouldn't want to get on the wrong side of Mrs M,' says the customer. 'But Crossways will be less interesting with her gone,' she chuckles.

Stacey must have got her wires crossed. Unless Joely is lying? Or Stacey? Or Mrs M told Stacey it was all Joely's fault for messing up all her plans, and that was a lie?

Here I have conflicting reports and evidence, where everyone is saying something different. Which version of events is true? I cannot help but want to puzzle it out.

My brain does a little dance as I try to sift through the possible explanations, and I cannot leave it alone. Who's made a mistake? Who's got their wires crossed? Who's deliberately lying? And why? I guess I've spent too much of my life interviewing witnesses. I'm too trained to log discrepancies; it is hard-wired. I can't help it.

'Mrs M changed the appointment?' I say. 'Did she say why? If she insisted on another quickly?'

'Told me how she has this very important meeting,' says Joely.

It runs through my mind that now there are several things that don't add up about the day someone had a nasty accident and died. Of course, Stacey admitted her mother was getting a little confused and forgetful. There was no calendar on the wall, and I didn't see anywhere she could write down her appointments. There was a notebook. It was in the sugar caddy.

I've already logged one discrepancy in what Stacey said – that letter from the landlord's agent couldn't be right because Mrs M's rent was going down. Was that Mrs M lying? Or Stacey getting her wires crossed?

Joely could be lying. But as reliable witnesses go, I've no reason to doubt Joely. And there is one person here who stands out as a manipulative liar.

The evidence is there that Mrs M made up things – that makes her a very unreliable witness. But why would Mrs M want to lie about her rent not going up? Why would she change a hair appointment she really needed? But these are small points, and of course, I am not getting involved.

I'm leaning towards the conclusion that Mrs M did call Joely to change an appointment she really wanted to keep, put off Stacey's visit to the afternoon, and blamed Joely for disrupting the day.

One thing about good liars is they are often good because they stick close enough to the truth not to trip themselves up. She told Joely she had an urgent meeting.

Does that mean Mrs M really did have a sudden, urgent meeting? Was it a meeting she didn't want to tell her daughter about?

'Mrs M phoned you to change her hair appointment because of an important meeting?' I say. 'Did she say what it was about or who it was with?'

The words are out before I can stop them, but this is just me, taking a kindly interest. This is not me getting involved. Although, maybe I can admit I am slightly curious about how there are so many discrepancies about exactly what happened on the day that, sadly, Mrs M fell down the stairs and died.

Joely shakes her head.

What does it matter what the truth is? Mrs M is dead, there's nothing I can do.

No, there is something I can do. I can make the correct decision and walk away.

I came here to deliver a kindly warning. That's done.

If I've come away with the shocking discovery that it sounds like Mrs M might not have been alone when she fell down the stairs and died… Well, it's got nothing to do with me.

11.

I can't help it. I am bothered by knowing I'm the only person who even suspects someone was with Mrs M the morning she died.

Particularly as she kept who she was meeting a secret from Stacey. And she upset people. And Joely told me she was scared of Mrs M spreading damaging stories. And there's that grim letter she received from Minty. Luckily, it's easy to remind myself this is Crossways. In Crossways why would anyone push an elderly woman down the stairs?

Even so, I'd love to talk to Liv about it.

I try, but Liv's got her own worries. In this case, not being hugely late for an anti-dry-January cocktails and champagne party that she's already a bit late for.

'You are off to a party with no alcohol?' I say. 'That doesn't sound very you.'

'It's an *anti*-dry-January party. It has proper cocktails and champagne, which, in my opinion, is exactly what everyone needs in January—you should come, instead of going from here to your horrible flat and more books.'

'Well, luckily I do like spending my evenings reading, and I expect I'll be busy putting together that events schedule, don't you?'

*

I didn't get far with the events schedule last night. But the day starts well, with actual sales. Mostly to children off sick from school. It's great that they want to find things to read, all spending book tokens they got for Christmas.

I get a real buzz when young people come in and I can talk to them, rather than adults choosing for them.

I just hope they won't be too generous in sharing their off-from-school germs.

Cady drops in on her way to some event in the village hall, telling me she's spent a fortune on cheese.

'Not for the thing at the village hall. The cheese is for me. I can talk to your customers if there are things you need to do. But I'll need to just pop this cheese in your fridge. But don't let me forget it, will you?'

'Why didn't I open a cheese shop instead of a bookshop? People eat it in one evening. It can take more than a month to read a book. I guess my being a vegan means I can't get very enthusiastic about cheese. Why do you need a lot of cheese, Cady?'

'There's already a cheese shop in Crossways,' says Cady seriously. 'We needed a bookshop. A bookshop is lovely, particularly when you invite all those famous authors, Liv says you are going to have here for events.'

'Yeeees…'

'And I get to come in and help here! It's so cosy and people chat about books and they have that smell, don't they? The cheese is to do with a favour I'm going to ask you.'

My mind shuffles through the sort of possible favour I can do for Cady. 'Is it the parish council approach? You want me to say no on your behalf? But no, that's not something you need cheese for.'

Cady gives me an impossibly grateful look. 'Would you do that, Keera? Really? I'm hopeless at saying no to people. Actually, I've got a little good news.' Cady plays with her fingers. 'I'm setting up a special occasion to announce it.'

Is this it? The news Liv and I have been waiting for, that she and Rick are making a go of it? But she would hardly announce that so close to the anniversary of Helena's death. It could be that the Cravens are finally packing up and heading back to their place; I'd certainly celebrate that. Cady probably wants to regain her peace.

I hope it's that she and Rick are getting together. It would provide some great stability for Alys and Pip.

The Cravens' old home was tiny and not in a great part of town. Helena had longed to be able to afford to move out of that house. And I know Helena and Rick argued about never moving on.

Rick's approach was that work should be on his terms, and his terms were that work should be fun.

'The favour I want to ask is, could you come for dinner on Friday?' Cady says.

'Friday? Sure.' I answer quickly and with guilt that she's had to screw up her courage to ask me. 'Sorry I haven't been over much lately. How are things?'

'Oh well...' Cady reties the loose bun of her hair. 'You know.'

I think we are all guilty of taking advantage of Cady. Scatty-Cady has to deal with the Cravens full-time.

I've been as guilty as anyone of wanting to assume that everything is basically all right. But it's only been a year. Why should it be?

Pip is still barely coping with his mother's death. Alys is in sixth form but has just started working at Halfway, the newish cafe along the high street with a modern outlook and a large selection of vegan meals, so a good fit.

'Rick's got some good news to celebrate,' Cady says.

'Great!'

I wait for her to tell more, while thinking the timing for a celebration is unfortunate. So close to the anniversary of Helena's death.

'Rick's gardening business just won a big contract,' announces Cady with so much pride in her voice.

She starts biting at the skin around her thumb.

'He found out a while ago. But I wanted to wait until after the anniversary of Helena's death… Biggest job he's ever had. He's going to need staff!' Cady practically squeals.

I want to say to keep it low-key, not turn it into a party, but Cady's bursting with excitement.

'It would be lovely to have you there when we celebrate,' she says.

'Friday? Of course.' It will be fine. As long as Cady doesn't go overboard. As long as Cady's not cooking.

'I've got champagne all sorted,' squeals Cady. 'I'm cooking!'

Who wants to be the person pouring cold water on someone else's happiness? Anyway, Liv arrives, as if the very mention of champagne has manifested her.

'Champagne? What are we celebrating? You sorted things out with your landlord, Keera? Funnily enough, if you'd have asked me, I'd have guessed you haven't even been around to talk to her yet.'

'Problem with Minty Carstairs?' says Cady. 'Good luck with that. I've heard she's as tough as they come.'

'No problem at all with Minty Carstairs,' I say smoothly. 'Cady and Rick are celebrating. Rick's won a contract and will be taking on staff.'

'Well, that's better news than Keera landed on me yesterday. She's getting all worked up that there's something suspicious about Mrs M's death. I knew bookselling and Crossways would be too dull for Keera, so I'm glad you're keeping her entertained.'

'What do you mean, something suspicious?' Cady asks. 'Did the police find something?' She looks at Liv because Liv's son, Elliott, works at the local station.

'No, it's Keera who's all suspicious,' says Liv.

I quickly explain about Stacey complaining how her whole day had to be rearranged because Joely upset Mrs M. But that Joely claimed Mrs M was the source of all the rearranging and the urgent meeting. 'Tea?' I add.

Cady writes details of the next bookgroup book and meeting on my impressive-looking new chalkboard. 'Not that I'm saying anything against Joely, but she and Mrs M had a little history.'

'Mrs M said something unkind about Joely just as she was trying to move to bigger premises. So Joely went out of her way to keep on her right side,' I call from my cupboard where I'm making tea. 'I believe her when she says she wouldn't have rearranged that appointment.'

'Crossways has a terrible reputation for gossip,' says Cady. 'I'm not completely sure you should believe everything you hear.'

'You're right. Maybe I am making something out of nothing.'

'You think?' says Liv. I can practically hear her raising an eyebrow at me. 'I thought a suspicious death that hinges on a cancelled hair appointment sounded pretty conclusive – it has to be murder.'

'Murder!' cries Cady as I bring through two cups of green tea and one builder's.

'Well Keera's convinced me,' says Liv. 'Convinced me life as a bookseller is not as exciting as your past working with criminals. Not hugely surprising you've stumbled on something where we need someone to come in all guns blazing and clean up Crossways.'

'Well. Poor old Mrs McFlintock definitely received an appalling letter from Minty at Key Keepers about a massive hike to her rent. That letter was pretty shocking to a vulnerable old lady living alone. Minty's a piece of work.'

Liv smiles at me indulgently. 'It's poor old Mrs McFlintock now, is it? And if you're taking on Minty, don't forget you're on a charm offensive to stop her putting your own rent up.'

'You think maybe I'd be better spending my time teaching myself how to return unsold stock than worrying about what happened to Mrs McFlintock?'

'Do you really need to ask if that's a maybe?' says Liv.

'But that letter would have been so upsetting to Mrs M. She would have been flustered and distracted,' says Cady. 'Then she had that unfortunate fall.'

'Now a valuable riverside property is empty,' I add. 'One that Minty wanted Mrs M out of.'

'Lucky, then,' says Liv, 'that in Crossways, old ladies do not get shoved down the stairs.'

'No! Is that what you think happened, Keera?' asks Cady.

'Next you'll be asking me if I can have a quiet word in Elliott's ear about Mrs M having a mysterious meeting the day she died,' says Liv, before I can attempt an answer.

In my old life, I would never have asked favours of the police. But here, everything is connected and Liv's son could find out if there's any police interest.

'Could you?' I hear myself saying.

'Absolutely no chance,' says Liv emphatically. 'Elliott would rather be locked overnight in one of his own cells than discuss cases with me. Now, the events schedule!'

'And I have to go too!' says Cady. 'See you Friday.'

'Looking forward to it,' I say.

'And I am looking forward to our next Malice and Tea at four-thirty,' says Liv. 'I wonder who we can speculate about next. Next time I should bring cake.'

'I'm happy providing the tea,' I say.

I remind Cady to not forget her cheese.

'But,' I say, 'I will leave the malice to everyone else in Crossways.'

'But that letter, Keera,' says Cady. 'That awful, greedy Minty. Someone should do something about her.'

'Oh, Keera is definitely talking to Minty,' says Liv. 'An even bigger priority than conjuring this mythical events schedule into being or learning to do returns. Keera is not going out of business before we can do anything. You absolutely do not want to suffer this outrageous rent hike. There's quite a lot of blood-sucking you can do if you own property in Crossways. You need to make sure you're not a victim.'

'You make Minty sound like a vampire!' giggles Cady as she leaves.

I grin too, until Liv says in her decisive way: 'I'll look after things here. Go!'

'You can't mean face the awful Vampire Minty now?'

'Why can't I mean that? And why are you seeing Cady on Friday?'

'Celebrating. At Cady's.'

'Celebrating? That sounds a terrible idea. She's not cooking, is she?'

My silence says it all.

'I think Cady's approach to cooking is keeping her fingers crossed, and ignoring it if things aren't right, like she approaches her whole life. Why can't she just follow a recipe like normal people? You will need all the luck you can get. And *celebrating*?'

I am getting a bit too used to relying on Liv and doing exactly as she says, as I get ready to follow Cady out the door without even arguing.

Of course, I would have gone to see Minty anyway. I remind myself to focus. Minty might be very top of my list of candidates who might have been with Mrs M the morning she died. But no. I absolutely will not be bringing that up. Minty has the power to put me out of business. I will be nothing but nice.

'If Minty does attack you and take all your blood and money, you can look on the bright side,' Liv says in a low voice and with her signature quirk of a single eyebrow as I leave. 'At least it'll get you out of having to suffer Cady's cooking on Friday.'

12.

Today, there's a muffled response from an ancient intercom at Key Keepers. I announce myself, a buzzer sounds, the door unlocks, but it's so swollen with winter rain, I have to shove it hard to get in. *Visitors not very welcome.* I climb dusty stairs.

I've only met vampire Minty, with her aggressive signature and blood-sucking rent demands, a couple of times, when I was doing all the many things necessary to take over the premises for Between the Lines. I've never been inside the offices before.

What should be on my mind is making a great job of smoothing Minty's ruffled feathers and making her see what an incredibly valuable feature my bookshop is in Crossways. And why she absolutely does not want to raise my rent.

Of course, what I am actually thinking is whether she rowed with old Mrs M and shoved her down the stairs.

Supportive Mum, with her never-ending list of warnings, never once mentioned not bringing up the potentially suspicious death of a customer when going to negotiate a rent hike. Although I'm sure she'd have plenty of advice.

The last thing I need to be doing as I prepare for a battle with a vampire is to be running past conversations with Supportive Mum in my head.

So why do I have to start thinking about her prediction of my getting into debt. She gave my bookshop plan a year. *No, two, because you never know when to give up, Keera, so you'll stick it out long after you should have given it up. And then you'll end up with debts as well as regrets over abandoning a promising career. You must be one volume short of a complete set of Dickens' novels.'* Always the one for the pep talk is Mum.

I do keep trying to convince myself I'm really not sticking to this ill-advised bookshop plan just to prove my Supportive Mum wrong. Even her prophecy that I never would leave my troubles behind by walking away, as the one thing I couldn't leave behind would be myself. Especially that one.

'Keera, how very charming of you to drop in.' Minty surprises me by being ever so friendly the second I reach her office on the first floor.

Minty showed me around my premises when it was a baby boutique (not selling babies, but very cute, upmarket small clothes). I had imagined a country land agent would be old-fashioned, a bit tweedy, a bit dusty on the shoulders.

Minty is taller than me, and she's wearing heels that cannot be practical for stomping around rural mud or even negotiating stairs. She's super sleek. Today she's wearing a suit in a muted green and a white blouse with a pussy-cat bow. Her hair is bleach blonde and arranged so it sweeps up elegantly and confidently with a gravity-defying upward flip that reminds me of a curl of vanilla frosting or a Mr Whippy ice cream. That must take a lot of time in the morning, time that could be spent lounging in bed. But then I haven't got Minty figured as much of a lounger.

'It's so peachy to see you. I hear nothing but good about your cute bookshop.'

Obviously what I should do is seize this moment to point out this is exactly why she should care about my business. But I'm instantly on the back foot. I came here all bristling, wronged-tenant and now she's busy joyfully telling me how well received the bookshop has been, how delighted she is with the part she played in bringing it to Crossways.

I find myself thanking her, as if any bookshop success is mostly down to Minty. So far, Mission: Getting on Minty's Right Side is going well, I think.

She gestures to a hard chair at a glass desk on which there is a shiny laptop and a pile of papers neatly in place with a steel paperweight shaped like the Eiffel Tower. I take the seat and have my back to the window. Her view would be of the chocolate-box niceness of Crossways' high street, but she doesn't sit.

'I'm sorry I haven't been in,' says Minty.

'Not a reader?'

'Never seem to find the time.'

Minty retrieves a document from a metal filing cabinet (green, she likes green). 'Prices are rising shockingly. But luckily bookshops are quite the high street success story, aren't they? Bookshops are quite the desirable business.'

Minty finally takes a seat. 'I hear they are opening all around the country.'

She slides a printout of what must be my lease in front of me, taps it with elegant fingernails painted a sugary pearlescent pink like the frosting on a Mr Kipling cake.

Contracts are not my expertise. But I'm sure I did actually read this. Must have done.

'I think you'll find there's a clause that allows for a rent negotiation once in the first three years of your lease, in case of unexpected events.'

'Unexpected event? Has there been one?' I say.

'No one could have predicted this cost of living rise. If I'm not making sure everyone's getting what they want out of the deal, I'm not doing my job,' says Minty.

What I want out of the deal is to stay in business. I know prices are rising – all my costs are going up. But with Minty waxing lyrical about what a high street success story bookshops are, I can hardly admit I'm struggling and a poor risk as a tenant.

Minty cups her hands around a green mug that is a similar colour to the filing cabinet, and I guess is still warm. She doesn't offer me one. 'I think we both know retail spaces in Crossways are in huge demand. It's a valuable asset my client wants to make the most of. Lucky for you that everyone loves bookshops, don't they?'

Minty's already put me in an impossible position and thrown in that replacing me would be easy. She regards me coolly across the desk. I think we both know she's winning the opening round of this negotiation.

I feel stupid and under-prepared. Too late to try (and fail) not to feel intimidated. Too late to walk out and ask if we can start this again tomorrow.

Did I really naively walk in here thinking I could simply soft-soap Minty? Appeal to Minty's better nature?

Do vampires have one?

But I don't mean to let her have it all her own way and that means I have to think up a strategy on the spot to persuade Minty to give a sparkly fuck about my business.

'The rent I agreed was considered good enough,' I say smoothly. 'Funnily enough, the price of books almost never goes up.' I lean in closer. 'But it's never just about money, is it? Like you say, your job is to ensure everyone is getting the best out of the situation, and my bookshop has been very well-received. It's in your best interests to give a popular new business a chance. How does hiking my rent already help here?'

'You want me to go back to the landlord and say you think they should be penalised by the fact your business is struggling?'

Minty folds her hands in front of her. There is one other desk, but it's covered with a load of filing boxes. Another business that needs a lot of boxes. That sign on the door yesterday said the office was closed because staff were all out – I'm picking up signals that it's just Minty here, running things alone.

'I understand you're not the bloodsucker who sets the rents. I've never even met my landlord,' I say. 'He's the one expecting you to do all the hard work. We should be on the same side, you and me. I work alone, trying to do the right thing. I can see you're trying to do the right thing, make popular choices for our little community, like giving my little bookshop a chance.'

I'm not sure chiselling away at that tough exterior, hoping to reach Minty's better side, is any kind of strategy, but what else do I have?

'Working alone isn't much fun, doing everything yourself. I have lovely customers to talk to. You're doing all the work, someone else makes all the money. Maybe I need to talk to the landlord directly,' I suggest brightly.

'They do not want to get involved in the day-to-day.'

'Exactly. They're not the ones writing letters, demanding rent increases.'

Luckily, I might have hit the mark as Minty's shoulders relax just a fraction, and she allows herself a little moan about her job and how she did have an assistant, but it didn't work out.

She sighs. 'Like I say, my landlords don't like to get involved in the day-to-day. I might be *persuaded* to try to negotiate this down for you.' Minty's gaze meets mine full on. 'How much could you get together?'

Now I feel even more out of my depth. The way she just put it, with that piercing look across the desk, makes it sound like she's conveying some hidden message... There's something off here, and I have to swallow down the urge to ask inappropriate questions. Is she saying that if I make it worth her while, if I pay her directly, she could make this go away and the rent won't go up?

Where I come from, we call that a bribe.

Is Minty expecting a payoff? If so, she's going to have to make it a lot clearer what the deal is. But I can hardly say that. I'm not sure what to say without making it super awkward if I've misinterpreted things.

'I really haven't been in business long enough to work out the balance sheet,' I say carefully. 'There will be money coming in. A little further down the line.' I now feel like a poor-risk punter asking a loan shark for more time.

I can easily imagine Mrs M getting belligerent and rowing with Minty, who I've decided is more shark than vampire.

Does it even help if I let Minty think I'm up for offering a bribe when I can't even afford the price of upmarket pastries? Any money coming down the line is as much a complete fabrication as my non-existent thrilling events schedule of celebrity authors. Even so...

'I'm planning an exciting events agenda. Bringing a little bit of celeb glitter to Crossways.'

I've fallen back on the thing that everyone but me seems thrilled about. Can hard-edged Minty be swayed by the prospect of book-writing celebrities?

Minty's face takes on a little moue that could be amusement, doubt, or just disapproval. I've met plenty of judges who have that same look. But I don't think Minty's getting all excited about celebrity authors. I might even agree with her.

I'm out of negotiating tactics. But I can't help remembering what Stacey said about Mrs M having a special relationship with her landlord, how Mrs M was apparently sitting on low rent on a prime property that could be run as a lucrative Airbnb. I'd asked to be let in on the secret and now I'm wondering. Does Minty always act in her landlords' best interests? Does some money find its way into Minty's back pocket? And did Mrs M know something about Minty that helped in her negotiations?

I cannot mess this up by bringing up Mrs McFlintock now. I really can't. It would be a terrible move.

But my mouth just takes over. 'I'm sorry about the news of what happened to Mrs McFlintock. She was one of your tenants too, wasn't she?' I say. 'Thought she'd be around forever. Such a sudden, unexpected death.'

I cannot help it. It's not so much that trouble follows me around, it really is my mouth – it's like it has a life of its own. I have these thoughts, and out they come.

'Mrs McFlintock, I know, what a shock,' says Minty, finally draining the dregs of her coffee. 'Our longest tenant.'

'Those long-term tenants can be tricky, can't they? Agreements drawn up with ancient clauses you'd never include now. Locked into below-market rents. Painful in Crossways when there's so much demand for property and those lucrative Airbnbs.'

It wouldn't be so bad if I could just shut up now. I thought I wasn't actually doing terribly fighting my corner, but now I've steered us away from the subject without getting any answers about my own rent. So much for getting Minty onside. So much for that whole advice about quitting while you're ahead. I'm still here, and we're well away from talking about the important subject of my rent and on the one subject I was determined to avoid, and somehow, I still cannot stop.

'And those ancient buildings cost you a lot to keep in a good state of repair? She told me you were so understanding, how you had a special relationship.'

'Special relationship?' echoes Minty, and her eyebrows rise in a way that shifts the entire complicated uplift of her hair and brings the frost back into the room.

I hear Liv's voice in my head, telling me I need to use this meeting for one thing – my chance to plead for a reasonable rent and stay in business. I am about to screw things up, but still I cannot help it.

I know what it is. I suspect Minty of being there when Mrs M died. And if I don't ask questions, who else will?

'Her rent went down last year – how very kind. Although it does make me wonder what her secret was?' I give a little chuckle. 'I guess this special relationship is why you visited her the day she died.'

13.

Minty looks frosty. More than frosty. Glacial.

'I haven't talked to Mrs McFlintock recently.' Minty's words are as clipped as her heels as she goes across the floor to the filing cabinet and pulls open a drawer.

Is Minty retrieving Mrs M's lease? Maybe what I said about ancient tenants, old leases, and even more ancient buildings hit a nerve. Or was Mrs M's claimed low rent more about a special relationship with Minty?

How I'd love to take a quick squint at what's in that lease.

In fact, I'm so burning with curiosity to see the contents of the tatty old file Minty has retrieved, I get up too, moving to read over her shoulder. The second I sidle up to her, she closes it again and fixes me with a stare that convinces me she could drain blood with that glare alone.

It certainly brings me to my senses, because I can imagine getting a similar stare from Liv if I report back just what a mess I made of this meeting.

I really am cursed and I look around desperately for a change of subject, something to bring this whole getting-Minty-on-side strategy back on track. Luckily, my gaze alights on a front-page newspaper article framed on the wall. I seize on this as a nice neutral subject because I actually know what that article is about.

'Oh, you framed that story about that mass litter pick along the river. That happened just before I opened my bookshop. Helena had her troubles, but she managed to do this huge thing. Organised it; got her firm to sponsor it. She was so proud.'

There she is, Helena Craven, with her distinctive dark corkscrew curls, beaming out of the framed front page of the local newspaper, The Harcourt Gazette. She's right in the centre of a big group of volunteers.

'Helena and I became friends, you know. She was so kind to me after I opened the shop. And it was the weirdest thing, because the way she talked about that day it made me sad to have missed it. Litter picking!'

I'm lost staring at Helena's face, smiling triumphantly at the camera, and it aches to be reminded of how tragic it was that she was taken too soon.

'That was exactly what I wanted to create with my bookshop. I mean, nothing to do with litter, obviously. The feeling. The community coming together to stop all the plastic bottles, food wrappers, fishing waste, and everything from overflowing bins, from getting in the water and being on its way to the ocean. I guess you know what I mean, because I guess you were part of that?'

'I've no idea what that photo is doing there.' Minty is quickly dismissive.

There's something about her glance as it flicks to the framed picture and away. Makes me feel Minty is being evasive. But let's be honest, what can anyone be hiding about something so community-positive like a litter-pick?

The clear and sensible reaction would be to let it go.

'But it's on your wall, Minty.'

It wasn't supposed to come out like an accusation.

But there's no doubt that Minty's expression has turned from glacial to arctic as Minty shuts the filing cabinet drawer. That was a definite slam.

I've been scanning the accompanying newspaper story and a name leaps out at me.

'Oh, Key Keepers is mentioned in the article. You sponsored it. That's so great of you. So yours was the firm that sponsored it? So kind of you.' So Minty was involved.

If you speak to a lot of witnesses, you learn to recognise signs. Often it's hardly more than a flicker. It's mostly intuition, but that's when you push. That's when you find another question to ask, right away, before you give them a moment to get their thoughts together and plan how they are going to answer.

Of course, Minty is not a witness, and I came here to save my business, not to be nosy, not to satisfy my curiosity, and absolutely not to ask a lot of questions that are none of my business. But it's too hard-wired, this wish to get at the truth.

Because that litter pick was at Harcourt Pools where Mrs M lived. And now I've spotted another connection and it makes me feel I'm seeing signs that there's something here, something that doesn't feel right. Now I just want to dig.

'You knew Helena? You must have done if she got you to sponsor it. Ah, she got her firm to sponsor it. So she worked here? Helena put that picture there.'

That empty desk. And Minty said she had an assistant.

'Helena was the assistant who didn't work out?'

'Yes, we did sponsor it. She did work here. Only for a very short while.'

I give myself a stern reminder to stop seeing connections as suspicious – this is Crossways; this is my new normal. Also, I should not be surprised that Helena had a stint working here on top of all the other places she tried that didn't work out. One thing I learned about Helena was that she never stuck at a job for very long. Also, I need to stop myself from firing questions at Minty.

For once, I need to do the right thing before I reach the stage where I might have actually made things worse, because I really do have that gift. No, I have definitely already made my situation worse. I need to leave. In fact, I need to draw a line under the complete mess I've made of this. I need to leave right now and come back another day when I have better control of my mouth.

'Well, thanks, Minty, you've been very kind. Thanks for saying you'll do what you can about my rent.' Minty did not say that. We came to no agreement at all, apart from me suspecting she was hinting that a possible way out for me might be a backhander. Did I imagine that? I don't even know.

I know my next ordeal is going to be even worse – I've got to explain to Liv how well I did with Minty.

14.

'So, success?' Liv asks me brightly upon my return to Between the Lines. 'Did you persuade your horrible landlord not to put up your rent?'

'Cady came back?' I ask, pointing out a takeaway coffee mug on the counter. Are you working shifts or something?' I ask. It's pretty obvious I'm sliding around the question.

'Working usually has at least the hint of getting paid about it,' Liv responds dryly. 'Cady popped back with two cappuccinos. But I could not promise she remembered to ask for oat milk in yours, and you were away so long, I drank both.'

'Fair enough.' I check sales through the till. A popular nature-writing book and an iffy history book that didn't even sell at Christmas. 'Great sales, thank you, Liv.'

'Cady mentioned a haircut, and a deep need to get to the florist. Sounds like you've let yourself in for a big deal on Friday.' Liv crooks a single eyebrow at me. 'Champagne this close to the anniversary of Helena's death?'

'Cady's not great at thinking things through practically. She just fizzes through life and thinks things will work out, which seems to work for her. She was so excited! I will have to find the right moment to talk her out of the champagne.'

'I guess by the way you are avoiding the topic, your meeting with the joyful Minty went badly. How badly?'

I mumble my way through an account that sidles around me admitting that I put most of my effort into quizzing Minty about her deal with Mrs M, her relationship with Helena, and whether she'd visited Mrs M the day she died. And how Minty ran rings around me about pretty much everything.

'Vampire Minty said she'd put in a good word for me with my landlord.'

'Well, that's you playing hardball.'

'I didn't think being a bookseller was going to involve playing hardball.'

'You're an under-funded high street retail business in a cut-throat internet world. Of course you need to play hardball.'

'You are right as usual, Liv. I need to speak directly to my landlord, don't I?'

'Either that or trust Minty Carstairs to do a flawless job of representing your best interests to your landlord—who is paying her wages.'

'Maybe I should have sent you to do my negotiations. Get you to do everything.'

'Helping you out here, stepping in, that's fine for me. Being here day in, day out—no, thank you. Are you needing some good news?'

'Do you have some?'

Maybe Liv's good news involves Elliott letting some insider information slip. Did Mrs M's cottage even get close to being declared a crime scene? Maybe they did find something unusual and I'm not alone in my suspicions about Mrs M's death. Was there evidence that she wasn't alone when she died? Is there evidence Minty was with her? Minty is very firmly at the top of my list.

'I looked over the returns paperwork you'd started,' says Liv.

It takes a moment. 'You did…? Ah. Right! That's your good news? Sorry. I mean, of course, I'm hugely grateful. I haven't really taught myself that side of things.'

'I've discovered the most fantastic way you can get these untidy boxes out of the shop! You can send them back in exchange for actual money— Well, credit. Publishers are so desperate for shelf space in a real-life bookshop, they will take back all the books you rashly ordered that no one actually wants to buy. It's like a little bookshop miracle! Seems churlish not to take them up on it.'

'You are officially amazing! Tea?' I head to the kettle. 'Making the tea seems a valuable contribution I can offer. Maybe the only one,' I mutter.

'You have to give yourself time to find your feet. And you do get easily distracted.'

'I don't know about my feet, but I've just found I have something else to thank you for. I seem to have supplies of tea, oat milk, ginger nuts, and I have bread to go with my go-to snack of peanut butter.'

'All Cady. We worked out you must be eating the peanut butter from the jar.'

'Wouldn't want to be caught with a sandwich if a customer comes in.'

'All we have to do is locate this list of books on your shelves,' says Liv. 'Get the publisher to approve the list. Then we box them up and send them back for this credit that sounds too good to be true. Let's do it before the publishers change their minds.'

'Thank you Liv.' I can't stop the feeling that I'm the newbie here and Liv's the smart and successful business owner. But I'm learning to trust Liv's opinion on most things. If I'm going to do anything before Mrs M's death gets written off completely as an old lady having an accident, and everyone moves on, I'm going to have to tell someone my suspicions. And they are mostly about Minty.

'Have you heard any rumours about Minty?' I hand Liv her green tea. She has filled a box already.

'Now that is a perfect example of what I mean about being distracted.'

'I rely on you to give me all the insider info, as you know everyone and everything about Crossways. What you got on Minty?'

'As in your strategy with Minty is now to blackmail her?'

'If you're right and I get credit for returning all this unsold stock, there's a chance I can pay my bills this month. All I need is to stop Minty spiking my rent, and I might even stay in business.'

'I pass on advice about the local people you should be friendly to and who to avoid while you find your feet. I actively avoid passing on gossip, especially with no evidence,' says Liv acidly.

'I think that is the definition of a rumour, and you are making it sound like you *have* heard something about Minty. Because at one point, I felt like adorable Minty was dropping a hint she was open to a bribe. If you've heard anything, do spill.'

Liv starts to fill another box.

'It would be a neat little scam,' I say. 'Minty gets a handout, the tenant gets the landlord to back off on the rent increase. I can see how it might be popular.'

I will build up to voicing my suspicions that maybe Mrs M was rather too-well aware Minty was open to a bribe. And Mrs M was the last person you'd want to know your secrets.

'Anything at all on our friend Minty? I'm just nosy,' I press. 'Not for the purposes of blackmail.'

I don't think Liv's going to answer.

'I might've heard a sweetener or two going in Minty's pocket can smooth things,' she says eventually. 'I might also have heard Minty's got a little cashflow crisis of her own. Rumour has it that Minty saw all her landlords making a killing and jumped on the gravy train—only, plot twist! Her timing was bad. She borrowed big at the wrong time, and the debt quickly accumulated.'

I chew on the peanut butter sandwich I've made and drink a mouthful of tea.

'I do want to ask your advice, Liv, as you are right about everything. If you were me, would you find a way to use a bit of leverage to get Minty to back off?'

Liv gives me one of her forensic stares.

'A quick fix for a problem does buy you time for a longer fix,' I add.

'You want my advice on whether you should offer a bribe?' Liv's eyebrows shoot upwards.

'Oh no. Don't worry, I've no plan to offer a bribe.'

'Is that only because you don't have any money to offer?'

'Well, I—'

'I will give you my advice. Surely the best approach is to talk to your landlord directly. If you think Minty's trying to line her own pockets, you need to check where the request for more rent's coming from. Now, let's get these returns processed. Then we can move on to fun things.'

'Like trying to work out if Mrs M had something on Minty. Did she have her own way of doing rent negotiations that kept the rent low and stopped Minty being able to make more money doing holiday lets? Then Mrs M happened to fall down the stairs.'

Liv gives me a look that is scarily similar to the ones Minty gave me. 'Like, if we want to tempt a big-name author to visit, we need a venue.'

'Oh. Well, I guess we could squeeze ten in here at a pinch. Or did you mean village hall?'

'Ten is not what I mean by a big name or more ambition,' Liv says dryly. 'And somewhere the heating's flaky, the roof needs replacing, and the toilets block regularly is perfect for a big-name author?'

'The village hall also smells of Play-Doh and crisps from when it's used by the pre-school,' I admit. 'Where then? Also, I found out another of those surprising-not surprising Crossways connections.'

'My saying we have at least another twelve boxes of returns to process isn't going to stop you telling me, is it?'

'Helena Craven worked at Key Keepers, with Minty. She lost a job not long before I moved here. Was that the job? Tight finances were one of the things that were hinted at as a reason she might have killed herself.'

'Do you know the meaning of getting distracted? You're also forgetting, I didn't know Helena. If she had worked there just before you moved here perhaps it makes sense that maybe that's why she took an interest in you and getting your business started. Or maybe she could just spot a lost soul.'

'Was I a lost soul?'

'Was?'

I ignore this. 'Do you think it's even a little strange how Minty's connected again?'

'Again?'

'Well, there's Minty being open to a bribe. Mrs M having an urgent appointment and claiming her rent was going down. You've also got Joely giving Mrs M discounts and saying people were afraid of her, even though she was short and wore flowery trousers. You have also got Mrs M getting confused and forgetful—there was a notebook in the sugar bowl. And I cannot help being bothered about how Mrs M messed Stacey around and what Stacey said.'

'What did Stacey say? And what about the sugar bowl?'

'Mrs M had enough money for a shiny BMW, but made Stacey drive her everywhere in a little old car. Stacey wanted a fancy coffee machine. Her mum had one she never used. Stacey said, *"Well, I guess it's all mine now."* But what is? Not the house. Because Mrs M didn't own that.'

'This is you concentrating on saving your shop?' Liv says. 'I know you've been dealing with trauma, and you are clearly running away from something. I know you moved here because your past life was full of crime, and you're hard-wired to see crime everywhere. Helena was the first friend you made in Crossways. You feel guilty you didn't give Helena the time she might have needed. But it feels like you're looking for trouble to solve. Tell me I'm wrong.'

'Or looking for a distraction from the possible crippling rent hike, a possibly corrupt agent, a lack of customers, and no authors who want to come here for an event? You're right, Liv.'

'I usually am.'

'Partly right. Because things were never fully resolved about Helena. No one was entirely sure what happened the day Helena died. There was that unexplained note.'

'She didn't leave a note.'

But there was a note.

In Helena's writing: *4.30 Harcourt Pools.* Nothing else, no name, no date. It was on the passenger seat of her car, which was found in the Harcourt Pools car park.

Not the sort of neat note people would prefer. It could have been there for days. But four-thirty was when she'd have been there. They think. There's no CCTV to speak of around here.

'The simplest explanations are usually right' says Liv. 'The simple explanation is that everything and everyone seems connected—because they are. Because this is Crossways. It's such a small place, we're used to everything being connected.'

I'm saved from Liv delivering a bigger lecture as one of my bookgroup, Clarissa, arrives, shivering, even though she has a furry hat over her glossy dark hair. Even though she lives practically next door.

'I've just noticed the time. We'll finish those returns another time,' says Liv, sidling out with a wave. 'Seven o'clock suit you?'

'Sorry—what have I missed? Not another party you're trying to tempt me to? What is it this time? Blue January themed cocktails?'

'No, I have a far more interesting project than themed cocktails. I'm calling an emergency meeting. This evening. My place.'

'With who?'

'I have heating and I also have wine. You can walk.'

'Wait, *I'm* your far more interesting project?'

'Oh yes, Keera, whether you like it or not, you are definitely my interesting project.'

15.

Pip's 'This is supposed to be helping' journal
Broken Pieces, Day 255,
Simple challenge – just get through a family meal

In the Craven household, the trigger word was *lasagne*.

Just the smell of it made Pip want to be anywhere else. The dread of that watery flavourless sauce, pasta the texture of wet cement (Alys's analysis; Pip couldn't disagree), a layer of white slime, a query over whether that grilled cheese was really vegan, and Alys passing him the spoon and looking him straight in the eye. Because in Alys's world, someone always had to be punished, and in this game, it was always him.

Pip must eat whatever's on his plate quickly, ready for the moment Cady looked away. Plates would be swapped. The rules were that his plate must be clean enough for Alys to present to the world, and then he had to eat a whole second plate of whatever she passed over to him.

At least this was a game whose rules Pip understood. Hardly anything in his life contained rules that he could understand anymore.

Alys was always in a snarler of a mood, so it never mattered that her face was impossible to read, particularly under her long tangle of corkscrew curls, hair she got directly from their mum. But she must really be off when she loaded up a plate so big Pip's stomach squeezed, a little queasy.

Two portions of beyond terrible lasagne were bad, but what he couldn't stomach was it wasn't a game at all. At some point, someone should address the fact that underneath her clothes, Alys had become as empty as a featherless bird. And the truth was, it was probably going to be him.

Because Alys was never going to take any notice of anything Cady said, and Dad... well... the centre of Dad's world was charming, always genial Dad.

His superpower was an amazing ability not to see anything that might turn out to be difficult, let alone face it. He sailed through life in a way Pip could only admire.

Dad reached the table first as if actually eager, tugging off his tie and straight into entertaining them with some cheery story from another endlessly buoyant Dad day.

Pip barely recognised New Dad, who kept regular hours, who barely needed to do more than remove his tie before being ready to sit down to enjoy a family meal.

Where were the mud-splattered jeans and the endless scrubbing of dirt from under fingernails?

Also gone were the, 'But you knew when you married me the only thing I'm good at is gardening' arguments, and the late-night rows, mostly about, but not restricted to money.

Those arguments weren't missed, but new-Dad was so different sometimes it felt as if he'd lost both parents.

But mostly Pip thought if becoming new-Dad was that easy, why hadn't he done it when Mum was around? That would have saved a lot of arguments.

When he was an adult, Pip was going to try not to be a stupid one. Cady was not stupid, yet at family mealtimes she silently bit her lip, not quite able to understand, could not get why she's still way behind in playing this game of Craven Family Fortunes.

All Cady wanted was for things to be simple.

Cady thought their problems could be solved if she wrapped what remained of them in a big, kind blanket. No one liked to spoil her illusion that life can ever be simple. So they all pretended. One consequence was that here they all were, nearly a year on, and no one even able to tell Cady they can't stand her lasagne.

'So, how is everyone? How is the lasagne? Ok?' Cady asked nervously, hoping someone would give her a compliment.

Pip would love nothing more than to push back his chair, push back against playing any of these games. Why didn't he just stomp out? Probably because Alys already had that role: *Stroppy teenager*. Unluckily, all the good roles have been taken. Dad's *genial problem avoider*. Pip's left with a role no one wanted, one he'd never asked for: *family peacekeeper*.

There was only the sound of knives, forks, and expensive china. No one paid Cady the compliment she was seeking.

Dad coughed. 'Do you know what the biggest mystery about our lives is?'

For one insane and wildly over-optimistic moment, Pip thought they were actually going to have a conversation about why Mum died.

But Dad was scrutinising the end of his fork. 'It smells so great, this lasagne. But yet it's another of your incredible inedibles. Only you, Cady! Is there no end to your surprises?'

Cady's face registered a fleeting puzzled reaction. Then she burst into delighted laughter. 'I should have just got pizza.'

Dad got away with it. Again.

Mum always said that Dad, with his chiselled cheekbones, still boyishly floppy fringe and those hypnotic blue eyes, could get away with anything, even murder.

Cady reached for Dad's hand and squeezed.

Alys's swearing was emphatic. She scraped back the chair so it crashed into the wall, out of the room so quickly she'd vanished before there was even time for Cady's: 'Are you going to let her talk to me like that?' look directed at Dad. For all the good it would have done.

Dad just examined his plate.

Now Alys had beaten Pip in their silent, who can leave the room first game. Damn. Should have gone when he first had the thought. Now he was trapped.

Dad took another tiny forkful of lasagne and shrugged. 'Teenagers. No one tells you, do they? They never warn you. It's a worse responsibility than keeping a giant panda in the house.'

16.

I try to follow Liv's good advice, at least for the rest of the afternoon. She is right. I do need to focus. Her idea of evening events, making a bit of a party around books, is a good one that could really make a difference for me.

I have a customer. She tells me she didn't finish the last few books she bought and wants advice on what to read next, and this is where I like to think I shine.

We chat. I find out which authors she likes. I recommend Matt Haig's The Midnight Library.

People often say how lovely it is to talk to an expert, to save wasting time on a book they don't enjoy.

At the counter, this customer asks me how I can charge proper prices when she could have bought it elsewhere.

My real triumph of the afternoon is that I don't blurt out a rude remark. Not even about her having a carrier from the artisanal cheese shop (imported organic pecorino, she told me) when a book will be with her for much longer and be way more satisfying than cheese.

Maybe I am finally learning from my mistakes. My two closest, very friendly and supportive local bookseller buddies say the ratio you need to make up for one snotty customer is ten nice ones. But I cannot stop my spirits from drooping. Then, luckily, my next customer is lovely.

He makes up for any unpleasantness all on his own, by his cute smile, kind eyes, and by smelling nice and being expensively dressed and asking for recommendations for his mother. He's like the whole bundle of the wholesomeness I'm craving.

'She's not so well at the moment,' says Sully. (We even get chatty enough for me to find out his name.) 'I'm here looking at care homes. But she loves to read.'

He knows his mother well enough to identify her tastes and favourite authors. Close to, his heavy, dark coat, it smells a little of woodsmoke as if he spent yesterday evening outdoors, wild camping next to an open fire.

'This bookshop's not been here long? Or have I just been blindly missing it for years?'

'Just over a year. Still finding my feet. So you're local?' I hope this doesn't come across as: *Will I see you again?*

'Mum is. I tend to be on the move.'

'Sounds just like my adopted bookshop cat, who sometimes disappears for days,' I say as Jackson Brodie sits outside the door with his over-loud miaow and constant hunger. Jackson struts in. 'He is one of the ugliest tabbies I've ever seen. I think he must have had a hard life with one too many fights. That's the way it is for some cats.'

Sully grins. He tells me I've got a really interesting selection of books. It makes me want to purr, and I feel like maybe I'm not so utterly terrible at this bookselling business.

'I hope Crossways appreciates how wonderfully rare it is to get proper recommendations from someone who knows what they're talking about. You seem to have read everything. And how lucky it is to find a bookshop in such a small place. I hope things are going well?'

'As well as expected.'

'I'd have expected running a bookshop in such a small place might be...'

'You think opening a bookshop where the population is the size of a large school might be a terrible idea?'

He's well-dressed, so not broke, handsome, his fingernails are clean, he loves his mother. And he seems kind and interested. I think that's why I end up being honest. I don't admit to many people just how precarious my life is.

'My friend says I should have called the shop after The Graveyard Book because it's freezing in here and quiet as the grave.'

'Sorry it's quiet as the grave.'

'Ah, well, I didn't come into it to be retiring early or enjoying luxury holidays. Who wants to do those things? So lucky, hey?'

'You're following a dream,' Sully says seriously. 'Plenty of people talk about doing that. I think it's brilliant. But you're taking a risk, so some bits are bound to go badly. Are you enjoying the bits that are going well? Some bits *are* going well?'

'I should introduce you to my mum so you can tell her not everyone thinks I've made the stupidest move possible, giving up what she likes to call a "promising career." I worry I may be sticking it out just to prove her wrong.'

'You gave up a promising career to sell books in a village? You are so intriguing. I'm guessing, troubles, so you ran away?' He's smiling at me in a perceptive and understanding way that's also very cute.

'I usually find that is the best thing to do, don't you? Facing trouble head-on is so last year. My big life ambitions are now how to pay bills *and* eat. That's what's keeping me awake at night. So many mistakes! Even the name, Between the Lines—I'm constantly having to explain it.'

Over-sharing is really not me, so I try to get the discussion away from me. 'Is that a local care home you're thinking of moving your mum to?' Unless that came across as an attempt for more sales or flirting?

Sully nods. 'We've family near here who can call in on Mum, so she should stay here. I'm not sure how it'll all be paid for. But that's my problem that will be keeping me awake at night, rather than a book I can't put down.'

He twinkles at me in a way that I would like to think is flirting.

I need to avoid sticking my nose into trouble. I need to stop blurting out the wrong things at the wrong time.

But I am definitely leaving behind any involvement in any kind of romantic attachments. So I'll just pretend I'm not getting this uncomfortable blip low down inside of me or any feeling that I would not say no to being connected to this man in a way that may not involve books. Also, hitting on your customers is not a good look.

'So, seriously—I hope it is going well.' We narrow his choice down to a stack of three, which involves getting close enough so I get a hint of a woody aftershave, or maybe the shampoo he uses. 'And I'm still waiting to hear where the name Between the Sheets comes from. Between the Lines! Sorry!'

We both laugh. Our eyes had locked at just the wrong moment, so I quickly stammer out a reply to cover my embarrassment.

'You know, it's that the best bits of books are between the lines. Everyone thinks it's a quote. But I thought it summed up what I like about reading.'

'That's… I really like that. It's beautiful.'

I feel myself flush and definitely need to switch the subject.

'I hope your mum enjoys these and needs some more to read soon. Let me know, because I could always do with more customers! And of course, if you want any recommendations for yourself…'

Now, that sounds way too much like an invitation to keep flirting. I never imagined I'd ever be open to even the prospect of entanglements. Am I really so incapable of learning from my mistakes?

Luckily, he laughs, but I note he avoids answering if he's a reader, which makes me suspect he isn't, and I try not to find that disappointing. Although if he'd said he'd just read the latest Leigh Bardugo, he might have been in serious trouble of not being let back out the door. I cannot believe I even thought that.

'I hope it works out,' Sully says, as I put his purchases through the till.

'Let's hope.' I try not to meet his eye, and that is the only reason I notice he's not wearing a wedding ring. 'Because knowing nothing about running a bookshop and taking that step in the dark wasn't in the least bit smart. So let's hope the running away part was the smart bit!'

'Sounds exciting!' he twinkles at me again.

I open the door for him, where the January wind and early afternoon darkness already await.

He shuffles a bit at the door, but another customer comes rushing in on the arctic chill. Grant Michaels, my friendly local estate agent, keen to buy a book (or more likely, after gossip).

And Sully Blake is gone (I'd noticed the surname on his credit card).

'What's the next bookgroup book?' Grant asks me. 'I don't think I've seen tall, dark, and handsome around before.'

I watch Sully's back, broad shoulders in that expensive coat, and I wish I could convince myself I was never considering complicating my life even more.

I think Grant might have just saved me from making at least one poor decision today.

17.

Liv lives alone in a very lovely, very modern house with big windows looking uphill towards a wood, but with an immediate view of sheep (I thought you'd have to go as far New Zealand, or at least Wales, for the number of sheep that surround Crossways).

Liv's smart, organised, and a great networker. We are complete opposites.

What we do have in common is that she lives in what would be my ideal house. I'm trying to learn from my mistakes, so when I went over there last night, I managed to curb my curiosity and not ask a bunch of intrusive questions. But that just leaves me wondering.

She can only be in her fifties. She never talks about some previous high-flying job, but I can guess at one. An early retirement?

She lives a brisk walking distance (just). And I was very glad to be free of spending my evening in my litter-strewn part of Harcourt. Why do I have to live where it's all about the takeaways? Living above a florist would be perfect.

I daren't even dream of living somewhere like Liv's, where everything is tasteful, down to the choice she offers me between her favourite local artisan Ox Gin or expensive wine. Even the very fine, very big glasses. Dreaming would just emphasise my own, stark reality.

I do, however, blame the very big glasses on why I have vaguer memories than I should about last night.

And I thought I'd been smart turning down the gin.

No wonder I opened up this morning with a teensy bit of a hangover and in a good position to fully appreciate Cady's shopping for me yesterday. I make myself a strong tea, grab the jar of peanut butter and a spoon, and brace myself for customers. Perhaps luckily, no customers arrive. I find myself looking at the list we apparently put together last night, all in Liv's neat handwriting.

Liv says she writes everything down, which is just as well, as I don't remember half of this. Looking at it I have two questions: Am I really in this much trouble? And has Crossways turned me into a massive over-sharer?

1. Stay in business – <u>number one priority</u>.
2. Cut costs. Action: Go back to Minty immediately – if no movement on rent, demand to speak to landlord directly.
3. Consider source of additional funds to see through bad patch, eg bank loan or Supportive Mum (unless you have other secret sources of wealth, but I'm guessing not)
4. Find new income streams from shop, eg source bestselling author for giving lucrative talk, high demand for well-priced tickets, finding new readers/customers/supporters (win, win). Action: <u>Need list of potential guests and venue</u>. Urgently!!

5. Talk to Jaxx and Maya at Halfway. They might want to host joint event.

6. Find a way to check in on Pip and whether Cady is coping with the anniversary of Helena's death (all right, we already suspect she isn't – how bad is it? And are she and Rick **ever** going to make a go of it? Find subtle way to dig).

7. **Do not** waste time speculating ways to discover who Mrs McFlintock had a sudden and urgent meeting with on the day of her death. Or even if anyone actively benefits from her being out of the way (you'd be making a list of half of Crossways!).

8. Hope Sully comes back in to buy more books (why did you let him leave? sounds like there was a spark there). He sounds well worth following up on. Because you never know what will happen in life, and you may think now is not a great time for a new relationship, but why the heck not? You cannot let past mistakes rule your life.

9. Trust your instincts. No, first, learn to trust yourself. Oh, and other people. You really cannot be sworn off getting close to people forever.

10. I could not think of a tenth, so I only put this number here for roundness because we were supposed to get onto speculating about Cady and Rick, but you fell asleep.

I'm shocked that I shared so much, even the dodgy fact that I was slightly hitting on a customer who I might have been having mild fantasies about. (Does Sully really stay out in the open with a campfire?). But I am definitely sworn off men, that has not changed.

I was way too indiscreet. Actually, that's a great suggestion about approaching Jaxx and Maya at Halfway about hosting these dreaded events.

But still the main task to drag my business from the black to the red involves appealing to Minty's better side. I'm still not convinced she's got one. But I have to find a way, or Supportive Mum's prophecy about my spiralling into debt is going to come true. Vampire Minty made it clear there won't be a shortage of vultures waiting to swoop in on this nice little Crossways high street location.

The first customer of the day arrives before I've even checked in my box of new stock, before I have a chance to have a sit in the cosy reading chair and have a sneaky flick through the first chapter of any of them.

'I got twelve books for Christmas and I don't want to read any of them,' confesses Mr Baxter, one of my regulars, an upright ex-army white guy whose family clearly thinks he should adore military history. He leaves with a nice Val McDermid paperback, Past Lying.

Even in the dark days of January, people have birthdays and need gifts – or just a good book to curl up with and the fact that I get a few customers gives me hope, despite the teensy hangover.

Having a friend like Liv brings renewed optimism, along with the fact that I have tea and peanut butter.

Liv keeps her promise. She arrives before lunchtime in a chic black and white coat and a waft of Dior, with a celebratory vegan blueberry croissant and instructions that I kick-start our action plan right away.

'I haven't even finished unpacking my delivery yet.' And I have not shifted that teensy hangover.

'That's because you keep stopping to read the books.'

'Reading the books is what this job is all about.'

'Selling the books is what the job is all about. The clue is in the title: bookseller. I will finish unpacking the stock. You talk to Vampire Minty. And no letting her run rings around you this time.'

Thanks to Liv's list and her fortifying belief I can save my business, a celebratory vegan blueberry croissant and quite a few spoonfuls of peanut butter and mouthfuls of tea, I arrive at Key Keepers convinced I'm going to do this.

I'm so fired up, I'm disappointed Minty doesn't respond to my buzzing.

This time there's no note on the door saying all staff are out. I now know, of course, that 'all staff' is just Minty and she could well be in there and not answering for reasons of her own. I'm not going to give up that easily.

Last time, the door wasn't properly closed. So I give the door an experimental shove.

And after one more heftier shove with my shoulder, it opens. That door needs replacing. Minty should get the landlord onto that.

When I step inside, I hear raised voices.

Of course, the right thing to do is to step away; none of my business. On the other hand, I recognise Stacey's voice, and my curiosity takes over.

107

'And she slipped and fell down the stairs the very morning she got your upsetting letter. You need to be made to own up to your responsibility.'

'That almost sounded like a threat,' Minty retorts.

'It might be. Depends.'

'Depends?' Minty is sounding far calmer than Stacey, who's building up quite the head of steam. 'On what?'

'I have rights to that property. I have given you a chance to play nice, but I will get what's rightfully mine. Even if I have to drag you through the courts.'

'I am sure if you just sit down and calmly—'

'If you offer me another cup of coffee, I think I will scream.'

'I wasn't going to offer coffee,' says Minty. 'And you are not going to scream. Or take me to court. That is not in either of our best interests. The only people that ends well for are the lawyers.'

Sounds like they've been at this for some time.

'Don't you dare sit there smugly and tell me what you think are my best interests. You must be crazy if you think I am going to take advice from you. By rights, that lease now passes to me. Don't think I'll be a pushover. I learned a few things from Mum.'

'I'm not sure you quite understand what *by rights* actually means. And you'll regret it if you go up against me.'

'Now you're the one making threats.'

'Might be. Depends.'

I'm taken by surprise by a sudden clomping sound that warns me Stacey has decided this conversation is over. I turn and fumble for the still partly open door and step outside, shutting the door behind me and not a second too soon. Stacey comes flying through and collides with me before I can even pretend I wasn't here.

'Oh, Keera, so sorry, I am so flustered, I didn't mean to… I almost knocked you over!' She pushes her heavy glasses up her nose.

'No harm done. You seem very upset.'

'I did exactly as you advised, Keera. I challenged that awful Minty about that letter—you know, the upsetting one Mum got the morning she had her fall.'

'Yes… I'm not sure, did I…? What did Vampire Minty say?'

'You're so right. Minty's got a lot to answer for,' Stacey says. 'Mum always said she had things I'd benefit from one day, and I'm not missing out on that.'

I want to say Minty's advice is probably sound – the only thing fighting a legal battle will guarantee is a huge bill. But Stacey is way too steaming to think logically.

'Minty tried to squirm out of everything.' Stacey grins suddenly. 'What did you call her—Vampire Minty? Spot on, that is. She's not getting away with it. Mum'd lived in her home years—decades. She knew she was sitting on a cushy number and told me everything would pass to me. Only, I couldn't find that lease, could I?'

'It's all yours now?' I realise I'm echoing something Stacey said before. 'There was something in your mum's lease that meant Minty couldn't get her out?' I cannot help but be curious, thinking of that tatty folder Minty had that

I tried to sneak a look at, which I'm even keener to read now.

I want to add a warning that she shouldn't trust anything her mum had said. Mrs M was a habitual liar. Worse, she made up stuff to upset people because she found it entertaining. Then there were those little signs; that notebook where the sugar should be. Mrs M was also starting to get a little mixed up, a little forgetful.

I did not blurt out any of that.

'All I do know is avoiding lawyers is usually good advice,' I say. 'Smoothing things over with Minty would be—'

'I gave Minty a chance to be reasonable.' Stacey pushes her glasses up her nose. She has that implacable look you see sometimes when people insist on not following good advice. 'Now the gloves are off, I need to watch out—but so does Vampire Minty. If I don't act quick, they'll have someone else in that cottage and I'll have missed out. I need to find that lease.'

'That would help. And maybe have an initial chat with a lawyer, get familiar with what your options and rights realistically are. Minty will have to give notice. If she gets threatening, if you want to, call me, I'd see if I could help.'

'That's so very kind! Minty moves to threatening pretty quickly.'

'And, this probably isn't important, but it was actually your mum who got Joely to change her appointment because she had a very important meeting. Any idea who she was meeting? The morning she had her accident?'

The question stops Stacey's full-steam-ahead anger. Her eyes widen. 'Mum had a… Someone was…'

'Well, I don't know for sure… I don't suppose you saw any signs … That your mum wasn't alone?'

Stacey puts her hand in front of her mouth. 'You mean Minty, don't you?'

'Well, I don't exactly…'

'That letter. Mum knew that letter was a try-on. Mum wouldn't waste time giving her a piece of her mind. You're right. Minty didn't just send a threatening letter, she was there! And she never breathed a word. What an awful—'

'Actually, I really didn't…'

'You spotted right off what this was. I can see it all now. Mum was in a state and not being careful on those stairs. Minty's absolutely responsible. Thank you, Keera.'

Stacey gives me an unexpected hug. 'This will be such a help. And I will absolutely be in touch the first sign of any trouble from— What did you call her—? Vampire Minty. Thank you for your offer of free legal advice too. Thanks *so much*.'

'Well, I didn't exactly…'

But Stacey's already climbing into her mum's BMW.

It won't get back to Minty that I put any of these ideas in Stacey's head, I'm sure. Because that just might mean things will get even more awkward with my planned charm offensive with that awful Vampire Minty.

18.

Broken Pieces, Day 359 (Pip Craven's this still isn't helping journal)

Daily challenge – get out of bed, get out of going to school

Pip discovered just how perfectly easy the not going to school part was.

Put on your uniform, eat breakfast, head out, go where you can quickly shove your uniform in your backpack and replace it with the clothes you are carrying. Freedom.

Do anything you want.

What do you want to do today? Hop on a bus and keep going?

Although he had to be home by four to give all the appearance of having spent the day at school so that no suspicions were raised, no one asked questions. And that way he could keep on doing what he'd been doing.

It wasn't that he stopped getting away with it. It was more that it just got so cold. All that walking. He was glad to be talked out of it.

Bumping into Keera. The unexpected offer of unpaid work at the bookshop. Her talking to the school. He wasn't so sure about the agreement to counselling, or the suggestion that writing it all down might help (it had been useful, but in a different way).

Today had been like old times. He'd put on his uniform and quietly left the house.

Freedom.

And what did he want to do? Apparently, what he wanted was to go and look down into the churning, boiling mess that was Harcourt Pools, reliving his mum's last awful, gasping moments.

He didn't want to think about it, but he also didn't want to forget. So he made himself go.

Pip squashed down his bag to sit and eat the kindly packed lunch Cady sent him off with each day, some sort of pre-sliced cheese in limp bread, a wrapped chocolate biscuit with over-sweet cream filling, a bag of crisps, and an apple.

He munched his way through the limp sandwich, allowing the uneaten biscuits to accumulate in the bottom of his bag. It felt like a lunch made for a much younger kid. Much of Cady's role she appeared to get from TV, like some 'sitcom mom'.

Like the way she'd often slip him money for 'extras', but never said what. The bottles the guys got someone with ID to buy? Presumably not for the vapes or edibles.

Once he became known as the boy whose mum died in a stupid accident, he lost the ability to do things he'd taken for granted before.

His friends gradually melted away, and that was before he'd slipped down to the year behind. Now his old friends were in the year ahead.

Any money from Cady just accumulated in the drawer of his bedside table. His getaway fund, he called it.

It had turned cold again. The world had moved on, slowly, relentlessly, as it always did. It was easy to slip back into old habits, eating his lunch, slowly freezing, surrounded by angry water, listening to the crash and roll of the torrent surging through narrow sluices, trying to escape, or trying to warn you to stay away? He could never decide.

The mist enveloped him. He felt like he became part of this whole grey mass of blurred edges, difficult to see where water ended and mist began. A fog as full of menace, as if it had drifted from a nearby graveyard, dragging a few shrieking ghouls along with it.

And he asked himself again: Why?

What had Mum been doing here?

Mum had loved it here. But she hated the winter.

Lots of mums brought kids to sit in summer sunshine, spread out picnic rugs, eat crisps, limp sandwiches and biscuits with a nasty cream filling, watch fish and sea birds swooping. Sea birds? Childhood memories were so not to be trusted.

He could have sworn there was a proper beach here that Mum had brought him to when he was younger, not just a scrap of second-rate grit, foaming dirtily with random waste.

Could she have gone to meet a friend? That's what the police asked again and again; sometimes the older guy, or he'd swap places with a younger one, or together, one asking questions, the other listening.

They hadn't been obviously playing good-cop, bad-cop, just put their heads on one side and asked the same questions over and over as if they were simply curious. They'd spoke to this person (witnesses they called them) who she'd spoken to that day. Would Mum have met them for a walk? Was Mum troubled? Family finances ok? Did she go to the pools often? Alone?

Sometimes the 'chat' would involve the whole family. Sometimes only Dad.

Or had she come here deliberately wanting a way out? No one could say for sure. But could Mum really have looked at this raging water and thought this would be the way she'd choose to go? Pip refused to think so, nor could he shut out thinking about her last moments.

What was worse? Accident? Losing her footing in the grey, not able to stop herself slipping? Trying to climb back out. The tug of the current would fight you and drag you towards one of the sluices. You'd disappear under the surface.

Would there be silence? Because right now, all he was getting was the roar.

Had Mum cried out? No one would have heard.

It was like a horror movie; once inside your head, it appeared in your nightmares.

Today it was sunless, freezing. No one here but him. The wind whipped across the place. He sat on his squashed-down bag as long as he could bear it, until he could no longer feel his fingers, or his face. He should move on.

Move on. He'd tried to do as everyone wanted. Really tried.

But no one had warned him how quickly it would become difficult to remember, to catch that memory of her face properly in his mind's eye.

And now he came here partly because he was clinging to any clear, strong images.

There was one. She was dressed up, heading for a girls' night out? No. She was dressed smart, so had she just got in from work? That new job she had.

Memories became unreliable. But he remembered it being in the kitchen, her leaning against the worktop, glass of red wine, pressing it against her cheek, her corkscrew hair loose. Her eyes were a warm light brown and crinkling in the corners as she smiled at him.

Lipstick, dark red. She wiped a smear from the rim of the glass.

'Pip, d'you know I think I might have cracked it. This time I'm on to something good. I might have a little secret.' She'd looked so happy, triumphant almost.

'Great!' he'd said. 'Are you going to share it?'

She'd put her finger to her lips.

He'd caught that memory. It was a good memory. She'd been happy. And that's how he was going to fight to remember her.

19.

Friday evening comes around too quickly, and I'm approaching Cady's lovely home with a lot of trepidation and a half-decent bottle of wine.

She has one of those wonderful, solid double-fronted houses like children draw. The sort of house where you want to believe that, behind that perfect façade, everything inside is wonderful.

But I'd bet on the fact that breezy Cady, who never complains, is covering up a lot. I also approach with a guilty conscience. I haven't called in for ages.

Cady closes the door behind me and picks up a bag slung on the hall floor alongside some platform shoes I take to be Alys's. Cady tidies them into a trunk that looks like it might be an actual antique and reties her hair, a sure sign she's nervous.

'No one ever puts anything away,' she groans.

On a side table in the hall sits a beautiful arrangement of fresh flowers that reminds me of a previous row, and I hope flowers are locally grown or at least organic, because I doubt Alys has lost any of her principles.

In the dining room, a dark wood table is set formally for five, starched napkins, sparkling cutlery and polished glasses. I wasn't expecting anything half so formal. Cady loves this kind of thing, setting stuff up to be perfect.

On a sideboard, in a silver bucket, sits champagne, waiting to be exploded. I find myself counting the number of people I actually know who have a sideboard. Guilt twists my gut. I never did get around to dropping that hint that maybe champagne wasn't such a great idea. It's a terrible idea. I really am quite a terrible friend.

Cady steers me to the kitchen. It's on the tip of my tongue to make a joke about a posse of drunk teenagers cooking the meal using every available saucepan with no more than a vague idea what they are doing. But the joke's taken away by the smell of burning.

'Got something in the oven?' I ask.

With a horrified look, Cady dives for the cooker, grabs ancient-looking oven gloves and retrieves a huge dish with a billow of smoke. A burned lasagne topped with a layer of blackened crust makes me want to make a joke about getting takeout. But Cady looks at me with such anguish.

'Do you think it looks all right?'

'It'll be fine. Is there a salad or something as well?' I hand over my bottle of wine. Will I soon be wishing I'd bought two cheap bottles of wine instead of one decent one?

'Ooh salad, that's a good idea. I'm doing a garlic bread.' Cady gives a stricken look towards a French stick. No signs (yet) of either garlic or (I'm hoping) vegan butter.

'If lasagne and garlic bread are everyone's favourite, it'll be fine.'

'I've no idea what everyone's favourite is because they never eat anything I cook. I wish I'd thought of a salad.'

'And I wish I'd thought to bring a salad rather than wine,' I say. 'I'd be happy to put one together for you. Make the most of this offer, because salad is actually one of the things I can claim not to mess up.'

'Would you, Keera? That's so kind. I'd better do this garlic bread.'

We both take an uneasy look at the lasagne.

'Could you cover it with tinfoil or something and put it back in a low oven?' I cannot believe Cady's so bad at this that even I'm offering cooking tips.

The whopping fridge is mostly filled with ready-meals. There is a soft cucumber and under-ripe tomatoes.

'Would you have a tin of something like kidney beans or chickpeas?'

Cady looks as bewildered as if she's the stranger in this kitchen, not me

'Oil? Any seasoning? Dried herbs?'

This salad is going to need a lot of optimism.

'I have a tin of tuna! That's good in salad?'

'It might be. If it wasn't for the vegans. That's Alys and me.'

'Oh, of course. I get so flustered.'

Is this the time to bring up the fact that a lot of pasta isn't vegan? What about that crispy (burned) cheese on top of the half-raw lasagne? I don't have the heart.

'I wanted everything to be perfect. It's almost as far from perfect as it can be!'

I stop Cady as she reaches for butter and hand her a vegan spread from the fridge for her garlic bread.

I try to imagine what it's been like for Cady, scooping up the desolate Craven family.

Failing to learn how to cook lasagne has only been a small part of her challenge.

'Shall I open the wine?'

I don't get a chance as I hear the front door open and close, and Rick Craven appears, wearing something I never thought I'd see him in – a tie. And a dark suit that is very well cut, which looks very good on him. I get a lovely sandalwood smell rather than damp earth and mulch, which I'm used to.

'Sorry this celebration greets you with the smell of burning and a disaster salad,' I say. 'But I guess things must be good as you are looking more "sleek French president" than gardener. You haven't given up the gardening, have you?'

When I first met Rick, the two words I'd have used to describe him were crumpled and charming. Now I'd say prosperous – but still charming as he greets me with a smile and leans in to plant a kiss on my cheek and he tells me how pleased he is that I'm here.

'Yes, something smells…' he sniffs the air and grins at Cady and goes to open a window. 'Smells like we need to order takeaway?'

'Keera says it'll be fine,' says Cady hurriedly.

I pop the garlic bread in the oven as I think Cady's forgotten. I think she's also forgotten the garlic.

'Everything Cady does turns out better than she gives herself credit for,' I say. 'I doubt I'd even still be here without Cady's help in the bookshop.'

'I think we can all say that,' says Rick. 'But you can't stop her. Now, is that wine? Do I have time to get changed?' He removes his jacket to reveal a crisp white shirt beneath. If he's doing less physical work gardening, he must be finding another way to work out.

I can't help but still feel slightly uncomfortable around Rick. I don't know what put that horrible idea into Mrs M's head that I've only helped Pip for selfish reasons, one of which is that I'm keen on Rick. He's the sort where he's so charming to everyone half the time it almost comes across as flirting. He's very handsome, whether crumpled and charming, or this new, prosperous and charming version. But he and Cady are the ones I want to get together.

'Cady loves your shop.' He opens the wine. 'Do I alert the kids dinner is go!'

'Pleeease, first just tell me how it went!' says Cady breathlessly. 'I cannot believe you are making me wait.'

'And there was me going to make the big announcement when everyone's together.' He turns to me. 'I did something very brave that I've never done before. I had a meeting with the bank. Me!'

I can tell from the way he's smiling and the buoyant energy flowing from him that it must be good news.

'Stop teasing! You wouldn't save a bad news announcement for over dinner. The bank said yes—didn't they?' Cady's unable to keep the thrill out of her voice.

'They said… yes!' Rick confirms.

Cady squeals and jumps across to Rick and hugs him, leaping excitedly.

Rick's life has really transformed, and now it sounds like the Cravens are properly on their feet. Will they finally move out of Cady's? I feel as sad and as depressed as my salad looks, and then I tell myself that's the wrong reaction. I should be glad.

I didn't know Helena long, but there was more than a hint that she took her own life because of financial stress. Now things have turned around. Only a year on and Rick's in a tie, with clean fingernails, having a meeting with the bank and celebrating his biggest ever contract with champagne. And Helena is not around to see it.

I tell myself sternly that this family has had so much to deal with in the last year, what they need is something to celebrate and a sign that life is moving forward. Life only ever moves on. It's right that Helena belongs in the past. But it hurts. And I find I'm angry at Minty too, because Helena lost that job just when the family was struggling. And it all led to Helena feeling everything was hopeless.

'Let's not wait to give the kids the good news,' says Cady, staring around at the destruction in the kitchen. 'Let's eat!'

20.

Pip joins us and hides silently behind his hair. Alys finally slumps in too, earbuds in, another who hides behind her hair – long, corkscrew curly hair. It wouldn't be hard to imagine Helena is sitting with us at the table. It makes my heart squeeze.

Rick is looking relaxed.

He's found time to change into blue jeans and a faded t-shirt, chattering on, oblivious to any tension around the table. Perhaps he's just used to it. Perhaps he really is just oblivious. Even to the fact that beneath a voluminous jumper, it looks like Alys isn't eating enough at all.

I watched how she put food on her plate, but the minute she could, she swapped her plate for Pip's empty one.

'There is nothing half-baked about your efforts, but only you could produce a dinner that is both burned and raw at the same time,' jokes Rick to Cady.

He puts down his knife and fork. I follow, gladly taking this as permission to stop pushing food around my plate

'All right, I won't keep you in the dark any longer,' Rick says. 'We have something to celebrate.'

The champagne is in my line of sight.

'No, we don't. I assumed the champagne was a sick joke.' Alys tears the buds from her ears. 'We cannot be drinking champagne on the anniversary of Mum's death.'

'I've won a big contract,' Rick announces, as if Alys hadn't spoken. 'It's all down to Cady, who persuaded me to pitch for this work.'

He grins at Cady. 'She helped me with all the paperwork, all the bits I struggle with. I got the news a couple of weeks ago.' He looks at his family. I think he is waiting for joy, or at least congratulations.

Alys's gimlet eyes switch to her father questioningly, but also manages to take in the way Rick reaches across to give Cady's arm a supporting squeeze.

'What big contract?' Pip demands.

'I get to look after a whole bunch of green spaces.'

'Is that gardens?' Pip asks.

'This is the brave new direction for the man who left a job because his customer wanted him to chop down her oak tree and replace it with a patio. Means he's sold out.'

'Even I'd forgotten that.' Rick's smile doesn't falter. 'I was arrogant. It was her garden.'

'You used to have principles.' says Alys. 'Suddenly, you're all about ugly low-maintenance shrubs and the sort of gardening that is the opposite of nature or beauty? You've won a contract to plant up a car park. And you want us to celebrate?'

'I won for my idea that every space can improve biodiversity if managed right,' says Rick, still smiling. 'Even car parks need trees. Have you noticed people always park in the shade? That was in my pitch; proud of that, actually.' He glances at Cady.

'You always told Mum you could never abandon making beautiful gardens in favour of just money. You said—why bother? You know, like that time you rowed about selling Mum's camera to pay the electricity bill. Or have you forgotten Mum?'

'You are right, Alys. It's a challenge. But I never had the confidence to go for work like this. Never thought I'd cope with the paperwork.'

Rick goes on. 'Suddenly, I can help a property company that maintains a lot of green space because companies are looking at their carbon footprints, so they absolutely loved our pitch! Today I met with the bank! They're advancing me a loan so I can take on someone to help me. But it doesn't change that I will always want to create beauty, even if I have to sneak it in. Honestly, what sold it to them was that I pitched about wanting people to feel like they aren't so much in a car park as in a green corridor.'

'What a load of crap.'

'Well, they bought it and are paying me good money,' Rick finally snaps, reaching to top up his wine.

Silence from Pip.

I totally get why Cady was so keen for me to be here. I want to do nothing more than get out of here, this is a family argument. But I owe it to Cady.

I feel I have to speak, break the head of steam Alys is building up.

'Well, this is absolutely wonderful news,' I say, injecting all the positivity I can muster and beaming at everyone. 'Congratulations Rick, I'm thrilled! What agency?'

'Key Keepers,' Cady answers for him.

My stomach plummets. If I didn't constantly remind myself that everything is connected, I'd be shocked, or see it as a sign.

Everything I've been worrying about rushes back in like a tidal wave of reminders of just how complex my life is now, how sucked into the community I've become. My dream of loveliness, calm, and remaining deliciously uninvolved, is in unrecoverable tatters. It feels like more proof that moving here was a mistake.

Alys looks like she's about to say something, and I'm guessing she won't be playing nice.

'Oh. Rick, then you know Minty,' I say quickly to divert her. 'But then, of course you do—Helena worked with her.'

I realise my mistake too late.

Cady looks tight-lipped that I've brought up Helena when this whole evening is about moving on.

'Rick gets on with everyone,' Cady says with a forced smile. 'Even Vampire Minty.'

'Your new business pitch sounds so imaginative,' I say, one eye on Alys. 'Blending the climate crisis with low-maintenance green spaces.'

I was hoping my words might at least give Alys time to pause, to think there is a positive side to her dad's news.

But when I slide her a smile, she gives me daggers.

Alys ends any chance of my feeble efforts smoothing things over. She throws Rick and then Cady a look that could kill. She exits, slamming the door so hard, expensive glassware rattles in the sideboard. She stomps upstairs. Another door slams.

'Well, that sounds a very satisfying door slam,' I say. 'Well practised. That might make her feel better.'

And then Pip, who hasn't spoken a word, follows, although with less of a door slam, more slinking away. Cady bursts into tears.

'Well, I think that went well,' jokes Rick, going to Cady and putting his arms around her. Her sobbing only increases.

About the only thing that went well is that I think I'm saved from having the eat the lasagne.

21.

I've put up a sign saying I'll be back in five minutes. It's Saturday. So I probably shouldn't. But it's also January. I don't think I'll be disappointing any customers.

Cady invited me to her lasagne party to smooth things over, and I don't feel I exactly played my part to perfection. I need to make it up to her.

I've not forgotten I need to make things up to Liv for my inability to focus.

Or that I need to make things up with Minty.

I hope Stacey's bid to dig in her heels about letting go of her mother's valuable riverside property doesn't come back to haunt me. Otherwise, my charm offensive to get Minty not to raise the rent is definitely sunk. Soon, my only option will be to find some money for a bribe.

But I have a cunning plan to drop in on Jaxx and Maya at Halfway and kill two birds with one stone. Cady will be grateful if I smooth Alys's ruffled feathers, and Alys has started working there. And Liv's events venue idea is a good one.

Halfway is much better than the village hall if I can talk Jaxx into it. I hope to get something to report to Liv. Why does it feel like she's my new boss?

Haven't yet worked out a plan to soften Minty's hard-edges, but I will get around to it.

Why is it to-do lists only ever get bigger? It's why I don't bother with them. Liv would tell me that bothering myself about Mrs M's death should be well down any priority list. And she may be right.

'Even with semi-skimmed, a large is three hundred calories.' Alys is serving, and it sounds like she's also dispensing free advice. 'Some people add syrup *and* whipped cream and for your average person, we are talking a quarter of your entire calorie intake *for the day* in just a single coffee.'

'Well, no. I guess…' A pause. 'I guess, don't bother with the pumpkin spice syrup.'

'Sure! Decision on the whipped cream?' Alys goes about making the coffee and carries on with the advice. 'Did you know Starbucks' best-selling flavours are the ones with the least coffee? It's like people don't actually like the taste of coffee, they just like the syrup and cream and shit.'

Jaxx appears from out back, and she definitely caught that last bit. 'Er, Alys, I think we have to remember…' Her pretty face scrunches into an anxious smile.

Jaxx is super-petite, super-efficient, and super-organised. When she's not working, she lets her hair down, which makes me wonder how she even tidies all her curly hair to almost nothing when she's behind the bar.

'I know, I know,' says Alys. 'We never, ever mention Starbucks.'

'And people get to order whatever they choose.'

'I know, I'm just saying.' Alys shrugs at the bemused customer. 'And don't forget tea. With semi-skimmed, tea is less than a hundred calories. Why don't Gen Z drink tea? Or herbal tea—that's full of benefits! You can add a bit of honey—that's good for gut health. Or do what I do, drink your coffee black, like my soul. And that is pretty much what we can call zero calories.' She finishes with an anxious giggle and puts the coffee in front of the customer, who looks at it as if she's no longer convinced she wants it. Alys half-heartedly squirts on some whipped cream.

Jaxx keeps on smiling, if grimly. 'But it all comes free of lectures if you come here again,' she reassures the customer, adding that this one will be on the house and adding a square of sticky flapjack on the side.

'Sorry!' says Alys as the customer takes a table. 'I'll do better, promise!'

'How about a career in nutrition rather than a cafe?' says Jaxx with a laugh.

'Enjoying your new job?' I ask.

'Yeah, nice to have something that's not school and not home, you know?'

'Sorry things are so tough at home.'

'I hope you're not here to tell me Cady tries her best. She really doesn't, you know, but you'll never see that— you're Cady's friend.'

'I hope I'm your friend, too. I do know that what you've been through is tougher than I could ever imagine. I wish I knew the right thing to say to make things any better. But I'm sure there's nothing that can—'

'Well, that's easy, tell Cady to get the hell out of our life.'

'I could do that.'

'But? I can feel a but coming.'

'You're heading off to uni soon?'

And Pip will move on. And Rick will be here. Whether or not it's Cady, Rick won't be single for long. And I really want it to be Cady. But I'm beginning to suspect why that's not happened, why that's never going to happen.

Not with Alys around.

I could tell Alys it's been a year, but she won't see that's nearly long enough for Rick to have found someone else.

'You'll have your own place soon enough.'

'Can't wait. September is almost a year to wait.'

And I cannot see the Craven household not imploding if last night's dinner was normal. 'It's good to want a place of your own, stand on your own two feet. Sometimes, you have to be patient.'

'Not normal to live with Mum's cousin and see the way she looks at him when Mum's only been dead a year. When did it start? Do you know?' Alys glares at me, a scary look. 'You were friends with Mum. Why did you not say anything?'

'I'm not sure…'

'Knew there'd be no point talking to you. No one listens because they just dismiss us as kids. Now, I've got customers. You ordering or not?'

I order my coffee (black, shamed out of my frothy cappuccino with sprinkles) and grab Jaxx for a quick word.

I have failed spectacularly to make a friend of Alys. But I want to have good news to tell Liv when she drops in later.

*

'So, I bring the audience, I keep the ticket money. Jaxx hopes to sell a bit of food and drink on the evening so she won't charge me for the space. No risk for either of us.'

'Keera! Amazing! This is just the boost your business needs. You start drawing up some lists of authors to invite. Hopefully it will take your mind off obsessing about terrible Mrs M and this urge of yours to want to clean up Crossways. You are so imaginative, Keera. Maybe you should write books, as well as sell them. Now, I'm on my way to a swim and sauna with a friend who needs a chat.'

'This is Crossways, and I have way too much imagination and I should let it go. I know.' I sigh.

'I've told you to learn to trust yourself and your intuition again. Your intuition should be telling you people in Crossways get irate over potholes, they don't murder gossipy old ladies. Please tell me you're not still obsessing over whether anyone around here is the type to murder? Even Vampire Minty.'

But my intuition isn't telling me that. It's telling me someone might have.

'Does there have to be a type? People in Crossways feel like aliens half the time, but of course they are just people. Everyone has secrets and grudges. They row.'

'You haven't said how last night went.'

'That's probably because it couldn't actually have gone any worse.'

'Sorry to hear that. Poor Cady.'

'Yes, poor Cady. There was one good thing about the whole evening and that is I don't think I was in any way to blame for the utter chaos and disaster, for once. Rick won this big contract. From Minty at Key Keepers.'

'Before you tell me this is more evidence of a sinister plot, I should remind you one of your first observations about Crossways was that everyone knows everyone else and their business. And I can see Rick easily charming Minty.'

'Helena worked for Minty.'

'You told me Helena worked for everyone at some point.'

'Do you know what would help me let it go? Has Elliott mentioned anything at all about Mrs McFlintock? Is it even a case?'

'At this rate, saving your business is mostly going to be down to me.'

Only a moment ago we'd agreed I'd taken a sensible move to turn my business around. I was close to getting Liv to think I'm not terrible at bookselling.

Now I've upset Liv. She's right, I am making all the wrong decisions.

Trouble is, I think I've got to find a way to convince myself this is all just my imagination. Because I cannot let it go.

22.

I return to the scene of the crime. Or rather, the place where I'm convinced a crime was committed. I could try to fool myself that I enjoy a winter walk as much as anyone, but this dank and horrible place is the opposite of anywhere I'd ever pick for a crisp winter walk. I thought the fog might have lifted finally, but it's more like a permanent mist that creeps from that churning water raging through the sluices. So why does bumping down a potholed, unlit road feel the right thing to be doing?

It's utterly dark. I don't know how Mrs McFlintock stood living out here. Alone for the worst, darkest part of the year. I guess she'd lived there for years and this was home. Still. It cannot be easy for Stacey to come here. The decent thing is to check on how she's doing and I do need to talk to her. And there's a chance she'll be here.

I definitely want to avoid the river. I don't want to look down at the water. I don't park in my usual place, I want to get as close as I can to Mrs M's empty cottage. Maybe the truth was I just didn't want to head to my under-heated, damp, and fragrant flat, not even to spend the evening reading. But I'm surprised when I'm right and Stacey's old Fiat is outside.

Has she come straight from work, still facing the grim task of clearing out, getting closure? I guess she has lots to do here. Maybe she's inside searching through paperwork to see if Mrs M was telling the truth for once, and Stacey has rights to the property? I should go and ask if she's been able to find evidence Minty, or anyone, was here, and hope she doesn't hit me up for any free legal advice.

I know that getting answers might simply be impossible. I very much doubt the police even considered that Mrs M's fall down the stairs wasn't simply an accident. Not in blinkered Crossways, where everyone wants to believe if you keep saying everything is lovely, you make it true. But Crossways is just like everywhere else. It has its unpleasant people. Take Mrs M. Well, I suppose someone did. There might be plenty the police missed, because they wouldn't have been looking.

Out of the darkness looms a dim, grey figure coming straight towards me and I nearly leap out of my skin as well as the seat. But it's not a ghostly apparition. It's a figure in a grey hoodie.

'Pip!' I wind the window down. 'What are you doing here?'

'What are *you* doing here?'

'Clearly, great minds think alike, and this is undoubtedly the best place to spend a freezing January evening. I was sort of on my way home and diverted here. Thought I'd check in on Stacey.'

'I was sort of on my way home and diverted too,' he jokes. Joking is good. Although he's not telling the truth.

Diverting here in my warm car is one thing. He is miles from home, and worry knots my stomach. Is he still such a lost soul? It's how Liv described me recently. Are we two lost souls? Is that what really drew me here this evening?

'I can give you a lift home if you like.'

He hesitates. 'Thought you wanted to talk to Stacey.'

'It's not urgent.'

'Nah. I can walk up to the main road, get a bus. I'll be fine.'

'Will you, Pip? I really hope so.'

'Course,' he says easily. 'I'm not coming here every day to work up the courage to throw myself in, if that's what you're thinking.'

'It crossed my mind.'

'You don't have to drive here every day to make sure I haven't jumped in.'

'I will probably stop when I can completely believe you, Pip. Last night was a shitshow, wasn't it?' When he doesn't respond, I press on. 'I think you're doing really well, under the circumstances, you know. You've coped in your own way and your mother would be very proud. I'm always here, Pip. Never forget that. Not just me. Everyone cares about you.'

'Right.'

'You've your whole life ahead of you, and you can make it anything you want. You are stronger than you know.' I pause. 'If this is turning into a speech from Rocky, you would let me know, wouldn't you? You do know Rocky? Or am I just old?'

That brings a smile underneath all that hair. 'I've heard of Rocky.'

'Giving inspirational lectures is something I might need to work on. Last chance for a lift?'

But Pip's not hanging around. He's already away. For a lost soul, he looks like someone who wants to be somewhere in a hurry. I'm left alone. It's completely dark.

If Stacey's inside going through her mother's things, why are there no lights on?

Sod having to rely on the weak light of the moon and stars getting through this permanent mist. There's a heavy torch in the boot, and I need to check she's all right.

I remember the doorbell doesn't work, so I knock loudly. But this time I'm not going to wait. Why isn't Stacey opening the door? I need to get inside.

Because look what happened to her mother.

23.

The windows are small, and even with the light of my big torch shining inside, I can't see much.

The sound of the water seems especially loud and threatening.

I let myself through the side gate and around the back. I go to shine a light through the window of the kitchen door, but there is no reflection, just a lot of jagged glass. My torchlight picks out a river of glass glinting back at me from the floor. Someone's broken in.

Are they still here?

Where is Stacey?

I picture her hurt, injured. If I'm going to climb through this window (I already know I am), I'd better be careful and make sure it's not me who's taken by surprise.

So I call my go-to person, who I appear to be turning to for help and advice about everything. Liv answers at the first ring, and in a whisper, I tell her what's happening. I'm still going to ignore her advice if it's inconvenient.

'You are not going in there.'

'I might be. I didn't phone for an argument.'

'You phoned so if you die, there's a proper police investigation.'

'I called you because you're sharp and you pick up on things without my having to waste time explaining that Stacey must be inside and needs my help. I have to go in.'

'You know the right thing to do is call the police.'

'The window's broken, but there are no lights. Why's the place in darkness when her car's here? I don't think anyone else can still be in there. I just want to check. I won't even have to kick down any doors.'

'Keera—no one ever goes in without backup.' Bossy as ever.

'You are my backup, Liv.'

'I'll make some calls. Stacey might be safely at home.'

'So why's her car here? You have her number?'

'I can get Stacey's number with probably three calls. Like you're always saying, everything in Crossways is connected. I am also calling Elliott.'

'No, you don't need to—'

She ends the call.

Liv calling Elliott is better than calling it in officially. But I can't wait. Someone probably thought they were breaking into an isolated, empty building. I have to check Stacey is all right.

Adrenaline rushes through my veins as I carefully climb through the window. Why did I ever think I could become a sensible grown-up, moving from the city into the peaceful countryside, navigating nothing more tricky than who on the parish council I needed to be nice to? Was Supportive Mum too annoyingly perceptive? Do I attract trouble? Or do I simply go towards it?

Even in idyllic Crossways, I am still standing with a torch in my hand, breaking into an isolated cottage where at least one criminal has been in ahead of me and where someone died a few days ago.

I arrive in an embarrassingly awkward heap and think an elephant could have landed more elegantly. So much for being quiet. I'm glad no one is here to witness it.

I don't cut myself too badly, even though there is glass everywhere. I pick my way through the kitchen and into the short hallway. More glass shines in the torchlight as I follow a trail I guess comes from the bottom of the intruder's shoes.

I flash my torch around the ground floor, glad it's a big torch, and I hold it ready, like a weapon, looking for any signs of Stacey, or anyone.

I shine the beam into the front room, pleased I've been here once before and know the layout. If this was a burglary, surely the place would be ransacked? The drawers in a bureau in the lounge are shut. If someone's searched, they've done it carefully. Nothing looks disturbed. Or they were disturbed? It doesn't take long to see there is no sign of Stacey downstairs.

I stand at the bottom of the steep stairs that brought the end of Mrs M. I hear myself gulp audibly as I feel the shadow of Mrs M lying dead on the tiled floor under my feet. If I'm going to do this, I have to go up. I take a moment to try to quiet my rapidly beating heart by inhaling some deep breaths.

'Stacey!' I call into the darkness. 'Are you here?'

No response. The place feels empty, luckily even of any ghosts. If anyone's here, it'll be Stacey, lying injured on the floor or worse.

Sod trying to do this quietly. I decide to switch on lights. I blink painfully at the sudden brightness, and go through, switching on lights in every room.

And then I'm ready. I shake a little as I go up those steep carpeted stairs.

It's my first time upstairs, but it's pretty much the same story as downstairs.

Luckily, Stacey is not here, lying injured, attacked, or otherwise. I would start to breathe easier, only... What's Stacey's car doing here?

Any hope this house would contain evidence of what happened to Mrs M evaporates. There's sparseness here, in the furnishings, the small pile of spare bedding on an unmade bed in the second bedroom. I take a quick poke into two wardrobes, which reveal mostly that Mrs M wasn't much of a hoarder, didn't spend big on herself, although there is quite the pile of flowery trousers.

Yet, there is that incongruous fancy coffee machine Stacey had her eye on, and the BMW. She could splash out if she wanted to.

I'm now regretting my rash phone call to Liv. How likely is it that Elliott will head out on a freezing evening to help his mum's friend, who's making the risky decision of going into a house that's been burgled? Elliott's very unlikely to respond to his mother's request for backup. But has this place been burgled?

There's been a break-in. But who'd be passing? The only person who comes here regularly is Stacey. I suppose me. Oh. And Pip. I'm suddenly struck by wondering exactly Pip was doing out here? It was late for him. He's normally here earlier. And another thought I should have logged more quickly. Stacey had her eye on the BMW.

Oh.

Stacey's Fiat is outside, but Mrs M's BMW isn't. Ah. Should have worked out right away that Stacey's car is here because Stacey has swapped cars.

So Stacey was never in danger of being here and being attacked. My mistake.

I work this out just as there's the sound of a car approaching, headlights piercing the gloom as a car rockets at a very unwise speed to crunch over those potholes, doing all kinds of damage to its suspension and undercarriage.

I'm pretty sure that's Elliott and I'm even more sure I'm about to look really dumb.

The car screeches to a stop right outside.

He's been quick, must have dropped everything and rushed here. Dragging him out in a freezing January evening on a wild goose chase, all based on the fact I didn't think things through. He's bound to be in a great mood.

Now I feel guilty, plus stupid. Stacey was never in any danger. As I go to open the front door, I'm thinking the biggest danger I'm in this evening is just how angry Elliott has a right to be.

24.

The kitchen is too small to avoid being glowered at.

'What are you doing here again?' Elliott asks, despite my showing him the broken glass. 'What am *I* doing here again?'

I had tried to explain that it was all a misunderstanding, but that didn't stop him barging in and checking no one was around, which I'd already done anyway.

'You shouldn't have climbed in through a window, as technically, you've just committed a burglary too,' he lectures.

I do know that. But I bite my lip, knowing I'm too much in the wrong not to deserve getting told off.

'And you certainly shouldn't have climbed in if you thought there was any danger.'

'I am so, so in the wrong, and I am sorry,' I say again. 'It was because of what happened to Mrs McFlintock and I thought Stacey was in danger—that's not breaking and entering, is it, if you go into a building because you think someone's in danger?' I cannot help but argue my case.

'But she's not even here, right?'

'No. That was her car outside, and the place was dark. So I—'

'Jumped to the wrong conclusion.'

I take a deep breath before I answer. 'Yes. I did that. Sorry. But there *was* a break-in.'

It's like being talked to by a teacher, which is annoying on so many levels, not least that I don't think he's any older than me. I bite my lip harder, reminding myself that I get rude when I get stressed. I have to try to watch what I say because he's Liv's son, and he's dragged himself out here to do me a favour. Well, do *her* a favour. He hardly knows me. And I am grateful, truly.

I've met Elliott only once. He's a reader, but came into my shop with the air of someone who was doing it to please his mother and bought a book under a feeling of heavy sufferance. I kind of guess Liv bosses him about like she bosses me.

'It doesn't exactly look like a burglary. The place hasn't been searched,' Elliott says with a scant glance around the kitchen. 'The window might not have been broken deliberately. It's windy. Things fly about. Windows break.'

'But do they?'

'The owner might be repairing that window all the time. But we don't know, do we? Because this isn't your house. You can't even tell me if anything's been taken.'

'You cannot be serious about a freak gust of wind. You know that's a terrible explanation.'

We both stare at the trail of glass. I wait for him to suggest it could just as easily have been my shoes that carried that glass from the back door through the hallway.

I feel myself getting stressed.

'All right, maybe I'd be grumpy if my mum ordered me to drive out here in the dark and fog. I can say sorry again. But there was a break-in. And even the owner can't tell you if anything's been taken, because she's dead. Died a few days ago.' I leave the comment there.

'It's probably kids,' says Elliott. 'You probably disturbed them. Makes it even more irresponsible to do what you did. Did you see anyone around?'

A guilty flush spreads up my neck, because of course I saw Pip. Actually, now that Elliott's made me think of it, this is even worse. I guess it's pretty likely it was Pip who broke in, which makes me feel even more stupid for alerting the police. Even an off-duty one in probably the ugliest jumper I have ever seen.

But why would Pip break in? Hoping to find something? Did he find it?

Elliott is waiting for an answer.

'How likely is it I'd see anyone here? On a freezing, foggy evening like this? And kids?' I scoff. 'Out here? Really?' I lie – convincingly?

My experience has taught me most people lie and keep secrets when they talk to the police. I think the police expect it. So it's fine not to mention Pip.

'We will, of course, let the owner know,' Elliott says formally.

'Already told you that might be difficult. I think there's even a dispute about this place, about who has a right to live here now—after the last owner *died*. Just days ago. You do know Mrs McFlintock, who lived here, just died?' I bite my lip to stop myself from adding *died in mysterious circumstances* like I'm in a bad spy film.

I did hope he'd see there's a connection here. He'd promise to go over what happened the day Mrs McFlintock died. And maybe find there was something suspicious about her death.

That hope is dying.

'Now there's been a break-in,' I say. 'But I do get it. It's just an old lady and a fall. Nothing's worth the effort of investigating without a chance of a watertight case and a conviction.'

Elliott rubs a hand distractedly through his sandy hair. He's kind of short for a policeman. I daresay some people could find something in him cute. But I've had the wrong kind of career and sat on the wrong side of a courtroom to ever really trust the police. Plus, he's wearing tight jeans with an awful chunky-knit jumper that belongs on a much older man, along with a cross expression, and a recent, too-close shave.

That raw look from a shave in the evening tells me I might have ruined his plans by dragging him out here.

I might possibly have ruined any chance of us ever getting on well. But that might be a good thing, since sometimes I get a sneaking suspicion Liv has a secret agenda and is out to play matchmaker.

Luckily, neither Elliott nor I want that, even though I did have wild imaginings about meeting up with Elliott this evening. They involved him being intrigued and how we'd end up comparing notes. That's gone out the window. So why do I plunge on in, trying to get him to see there's something here worth him investigating?

'Did you know the rental agent, Minty Carstairs, was trying to get Mrs M out so she could rent this place for shedloads more?'

He says nothing, he is not bothering to hide that he thinks I've wasted his time. But now he's here, I cannot help but try to push my agenda a little. Well, not *my* agenda – I am definitely not sticking my nose in – but is there any kind of investigation into Mrs M's death?

'I get it. An elderly woman dies, so I bet that meant no one even treated this as a crime scene. But she was fit and appeared much younger than she was. And throw in that I'm pretty sure Mrs M was sitting on a valuable property paying a below-market rent because she had something on Minty Carstairs. And now she's died there's a new battle going on as Mrs McFlintock's daughter feels she can prove she's got rights to this place. And, to be honest, everyone was a bit afraid of Mrs M as she was a terrible gossip. Worse, if she didn't have anything on you, she'd make it up. So if anyone was going to get pushed down their own stairs in Crossways, it would be Mrs McFlintock.'

I didn't mean to quite come out with all of that. Did it make me sound like I think I'm in a bad spy film?

Elliott rubs his chin thoughtfully.

'Well, lucky then we took crime scene photographs and had a full forensic team here dusting for fingerprints. DNA fragments are off to the lab. Plus, we took plaster casts of all the footprints left outside—there were plenty, as it's muddy. Now all we need to do is match it to a boot of one of our main suspects.'

His sarcasm raises my blood pressure, and I feel myself flush scarlet in an attempt not to respond just as rudely.

'She was the most unpopular person in Crossways.'

'Unpopular people have accidents just the same as the popular ones,' says Elliott. 'Even the ones malicious enough to make up damaging rumours. Even those people do not get murdered in Crossways, people just grumble about them. Sometimes quite loudly.'

Luckily, he walks away just before I get the chance to completely hate him.

I think that's it, he's leaving. But Elliott begins a lecture that involves questioning my actions in words that involve an uncountable number of unnecessary expletives, interspersed with a gist about *wasting time*. Both his and mine, I think.

'Well, you are a whole lot grumpier than I expected,' I say. 'I have apologised. Several times. I thought I was doing the right thing.'

'No! You did completely the wrong thing. I have a right to be about as grumpy as you might expect anyone to be whose evening was ruined by my mother insisting I drive to the back of beyond because the local bookseller has taken it into her head to break into a building where there is a high chance she'll be attacked! And who seems to think she's an amateur sleuth.'

'I should have been smarter and worked out about the cars sooner. My mistake. I am famous for them.'

'And it's very sad that an elderly woman died falling down some very steep stairs,' Elliott says. 'Maybe it's not surprising you got a bit spooked.'

'Spooked!'

A change of subject is desperately needed before I fall out with Liv's son completely. And he did drive out here.

'I can say sorry again if it helps. So, were you doing something special that I ruined this evening?'

'Actually, I was on my way to a…'

The way he tails off, the way he glances away from me and (I swear) blushes slightly, makes me wonder again about that close shave.

'For a minute, I thought you were going to say you were on your way to a date. But not in that chunky jumper! Sorry! My mouth. I swear it has a mind of its own. I'm stressed because I thought Stacey might be in trouble. She was the one who found her mother dead. I don't think Mrs M was alone when she died and… No, forget it.'

'It's fine,' he says. 'Mum did the right thing. It's you who didn't do the right thing breaking in here.'

'Yes, I've got it. It's ok, I don't need the lecture. Again. And sorry for the comments about your chunky knit jumper. It's my worst habit—I tend to get a bit rude when I get stressed. It's a very nice jumper,' I lie, and I hope this time it was convincing.

My apology makes Elliott seem a lot calmer. He must have been more worried about the jumper than I thought.

'All right,' he says, 'so you say this is all connected. So why did someone break in?'

I guess this is my chance to get him to see I'm not just some over-imaginative bookseller who thinks she's starring in one of her own books. I go over everything I've got, determined to offer something, and I've got nothing.

'What do you think were they after? Do you think anything's missing? Apart from a valuable car, which we have an explanation for.'

I glance at where the expensive coffee machine was, which is now an empty space. Burgled? Or did Stacey take that too, like she did the car?

My mind is turning over everything rapidly. I have to find even a shred of actual evidence to offer that backs up my suspicions. I must have something. I need something.

Facing a pissed-off policeman in a house I've broken into is not an ideal situation for thinking things through logically.

Even so, all I can come up with are things I absolutely cannot say, such as my grounds for suspicion started with a changed hair appointment.

I need to find the right thing. I want to look at least reasonably smart, trustworthy, and not at all like some panicky, over-imaginative, full of conspiracies and conjecture bookseller who reads too many books. And thinks they're an amateur sleuth.

I have nothing. Nothing to offer that's going to allow me to leave with even the smallest amount of my dignity intact.

25.

Elliott doesn't leave, but starts looking around again. I realise he's not assessing it as a crime scene when he appears with a piece of cardboard and some tape, and sets about covering over the broken window. Smart idea. Wish I'd thought of it. He also hands me a plaster for a cut on my palm that's still bleeding. I guess he foraged that from the bathroom cabinet.

'So what was the rumour Mrs McFlintock spread about you?' he asks me.

Too smart again. My flush returns.

'What makes you think she spread one about me?' I stick on the plaster and hunt around for a dustpan and brush. Do something useful.

He gives me a look with one raised eyebrow that he totally gets from his mum.

He's waiting for an answer, and I cannot avoid his level gaze or how he's so much smarter than that chunky-knit jumper makes him look. I can hardly refuse to tell him. Not after he came racing out here. Plus, it does prove my point about how poisonous Mrs M was.

'I helped out this teenage boy, Pip Craven, who was desolated by his mother's death. I thought he might be going to run away, disappear. The whole family was in pieces. I wanted to help, who wouldn't? Mrs McFlintock accused me of…' I hear my breathing get faster and can feel my blood pressure rising, 'having *unhealthy* reasons for helping Pip. I don't know exactly what poison was in her mind. She also accused me of being motivated by wanting to get in his Dad's good books. Believe me, she didn't put it that politely. Trousers were mentioned. She enjoyed spreading malicious lies. That's why I say the most unpopular person in Crossways had a fatal accident.'

Elliott digests this as he rips off a piece of brown tape with his teeth. 'I'm sorry about that. Surprised you care so much what happened to her if she said that about you.'

Elliott's doing a grand job of patching up the broken window against the weather. Where's a dustpan and brush? Unless Mrs M was so forgetful she put it back in some strange place.

'Thank you for being frank,' says Elliott. 'Now I'd like to be too. She wasn't young, lived alone, and had such bad stairs, even I wouldn't want to run down them in the dark, especially not with those hard tiles at the bottom. Why do you care so much about a woman who was seriously unpleasant to you? To come here on a freezing, foggy evening?'

It's a fair question. He may as well have said *sticking my nose in.*

'I've nowhere better to be, I guess. I've got a lot on my mind and the flat I'm renting is dismal. Plus I guess no one's treating her death as anything other than an accident, but she was poison. People were afraid of her. The rumours she spread about people were proper vicious. In Crossways, everyone knows your business, and you have to face people every day who have heard something shameful about you. I suppose I've got involved, even though I never meant to. Stacey was hunting through her mum's paperwork, I was curious if she found anything. I suppose I'm slightly guilty of looking for a distraction. And I am nosy.'

I find the dustpan and brush in the downstairs loo. Reminds me of the notebook I found in the sugar caddy; the sign Mrs M was getting forgetful.

How did she cope remembering all the stories she made up about so many people?

'And I have a habit of logging little discrepancies. And I suppose I have a strong feeling for justice, and if someone did shove her down those stairs—that's murder and someone's going to get away with it. '

'It's possible you read too many books.'

'No, I definitely do that.'

'And maybe you're finding Crossways a bit dull—a point on which you are completely correct, by the way. Why'd you move here? Crossways doesn't seem your sort of place at all.'

'I do not need to invent the fact that Mrs M's death is suspicious because my life is lacking in excitement. Believe me, the knife-edge of selling enough books to pay rent and eat is enough. Bookselling is living on a precipice enough for anyone.'

NICKI THORNTON

I wonder if Stacey found anything when she was looking for that lease. I wonder if Mrs M ever wrote any of it down, all her stories about people. Must have been tricky keeping track of all those lies she spread. I'd love to have something to show Elliott what a piece of work she was and it gives me an idea.

I lift the lid on the sugar caddy where Mrs M had put a thick notebook. Was that a mistake? Or…

The sugar caddy is empty. The notebook has disappeared.

Now I want to imagine that notebook was definitely hidden and contains a collection of Mrs M's best and most useful spiteful stories.

I so wish I'd read it when I had the chance, rather than dismissing it as being a sign that Mrs M was starting to misplace things. I guess I'll never know if it was full of all the dirt she was spreading about everyone in Crossways.

My phone rings, an unknown number, but I'm guessing it's Stacey, because Liv is bound to have succeeded in contacting her by now. It is Stacey, and I explain I dropped by and noticed the broken window and that Liv sent her son, who is in the police.

'What should I do about it?' Stacey sounds worried and nervous.

'We've used some cardboard and some tape and covered the window for now. I'd get a glazier to call to fix it. It was probably a chance thing; it doesn't look like anything was taken. I did notice the coffee maker's gone…'

'That was me,' says Stacey. 'Well I always wanted one.'

'I think you were just unlucky. It could have been kids. Or even just the wind.' I do not miss Elliott's smirk.

'Maybe you disturbed someone,' Stacey says. 'Thank you, Keera.'

I hate accepting thanks when I feel I've done nothing.

'Do you think someone might have been in before?' Stacey asks. 'I mean, since Mum died.'

'Why? Do you?'

'Mum had this really fancy phone. I can't find it anywhere.'

A couple of days ago, I wouldn't have marked Mrs M as someone who'd have had a fancy phone. Now, it doesn't surprise me. Joely offered her discounts to stop her spreading her lies. I wonder who else in Crossways might have been motivated to sweeten her up. It's getting easier to believe Mrs M did have a secret source of income.

Elliott can hear both sides of this conversation.

'Could you ask Stacey to check and notify us if anything does appear to be missing?' he asks stiffly.

I pass the message on.

Elliott's listening, but I have to ask, 'There was a notebook your mum kept in the sugar caddy. That's gone too. You don't know what happened to it, do you?'

'Mum kept a notebook in the sugar caddy?'

'Yes, she did.'

It's not difficult to interpret that cool, clear gaze as Elliott listens to discussions about a missing coffee machine and *a notebook in a sugar caddy*.

I'm still stinging from being called an amateur sleuth.

I think I have just lost any credibility that I do not suffer from an overactive imagination and see the sinister everywhere.

'I don't know anything about that,' says Stacey. 'It's not there now? Is it important?'

'Probably not,' I say. But it might have been. Have I let my one chance slip through my fingers of proving my suspicions?

I've failed to convince Elliott to take Mrs M's death even a little bit seriously. I've no way of proving any of it, I've really no option left. I have to do what I've been telling myself to do. The sensible thing. I need to let this go.

26.

Broken Pieces, Day 275

Daily challenge – Remember it's just an empty house

'Is it true our house is being sold?'

Alys chucked in the question as she was helping herself to peas.

Pip liked having a big sister who made people feel uncomfortable, mostly because he could never be bothered. And he would never dare to say the stuff she came out with.

All eyes went to Dad, who looked surprised that he should be expected to answer.

'Then I guess it is. Dad's selling our house,' said Alys matter-of-factly.

They were sitting around Cady's dining table, so polished and shiny the wine glasses were reflected in it.

When did they become a family that sat around in the dining room to eat? Had they become that family?

Everything was gradually breaking apart and setting them adrift from the life they had before, being remade as something different. Now it sounded as if that was happening to their home too. *Old home.*

Their house was being sold. Where did that leave the wrecked remains of the Cravens? How did he feel about that?

Homeless. Uncomfortably numb. It was happening too fast to even take in properly.

Alys was moving her fork through a pile of limp lettuce. Everything Cady served always seemed to be soggy. Pip waited for her to ask all the questions he wanted answers to.

What was going to happen to them next?

Cady had picked them up and moved them here in the blur. She'd stepped in and did the things Dad was too broken to even think about. Cooking, washing, cleaning.

Was this move to Cady's going to be permanent? Could Cady possibly want this to be permanent? But if their house was being sold...

Before-Cady had spare rooms and stillness. Now every space was gradually taken over by the Cravens, things flung in every corner. Damp towels dropped on the bathroom floor. Cady grumbled about all of it.

But Pip liked it here a lot better. It was better. Even though Alys occasionally said, '*But it's Cady's house, not ours.*' Pip had started to feel that this was their house too.

But what did Cady think? What did Dad think?

Alys chewed at the frayed ends of her jumper with more enthusiasm than she'd shown for her shepherd's pie, salad, and green peas.

'Shepherd slop,' she'd announced. *Who serves shepherd's pie with salad anyway?* She'd sat there, watching shepherd's pie dribble through the tines of her fork. *'Is it supposed to do that?'*

'It's our home,' said Alys. 'I think we should have been consulted.'

Pip looked at Dad, waiting for him to say something. Something proper, something real.

'You're being consulted now.' Which, of course, was a completely big lie. 'What you think is important, of course.' Another lie.

Dad's get-away-with-anything smile never worked on Alys. He put down his fork, looking glad of the excuse probably, picking up his wine with a lot more enthusiasm.

'Then if my opinion counts, I say no,' she said.

Cady reached for the bottle of wine in the middle of the table, topped up their big glasses even more. And gave a small amount to Alys, then hesitated and made it a big one. 'It's a very good idea, Alys.'

Pip considered their old house, sitting there empty, a bit like Dad's face right now. Pip examined his feelings and it didn't take long to reach the conclusion he'd be glad if they stayed at Cady's permanently.

But Cady... Would she want them? Her plan must have been that they would go back to the other side of town.

Then he felt torn, recognising he'd been worrying that they would have to go back, which made him feel disloyal to Mum.

When Pip met Mum in his dreams, as he did often, he had to remember all over again in the morning that she was gone. He still preferred that sometimes he could fool himself and expect Mum to walk right in. Even though that just meant a flood of pain when he remembered.

Sometimes, particularly if he was deep into his favourite game, General Oblivion, the one game that truly took his mind away from everything else, it could get so there was only the game.

Sometimes he did that thing of surfacing and went out of his room and reality properly swerved, spiralled, came back into focus. Because he had to remember all over again that this was the new reality. He wasn't even in his old room anymore, their old house. Mum was dead, and he'd never see her again. They could never go back. Was that why Dad was selling?

'So how do we stop it?' Alys asks. 'I do not want it sold.'

But if it meant they stayed here, maybe Pip did. Did Alys want to go back? Pip worried that Cady's niceness would come to an end. She'd want her life back. Cady would get fed up, bored, in the way Mum always got bored with things. She'd decide taking on two teenagers wasn't worth it. And if Cady got bored, they'd have nowhere to go back to. Cady, particularly, might not want Alys.

'Minty reckons it'll fetch a decent price in the current market,' said Dad.

'I don't know who Minty is, but I do know she should mind her own business,' snapped Alys.

'It is for the best, Alys,' said Dad.

'When people tell you they are doing things for your own good it usually means they don't really care how much it hurts you. And they mean they are doing what's best for them.'

'Your dad still goes over there to look after it,' said Cady gently. 'Homes need people living in them. Someone to live in it and love it.'

The garden was easily the best part of the house. At the height of summer, sweet peas tumbled over groups of wigwam canes. Mum would be there, a big glass of white wine, sitting on a chair on the smooth lawn and giggling as she fired instructions about what flowers she wanted him to plant. He could grow anything.

Pip was pleased he found that memory, because they were starting to slip away. She was starting to slip away.

He got a sharp feeling in his chest as he thought of another family enjoying that garden. Maybe Alys was right. Maybe Alys got that sharp feeling too.

'Alys. This is your home now,' smiled Cady.

Did she mean that? Could they live here, like, forever?

From the stony look on Alys's face she was not buying that Dad popping over to do a bit of gardening was any sort of reason not to keep the house. She pointed out (quite reasonably) that Dad liked nothing better than having a garden to potter in, and Cady's wasn't a pottering garden (true). Dad had created the perfect space for Cady. One that looked beautiful, but was functional.

'And also—' Cady went on brightly, her voice rising to prevent Alys from leaping in, 'think about what you'll do with the money.' Cady sounded like she'd finally played her trump card. And it was a big one.

27.

Liv shakes food in a bowl for Jackson Brodie, who also arrived early this morning. Liv was kind enough to bring me a breakfast pastry. She's now feeding me and the cat, who looks like he had a tough night.

Liv returns to nursing a hot cup of green tea, her butt firmly ensconced on the heater. She's reprimanding me about breaking in, although listening to some of my ideas, but mostly pouring cold water on them.

I give a deep sigh. 'I thought talking it through with you would be useful.' I rub Jackson under the chin.

'It is,' says Liv, raising one eyebrow. 'Because I'm talking you out of wasting your energy on the wrong thing.'

'Thought you'd be interested,' I say, a little too sharply. I don't want to piss off Liv. I need her to think helping me at the bookshop is fun, as it's not like she hasn't got another gazillion things she could do.

'I hope that sigh isn't because you'd rather stand here speculating than selling a book. Margot is approaching. She has plenty of money and could be persuaded to read a lot more.'

'It was you who said not to ignore my instincts if I felt there was something odd about Mrs M's death,' I say.

'I did?'

'In that incredibly long list of what Keera must do better, you wrote down to trust my instincts.'

Liv sips her tea and looks at me kindly.

'That was because I can tell you've lost your belief in yourself and your trust in the world. It was actually about trusting your instincts about not closing a possible door on a hot customer like Sully Blake. Not about becoming our sheriff.'

'I must look at that list again.'

Liv produces it from somewhere and waves it in front of me.

'I just need to let you and Cady write my blueprint for success?' I'm guessing Cady is going to join us soon since Rick Craven's gardening van parked up outside not long ago.

'Well, she has done wonders for Rick,' says Liv.

I remind myself of Liv's blueprint for my success.

1. Stay in business – <u>number one priority</u>.
2. Cut costs. Action: Go back to Minty immediately – if no movement on rent, demand to speak to landlord directly.

'Leave the customers to us. Go do your charm offensive with Minty. Get a meeting with your landlord,' urges Liv.

I don't feel any nearer ready to talk to Minty than I was for my last failed attempt. But Liv points out that if I don't succeed with Point 2, I will be forced to invoke Point 3, which is a lot worse.

3. Consider source potential for additional funds to see through bad patch, eg bank loan or Supportive Mum (unless you have other secret sources of wealth)

'I'm so lucky to have you, Liv; don't give up on me just yet. Minty it is.'

Last night I put aside the book I was reading and sat in my damp flat, thinking about how the black mould in the corner kind of looks like a flying seagull. And I tried to start a list: Authors who might come to Crossways for an event. But I could only think of another question: What was Pip doing at Harcourt Pools?

Did he break in? I guess I have to find a way to ask him. My life is suddenly full of difficult conversations I need to have. Did he steal the notebook? That would mean he knew it was there. He could easily have seen my headlights and got out of there quickly. Perhaps I really did interrupt the burglary. But was he coming from the path to the water, or from the cottages? I can't be sure.

Why did Pip visit Harcourt Pools so often? If I believe she had an urgent meeting with someone, the most uncomfortable question might be whether I have to include Pip as a possible visitor. He definitely chatted to Mrs M. It's easy to forget he's seventeen, almost an adult. Still traumatised from last year. Could he have got into an argument with her? Mrs M was an unpleasant person who could have got into an argument with anyone.

She had an accident and fell down the stairs. I should be content to leave it at that. Because I am beginning to realise if I do carry on trying to find out who might have been there, who might have given Mrs M a shove, it's going to include people I know.

I should listen to Liv, who's serving a customer – an easy transaction as Margot is just collecting an order. Liv's waiting for me to leave the shop, and to leave things alone. But I guess, if I go talk to Minty, I can try again to get her to admit she was the one Mrs M had the urgent meeting with the day she died. Then I don't have to consider Pip.

'Actually, I might even have one name for you,' says Liv, once Margot leaves. 'Someone who would find themselves at the top of the list if the police do investigate.'

'Sounds great! Are you going to tell me who?' I say.

'Someone she would have trusted enough to let into her home.'

Not Pip. I hope she's not thinking of Pip.

'Someone Mrs M was threatening to spread unpleasant stories about. Someone who recently fell out with her. Someone with a temper.'

'All interesting. Who?'

'Keera, sweetie, it's you.'

28.

'Now will you please put all of this obsession to one side,' says Liv. 'Go focus on what actually needs to be done.'

It's not far along the high street to get myself in a better frame of mind than last time I tried this. I need to be assertive, yet friendly. Get Minty on-side. I can do this.

I'm almost glad when I ring the Key Keepers' doorbell and there is no answer. But as I turn to head back to Between the Lines, I know Liv is right. And last time I was here, Minty was in, just not answering. Minty was arguing with Stacey. I got in just by giving the door a hefty shove.

If Minty's not in the mood for visitors, it might be a good time to catch her at a vulnerable moment. Plus I cannot face Liv if I don't give it a proper try.

I give the door an experimental nudge and it moves a little. I glance around before giving the door more than a nudge. It moves a bit more. Last time I put my shoulder to it. This time, I take a step back, glance around again, and give it a really good, heavy, satisfying kick. It slams back against the wall.

I really do like kicking things. Maybe that's why I'm so rubbish at bookselling – not enough opportunity to kick down doors.

This time, no argument is going on upstairs. All is quiet. Maybe I'm wrong and Minty simply isn't here? Well then… Who wouldn't be curious to find out more, if an opportunity happened to present itself? I haven't forgotten about that very tatty-looking folder Minty took out of the green filing cabinet. Mrs McFlintock's lease. It probably contains details of the deal Mrs M had on her valuable riverside property, the one Minty wanted her out of. And that Stacey now feels she has rights to. If Minty's not here. I might get some answers.

I tread quietly up the dusty stairs. I have a perfect right to be here. I call out. I push open the door at the top of the stairs.

Minty's right there at the desk. But I can see why she didn't answer. She has her back to me and she's slumped forward. Taking a wee daytime nap.

Even my kicking down the door didn't wake her. Do I try to sneak over to the filing cabinet? What I should do is wake the slumbering Minty and be assertive about my lease. This time I'm determined Minty isn't going to run rings around me. I put my shoulders back and tell myself I'm taking charge.

As I edge forward my brain finally registers what I'm actually looking at. Only slowly do I see properly and take it in. The horror as reality forces itself in. The metallic smell should have alerted me right away.

Blood. Blood matted into blonde hair. Blood pooling on the glass desk. Minty's dead. Her head bashed in by a heavy steel paperweight of the Eiffel Tower.

29.

I don't want to take in the horror.

I don't want to see this. I don't want it to be real. Why would anyone want to kill Minty? It looks like someone snatched up that paperweight. An argument?

I could have been standing there frozen for hours. But I force myself to cross the office floor, to get close. I reach for her limp hand. I try to find a pulse. I'm closer than I want to be to the bloody blonde hair flopped over her face. I try not to look too closely.

There's so much blood. There is no pulse. She's definitely gone.

I fumble for my phone. I'm calling emergency services and beginning to take things in properly. This can only have just happened. So while I make the call, I also do the sensible thing and nervously approach the only other door.

I fling it open, relieved to find an empty bathroom. Whoever did this has already gone. I force myself to look back at the grisly sight of her dead body.

Minty was at the top of my list of people who'd want Mrs McFlintock out of the picture. I could have been persuaded that Mrs M's death was an accident, but now... But where does this leave things?

Minty was my prime suspect. Now she's dead.

Then the final reality of what I am seeing slots into place. I take in what I should have noticed immediately.

It's not Minty.

It's as if reality spins, and I no longer trust what I'm seeing.

But it is definitely not Minty. Minty's far more angular.

I do know who wears those heavy-rimmed glasses.

It's Stacey.

Stacey's body is slumped across Minty's desk. What was Stacey doing here alone? I swallow down all the horror, and another question surfaces. Did whoever did this think that it was Minty sitting there? Was that what happened?

I've learned a few things in my previous life. Not all of them legal. Some of them make this next bit easier. I know what I'm going to do. I parcel the horror into a tight place inside me.

My very first day at my old job, my boss sent me to a crime scene. I had to take photos, collect evidence. Not throw up.

It wasn't such a bad crime scene. I guess my boss was gentle on me, although I didn't think so at the time. The body had already been removed by the police. You might say the police made more mess with their search, forensics, and taking all the fingerprint and DNA samples. Apart from all the blood spatter.

My boss was testing me, seeing how good I'd be at doing what needed to be done. Nearly ten years in my old job have taught me that you can tell a lot from a crime scene even if you're there only briefly.

I reckon I have less than twenty minutes before the police get here from Harcourt nick. And I need all the steely resolve all those years have taught me.

This is different – this is the first time I've known the victim. And I'm involved. I've been convinced someone pushed Mrs M down her stairs – that there's a murderer in idyllic Crossways. I've had suspicions. Now, Stacey is dead. Why?

I have no answers, but it looks like she was hit from behind. I hope she knew little about it. But I don't want to think about that. What was Stacey doing here? And where is Minty? Did Minty do this? Was Minty here? Or did Stacey sneak in the same way as I did? Was Stacey pleased to find the place empty? Looking for something?

I do know not to mess up a crime scene. I'll need to be very, very careful. But I guess it's time to be grateful that ten years of practise has hardened me into doing what needs to be done, because I've clocked that tatty buff folder – the one I saw Minty take out after we talked about Mrs M's lease. Didn't Stacey say she failed to find her mother's copy? What was Stacey looking for? What did Stacey find?

My curiosity overcomes everything else, and I edge forward, skirting the body, trying to get to that folder. All my mistrust of the police overcomes any lurking reluctance, because I'm still the only one who's even suspicious there's something very big and very dark going on in Crossways. I knew Minty was in this up to her soft, white neck. But up to her neck in what, exactly? I need to see what evidence is in that file.

I have to push aside that I know the victim, trying not to remember how recently I talked to her. How we shared tea and biscuits after her mum died. How I couldn't get any evidence so that I'd be taken seriously. Why I didn't voice my suspicions loudly enough over Mrs M's death. Because now, Stacey's dead.

That tatty folder might be my big chance to finally get the truth. Mrs M was hiding secrets, I'm sure of it. The folder is sitting on the desk alongside Stacey's right hand. Only partially sitting in blood, but still. I have to reach it. I have to read that file. I just need to get it open without getting my fingerprints all over it, and I think I can do it.

I take a pen from my back pocket and carefully lift the cover of the buff folder.

But I'm disappointed. The folder is empty.

I check around for any spilled paperwork on the desk or floor. The desk is glass and there is something beneath it. A thick envelope. That's going to be trickier to get to without messing up any evidence. Even so, I'd like to take a quick peek at what's inside, even better, take pictures of any paperwork so I can read it later. No sound of sirens, I figure I have a few moments.

I crouch and crawl, edging my way past Stacey's feet, under the desk and under the dead body. I'm not messing up crime scene evidence, not really. I was here already. And I've been here very recently. I touched Stacey while checking for a pulse. My DNA could be anywhere. But I get my excuses ready as I ease myself towards that envelope, my nose nearly touching the carpet. The thick envelope contains something.

I do another double-take. It's stuffed full of money. The sort of rolled-up banknotes I'd associate with deals for drugs or guns. I cannot tell how much is in here. But at a glance, I reckon over a thousand.

Then a voice behind me says: 'Stop there. Don't even think about moving.'

30.

'What the hell is going on?' says the voice behind. 'Is that… Is that Stacey? She's… Is she…?'

Crouching under a desk beneath a dead body and next to a haul of dodgy-looking cash is never how anyone wants to be caught. I recognise the voice, I don't even need to turn. As a reflex, I go for putting up my hands and try to get up, but only bump my head on the glass desk.

'Oh my God! What have you done? I'm calling the police!'

'Minty. I can explain,' I say, even though I definitely can't. 'The police are already on their way.' I need to think quickly. It's not the first time I've been faced with someone who looked at what they'd done, considered the consequences – and ran. But what's Minty come back for?

'Oh. My. God. It's Stacey? It is Stacey, isn't it? How did you both get in?'

Is this how Minty is going to play it? Surprise, shock, outrage.

'You've killed her!' says Minty. 'And in my office. What are you both doing here?'

I turn my head slowly. Enough to be sure Minty isn't standing over me with a weapon.

'Stacey is dead, yes, but she was dead when I found her. Guess you had a meeting with her? Did things get out of hand? I'm sure it was an accident. My other immediate issue is… Please, can I get up?'

Minty splutters. 'I'm not the one caught with a dead body. You are absolutely not putting this on me. And no, don't move.'

'I have explaining to do, I know,' I say. 'I can see the overwhelming circumstantial evidence. But the door was open.'

I don't mention the kicking part. I guess Stacey could have got in the same way.

'I can't get up and my leg muscles can't hold this crouching position any longer, and I'd rather get up than fall over. I think I can already hear sirens.' This is not true. 'I'm moving anyway.' I drop to all fours and crawl out from under the desk. Not my finest hour.

'Ok. Stand up, but slowly. Did you really call the police? I'm calling them anyway.'

'Sure. Do that.' I gladly shake out my cramp.

'Why have you… killed her? Did *you* have a row? But why in *my* office?' Minty is doing a good job of trying to accuse me. But then she would, wouldn't she?

Minty's smart. So what's her smart play here? Minty must have left to set up an alibi. Of course, I've handed myself on a plate here as an alternative suspect. I need to get her talking. It's how people give themselves away.

'When I first came in,' I say, 'I thought it was you. Stacey was sitting at your desk. Anyone you can think of who might have it in for you? If you claim you didn't do this—'

'Claim? I did not do this. Stop talking as if I did!'

'I agree things look far from ideal for me—but they also look bad for you. Maybe you should just tell me the truth.'

'How can it possibly look bad for me?' Minty scoffs.

'You think you can sell the idea you just happened to be out at a time when Stacey came in and someone killed her? And it's your office.'

My mind is racing, trying to make sense of what the real situation is as much as what it looks like. And what can I get out of Minty?

'Can you really hear sirens?' Minty pulls out her phone.

I stop her before she dials by pointing out the tatty, empty buff folder. I want to hear more of her story, before she has time to invent something that's going to sound extremely plausible and might leave me looking the dodgier of the two of us.

'It looks like you two were going over some paperwork, which I'm pretty sure relates to her mum's cottage—something you already rowed about.'

'I never had a meeting with Stacey,' says Minty. 'I've no idea why she's here.'

'And what's with the envelope of cash?'

Minty stares as I point at the incriminating envelope. 'What on earth is that?'

'I think the police are going to ask exactly that question. At least one of us is going to be carted off in handcuffs.' (Not a scenario even Supportive Mum had in her dossier of things that can go wrong when you open a bookshop.) 'That cash—that looks bad. I'd say worse for you than for me. Do you often need envelopes of cash in your office?'

'No, my business does not involve envelopes of cash, if that's what that is. You were the one I found on the floor next to it. I've been out meeting with a client. And you seem to know a lot.'

'That's because I'm very nosy.'

'You are trying to twist this. But I found you!' Minty is doing an impressive job of sounding outraged.

She quickly denied any involvement with the cash. Yet I was pretty sure when we spoke recently, she was hinting she'd take a bribe to make my rent troubles go away.

'Sorry, but I have to ask this, because I've heard you got yourself in a bit of debt and, if I've heard it, everyone's heard it—'

'Heard what exactly?'

'The rumour is that you're not above taking a few backhanders to dig yourself out of a financial hole. And as I'm pretty sure you don't take bribes on a credit card, the police might look at that envelope of cash and ask why Stacey was here and what you two might have rowed about.'

Now there are sirens, and we both turn to the window when we hear them.

'You told me property's a peachy premium around here,' I continue. 'And Stacey, well, I'm sorry, but the other day I heard Stacey threaten you, saying she's going to fight you over a legal claim to her mum's valuable riverside cottage. Then I find her dead with an envelope of cash.'

'You've done this!' Minty splutters. It's another impressive attempt at more indignation. '*You* were under that desk. Were you *planting* that? And you're going to tell the police all that?' Minty gasps.

Minty squeezes her eyes shut. 'You're going to say I'm open to a bribe?' Minty sounds even more outraged than when I accused her of murder. 'Why are you doing this, Keera?'

'The police are going to hear it all the minute they investigate anyway.'

Minty is doing a great job with the outrage. I pride myself on being pretty good at spotting when someone's lying. But some people are such very good liars. Being discovered with the body is never ideal, but Minty was too ready with that story that she was called away.

People will know she's been arguing with Stacey. It's not going to be too difficult to convince people they had a volatile meeting, which ended in a heavy paperweight with sharp edges being snatched up.

I also suspect she pushed Mrs M down the stairs. Mrs McFlintock's death might still be put down as an accident. But Stacey's end was far more brutal. No chance to disguise that as an accident. Then Minty scarpered and claims she wasn't here. It's a high-wire act.

'You say you weren't here because you were called out. Who were you with?'

That alibi. That's what everything is going to rest on.

'Well, actually...' Minty's poise is slipping. She's losing her confident demeanour. For the first time, she looks unsure. Vulnerable, even. 'Turned out to be a mistake.'

'A mistake?' I echo.

'Do you think someone got me out of the way deliberately?' Minty asks me.

This is the line Minty's going to take.

She was called away to a mysterious, non-existent meeting. That might make things very difficult for anyone to prove. I hear Supportive Mum's voice in my head, how I can never resist a sob story. Perhaps I should stop giving people the benefit of the doubt.

'That seems unlikely, if you don't mind my saying.'

'Someone's setting me up. This cannot be happening.'

Minty's determined to press on with her denials. 'This is getting scary. Someone lured me away. Someone's out to get me. Maybe you, Keera. Lured me away to sneak in here. But it's you they'll arrest. I found you standing over the body.'

'Well, hiding under the desk. And I called it in before you even got back.'

Minty looks at me through narrowed eyes as we both stand there, accusing each other, waiting for the police to arrive.

Who will they arrest?

Minty has set up an alibi that leaves me being the unfortunate one who was discovered with a dead body. Bad timing? Or just another example of my curse?

'The door was open,' I repeat. 'I just walked in and found Stacey. And why would Stacey bring me an envelope of cash? And to your office? Why would I argue with Stacey? Why would anyone, except you, Minty?'

'I've heard stories, things the police will find out about you too—you and Rick Craven and wriggling your way into that family with Helena only just dead.'

I feel myself flush. 'Well, that's not true.'

'Neither are any of those things you said about me.'

'And what about Mrs McFlintock? You were seen visiting her the day she died.'

Stating something you are only speculating about as an established fact is an obvious ploy. I do not expect it to work.

It's Minty's turn to flush. To me, she looks guilty as hell. She starts biting her immaculately manicured nails.

'Then someone's been spreading a lot of lies about me. The police will believe me.' Minty holds her head high. 'I have nothing to hide.'

I cannot help it. I believe everyone has a right to a defence. Innocent until proven otherwise.

'Minty, we all have something to hide. The police are not there to hold your hand, give you a cup of tea and sympathy. They will say that if you tell the truth, everything will be fine. But the police are only there to hold your hand, make you a cup of tea, and take down everything you say so they can build a case against you. Face it. Shit just got real.'

There's the sound of footsteps on the stairs.

'Whatever you've done or not done, you need to act smart,' I tell her. 'Do the smart thing. Say nothing. And get yourself a lawyer.'

The door busts open.

Minty looks terrified, but nods.

Elliott Trent walks through the door, followed by other uniformed police.

Our eyes meet across another crime scene. His eyes alight on the dead body. At least this time he won't be calling me out on my overactive imagination.

Although, with Elliott here, does that lessen my chances of not being led away in handcuffs? Or make everything infinitely worse?

31.

'So… All go well with Minty?' Liv raises a single eyebrow at me. 'Because my guess is it went even worse than last time. From the fact that you left here, less than half hour later there were blue lights everywhere, police dashing into Crossways, an ambulance blazing in. And you never came back.'

It's several hours later. I reek of police station, and all I want to do is go home and shower and pull a duvet over my head. But I'm bracing myself that there might be a lecture. Liv's still here, keeping my business going.

But Liv simply moves from the heater to turn the shop sign to *closed*. 'Tea?'

'Thanks for staying all afternoon, Liv, and giving up whatever better things you should be doing.'

I dive straight for my jar of peanut butter and start eating with a spoon. I count myself lucky I'm back here as soon as I am, rather than still down at the station. My hands might be shaking a bit.

There's a pounding on the glass door, Cady demanding to be let in.

'Someone said they saw a body being removed from Key Keepers?' Cady shakes her head in disbelief, loosening her already messy bun. 'Rumour is the body might be Minty. But someone else said they saw Minty being taken away in a police car in handcuffs. I was buying a jumper I saw in the January sale, and have been walking up and down the high street, desperate for proper news for *hours*.'

They both stare at me expectantly.

'Was there a body?' asks Liv.

'Not Minty?' asks Cady. 'Then whose?'

I mumble out about Stacey, but tell them I'm too tired to go through it again after being made to do so several times at the police station.

'I totally get that. Totally,' says Cady. 'What I think you need is… Just give me one minute.' Cady holds up a finger.

'To go home for a rest? A hot bath and a massage?' I say. 'With one of Liv's gins in a fishbowl-size glass?'

Cady disappears and returns about ten minutes later, clutching a stash of those mini cans of gin and tonic. They're even from the chiller. Without asking, she cracks one open and hands it to me.

'OK,' says Liv, taking one too, even though it's hardly her favourite local artisan gin. 'Keera, you've been saying for days there's something off about Mrs McFlintock's death, and I haven't been listening. You spotted something nasty was going on in Crossways. The rest of us missed it. Now her daughter's been murdered, and I feel horribly guilty. Please start from the beginning. If you're up to it.'

Somehow, I am. It's not like I'm going to be able to forget about finding Stacey. I need to make sense of it in my head. All of it. Liv's been on the side of dismissive when I've sounded out any theories that there was something dodgy about Mrs McFlintock's death. So I've kept some of it back. Quite a lot. I just can't remember what I've shared, knowing much of it was conjecture and imagination and likely to get the eye-roll from Liv. I try to go over everything.

'Mrs M had a secret about Minty. We think Minty was in debt and resorting to bribes. And Mrs M's secrets might have been written in the notebook in the sugar caddy?' Cady says, summarising after I'm done. She chews her lip and passes us all another tin. 'Minty argued with Mrs M, ending with a push down the stairs, and Stacey… Minty argued with Stacey, who knew the secret too, and was trying a bribe? You've worked out so much, Keera! Phew! Well, at least all this nastiness is over!'

'I hope so,' I say. 'But if Minty can prove she received a call, she could mess with the timeline; she'd have reasonable doubt.'

'I didn't understand a word of that,' says Cady.

'What Keera's saying is it'll be difficult to prove beyond doubt that Minty did it,' says Liv. 'And it might be difficult even for the police to get the whole story. Mrs M's dead, Stacey's dead. Anyone who has any pieces of this puzzle is dead.'

'But Stacey was killed in Minty's office, even if she claims she was called away. Keera doesn't have to find evidence,' says Cady. 'The police will do that.'

'But Keera's our sheriff. She finds it impossible to step away,' says Liv.

'But Stacey turned up with a bundle of cash to sweeten the deal with Minty and there was a row. Surely that's pretty clear.'

I wince at this. 'I advised Stacey that going through official channels would be expensive and how it's always best to reach an agreement if you can,' I confess. 'I told her to reach an agreement with Minty.'

'Keera, this is not your fault,' says Liv softly.

'But it's a very valid reason to feel guilty. I'll always regret that all I did was keep blundering about when I had suspicions about Mrs M's death.'

'Minty was getting desperate,' says Liv. 'I doubt she meant to kill Mrs M, and things just got worse when Stacey tried to get in on the action. And that tatty file was empty? Looks like she destroyed that piece of evidence, as well as setting herself up an alibi. You're dealing with someone very smart.'

'Maybe that's enough for today,' says Liv. 'Keera, you look absolutely terrible.'

'Cheers. Good to know.'

'I guess that wasn't your first dead body. But you knew Stacey. You're in shock. You're not as tough as you think you are.'

'I let someone who had killed think they'd got away with it. A murderer who thinks they've got away with it— they're one of the most dangerous people there is.'

'You've done well,' says Liv, giving my shoulder a squeeze. 'Don't take too much of this on your shoulders, Sheriff Munroe.' She squeezes even more reassuringly.

'None of this is your fault. You should go home. I'll drop you.'

Liv's right. I want a shower and my duvet. We might have to accept we'll never get all the answers, not with the two key people dead. I want to believe this is really over. But Minty is smart. It's possible the police won't get enough evidence to hold Minty, and that's difficult to feel comfortable with.

'Now you're the one who can't drop it,' I say quietly as I can see Liv's still thinking it through. 'Let's have it.'

'Just trying to make up for lost time from me not listening to you,' says Liv.

'In that case, would anyone like tea?' says Cady.

'Actually—' I reach for another of the delicious mini cans of G&T. 'I think this is helping with the shock. Then I'll go home and spend the evening under my duvet.'

But I want to know what she's thinking more than I want my duvet.

Also, maybe there's someone else holding pieces of the puzzle. Maybe I should go and talk to my other possible witness—I need to make sure Pip's safe.

Does Minty know Pip had chatted to Mrs M? What does Pip know? Is Pip in any danger? Maybe I need to stop blundering about like a fool and make sure no more nastiness happens.

'I confess I'm curious about a couple of things,' says Liv. 'Like, why take an incriminating document, set up an alibi... but leave a shitload of money on the floor?'

'Ooh, that's a good question,' says Cady.

'Maybe it depends on the circumstances,' I say. 'Let's say the circumstances are you've just argued with a client in your office, and angrily smashed them over the head with a heavy steel paperweight. Few people manage to be completely rational under those circumstances. Minty panicked. The money was under the far side of the desk, and she'd have had to get past Stacey to reach it. I'm sensing a *but* here.' I'm looking at Liv.

'Is Minty a panicker?' says Liv. 'Strikes me, she's a pretty cool customer. Did she panic after leaving Mrs M dead at the foot of the stairs? She managed to leave that crime scene with no one but Keera even believing there had been a crime.'

'Even Vampire Minty would panic, faced with a dead body on her hands. The second in a few days,' Cady insists. 'Even a cool customer's going to be upset they've stoved in one of their client's heads with a paperweight of the Eiffel Tower. It makes complete sense that she rushed out. Only then did her cool kick in, and she planned how to save her skin and invented a story about being called out.'

'Even Minty could be squeamish about being close to a dead body,' I say. 'Especially one leaking blood, because you wouldn't want to get any of that on you. Particularly because that would rather ruin the alibi.'

'Ooh, Keera, I can't believe you said that!' protests Cady, dunking a bourbon.

'Murderers aren't usually ready with a meticulous cover-up plan. Getting out of there was more important. To set up the alibi, she worked out she needed to pretend to find the body. She thought she'd have time to grab the cash,' I say.

We all think for a moment, slurping our drinks. I may not be the only one who wishes there were more biscuits.

'I bet she had a right shock to come back and find you there,' says Liv.

'Wow, you really are in the heart of this, aren't you, Keera?' says Cady. 'How do you manage it?'

'Just a gift, I guess.'

'Let's just hope this is the end of all the unpleasantness in Crossways and everything can go back to normal,' shudders Cady.

'Well, finding a dead body sure makes me look forward to Liv teaching me how to do the paperwork to return books to publishers.'

'You know that's not true, Sheriff Munroe,' jokes Liv.

'Minty's locked up now,' says Cady, 'and that's thanks to you.' She giggles. 'Our sheriff.'

The last thing I expect is a tap at the door. I'd happily ignore someone at the bookshop door, but I get a look from Liv that says she won't let me get away with turning down even one sale. Even after the day I've had.

But I'm glad I answered as the last person I was expecting to see was the guy in the posh dark coat, with that attractive twinkle in his eye.

'Sully!'

'Sorry, I didn't realise you had customers,' he says, spying Liv and Cady lurking. 'I saw the light.'

'These are not customers.'

'You're busy. I just called in to ask you… Well, I just wanted to tell you how much my mum appreciates her books.'

'That's very kind.' I find myself breathing deeply to see if he still has that comforting outdoors smell of woodsmoke. I want to add something, but have no idea what. But why do I say: 'I'm open again tomorrow and I really doubt I'll have that many customers.'

'There's that optimism again,' he twinkles and disappears off into the freezing dark night. I hope his campfire's a big one.

'I think he wanted a private consultation,' smirks Cady, joining me at the door to watch his elegant figure and broad shoulders disappear briskly down the road. 'Lucky you, Keera. He is very good-looking. I think he might have been after something other than a book, calling after hours,' smirks Cady. 'I wouldn't have said no.'

'You make it sound like I would hit on my customers.'

'I thought that's exactly what you'd been doing,' says Liv.

I make a note that I must be more careful of wine and Liv combinations.

'Come on, Liv, we've let you hog the heater because you've been sitting there thinking it all through,' I say, deciding talking about Minty is preferable. 'Anything else?'

'Well, I can't help but wonder what the argument was about?' says Liv.

'It was about the lease and the bribes because Stacey brought cash,' says Cady, looking puzzled.

'But if Stacey brought cash, she wanted to do a deal. Why argue? Why kill her?'

'Not enough cash?' suggests Cady.

'And…'

We wait for Liv to gather her thoughts.

'If there was an argument and Minty lashed out, how did Stacey end up with a blow to the *back* of the head?'

32.

Cady falls in with my suggestion that we pick up pizzas and head back to her house, which will give me an excuse to chat to Pip. I need to get him to talk to me.

I need to set my mind at rest that Pip isn't holding any dangerous cards that he found during his regular trips to the pools; that there's nothing Minty might know about or suspect he knows. Minty has efficiently removed everyone who's likely to be able to shed light on the deal she had going with Mrs M. This time, I'm taking no chances. If Pip knows anything, he's telling me – tonight.

Cady insists that anyone who eats pizza has to sit and watch a film with the family. Luckily, the argument about what to watch goes on for so long that the pizza issue literally disappears.

'Do you think film-makers actively make films for precisely those situations where no one can agree what film to watch?' I ask. 'Something no one actually wants to watch, but no one can strongly object to? The cinema of the bland.'

Pip snorts through his nose, biting into about his tenth slice of pizza. Alys already broke the rules and vanished, but I'm pretty sure she also smuggled out at least one slice of vegan pizza. Rick laid a calming hand on Cady's arm and stopped her from rushing after Alys.

I tried but failed not to nod off during the desperately bad film. I'm grateful to Cady that she told everyone I wouldn't be talking about what happened, because of course they already knew about Stacey and who found her body. Everybody knows.

Pip vanishes to his room the second the credits start to roll. The whole reason I'm here is because I need to talk to him. I'm learning from past mistakes, so not giving up.

'Are you making Pip a hot chocolate?' I say to Cady. 'Does he still like that? I could take it up.'

Hot chocolate in hand, I tap on Pip's bedroom door and after giving him a polite thirty seconds, open it when there's no answer.

Pip's sat at a computer, headphones on. I stand in the doorway and attract his attention, waving the hot chocolate. Relaxing, he looks even more all bones and pointy elbows. He's told me he finds computer games the ultimate way of switching off, so I'm delighted when he turns, sees me, and looks pleased. Although it might just be the hot chocolate.

When I think of him, I see his room in his old house. For a second, the world tilts on an axis of unreality as it feels like the walls have expanded, as if some sci-fi inter-dimensional shift has happened. There's the same single bed and slim wardrobe, even the duvet cover and the posters on the walls are the same. It's all just pushed back as the walls are further apart.

I'm pleased he logs out of the game and takes off his headphones, until he says, 'So Stacey was murdered! You found her body.'

Guilt knifes me in the gut. I feel so bad that I took him to talk to her, and now she's dead. I keep doing completely the wrong thing, poking around with no real purpose. I told Stacey to talk to Minty. I really messed up. Even more than usual. The Crossways Effect – I never truly saw the dangers.

I place the hot chocolate carefully on the bedside table, nudging aside the copy of Brandon Sanderson's The Final Empire I gave him. There's a bookmark about halfway through. It's a book I knew he'd love, and it pleases me enormously to see it there. I believe reading has a positive impact on anyone's life, and no more so than when your life is in pieces.

'Glad to see you're still reading. I can't fathom why there seems such a publishing-industry commitment to the narrative that boys don't read.'

'Maybe you're not so bad at your job,' Pip says.

'Think I should keep going?'

'I know you should keep going. You're not seriously thinking of jacking it in, are you?'

'It's not quite as I dreamed it would be. The things I like most—finding the right book to keep young people reading, supporting authors everyone should have heard of, but no one has—don't exactly keep money rolling in. But if I quit, it will be because I don't think I fit in here. It'll never feel like home.'

'Why d'you even want to fit in? How is not fitting in a bad thing? Who wants to fit in with a place like Crossways? Besides, you must fit in a bit, cos people'd miss you if you went.'

'And I would miss lots of people.' I remind Pip to drink his hot chocolate. 'Actually, the main reason I haven't closed might be because I'm too stubborn to quit and call myself a failure.'

'You are not a failure; you should always bet on yourself.'

'And that is exactly why I brought you hot chocolate— because you, at seventeen, Pip, are far better at the motivating pep talk than I am.' I watch him sip his drink. 'How did you get so good at imparting worldly advice?'

'Books, maybe? You're trying to be someone else. Look at how hard Vin worked to do her job.' He gestures at the book he's reading.

'I'm not in a fantasy novel where a group of magical criminals are trying to overthrow an evil dark lord who has ruled for a thousand years. I don't think bookselling is in quite the same kick-ass arena. But I do appreciate the comparison.'

'You're quite kick-ass. Cady says you've met murderers and things.'

'Ah, well, Cady is speculating. It's what people do for fun around here.' No surprise that Cady has been gossiping about me.

'You don't know any murderers?' Pip sounds wistful and disappointed.

'Know is a vague term.' But doing anything that impresses a teenager is remarkable, so I can't help but add, 'But I may have encountered a few.'

'OK!' Pip looks both eager and impressed. 'No surprise you found Stacey's body. You have a habit of being where there's trouble. Must have been horrible. And there was blood and everything?' He pushes his long fringe out of his eyes.

'That's a little ghoulish, Pip. Drink your wholesome hot chocolate.'

'I think everyone's allowed to be a bit ghoulish when there's been a murder.'

'Maybe. There may have been a little blood... and things.' Should I be talking to him about this? No, I definitely shouldn't. I am so the opposite of wholesome; no wonder I don't fit in. And I'm here with a hidden agenda to ask if he broke into a dead woman's house. Perhaps we are both as bad as each other.

'What things? Brains and things? How much blood? Did you faint?' Pip asks, after a pause where he finishes his drink. 'No. You've seen a dead body before.'

I wish Pip didn't have to know already that the world is a grim place. He's a mixture of being too wise for his years one moment, the next seeming impossibly young. He's already had more grim than many people will see in a lifetime.

'I couldn't possibly say.'

But then people gossip in Crossways in a way that makes me suspect they're craving a bit more drama in their lives. Maybe Pip can be forgiven for being in need of a distraction.

'I absolutely cannot confirm there was an envelope absolutely stuffed with cash.'

Pip's eyes widen, and he grins at me. 'There was an envelope of cash? And Minty's going to be my dad's new boss! If she murdered Stacey, does that mean she killed old Mrs McFlintock too?'

'I'm sure that was just a tragic accident.'

Pip raises his eyebrows. 'Yeah, but you don't really. That's why you don't fit in. Because everyone round here likes to pretend the world is a completely different place to what it is. Will Minty go to jail?'

'Everyone's innocent until proven guilty. That's the trouble with evidence, it can often be interpreted more than one way.'

'Really? I thought evidence was evidence.'

'Yes, that's the popular opinion. But not if you have a good lawyer. Talking of evidence and how it can lead to leaping to conclusions, can I ask you a question? It's about when I saw you near Mrs McFlintock's house the other night... I found the house had been broken into.'

'Wild! You found a burglary *and* a body. You really are a kick-ass bookseller.'

'You'd think being involved in two deaths and a burglary should tell me I was never cut out to be a bookseller at all. But I want to know if you saw anyone.'

'Me? Nah, missed all the good stuff, unlike you, who manages always to be right there in the action.' His eyes open wider with another question. 'Was that Minty too? What was she after? Trying to destroy evidence? And you are a great bookseller.'

'It's unlikely to have been random. Not even a car?'

Pip looks like he's trying hard and wants to have seen a car. Or something.

'Pip, I know you spoke to Mrs M. If she told you anything important, you need to tell me.'

'Because Minty murdered her, right?'

'Well, I think so, but there's a long way to go before she'll get convicted of anything.' It all makes perfect sense. It's neat. So why am I here, questioning Pip, feeling like there's something else, like he's involved? Because I don't like neat. Because life isn't neat, it's messy. 'If someone did see anything, or knew anything, or had been told anything—after two deaths—the sensible thing would be to tell someone. To keep themselves safe. What I'm saying, Pip, is that if you know anything at all, even if you'd done anything you felt I'd judge you for, you have to tell me.'

'Three deaths,' says Pip.

'What?'

'Does that mean Minty killed my mum?'

This comes at me right out of the blue. My breath catches.

'Killed your mum? Why do you say that? Pip, that was just a tragic accident.'

Even as I say the stupid, bland words, it goes through my mind that this is an echo of exactly what everyone was saying about Mrs McFlintock's death. And Helena Craven knew Minty. There it is again – a connection. I have to keep reminding myself I now live in a small place where everyone is connected. I have to stop being surprised.

'Pip, I don't think anyone's said—'

'You said there have been two deaths and a break-in,' says Pip. 'But it's *three.*' Pip's normally pale face colours. 'Three deaths in Crossways, three deaths you've been involved in. You're forgetting Mum. Never forget Mum.'

33.

Three deaths. Something nudges at my gut uncomfortably, like a reminder of something I should have remembered.

Everyone goes on about how nothing bad happens in Crossways. But Pip's right. In the short time I've been here, there have been three deaths. Bloody Crossways. I feel guilty again that I haven't taken things nearly seriously enough. Guilt that Pip's right, I'd forgotten Helena. Her death was never properly explained.

'I hope it's all Minty,' says Pip, yawning, 'and they get her to admit everything.'

'Why would you think Minty killed your mum?' I ask Pip.

Accident or suicide? That's all everyone asked themselves. I wanted it to have been an accident. She liked to walk on her own occasionally, and she liked Harcourt Pools. But she was prone to bouts of depression. She'd lost her job. Rick refused to settle into work with a reliable income. But surely she was used to that.

'They came around a lot, you know, the police,' murmurs Pip. He looks so tired it reminds me just how tired I am. 'This one officer was actually helpful, not intentionally. Probably talked a lot because she thought I didn't count. She told me they were doing this thing called a timeline. You've heard of timelines?'

'I've heard of timelines.'

That note in Helena's writing: *4.30 Harcourt Pools*. Nothing else, no date. It was found on the passenger seat of her car. It could have been there for days. But what else happened that day? Where else had she been? Who did she talk to?

'The police did a timeline. Of course, they would have done,' I say, mostly to myself. 'You think Minty was with Helena that day? But they'd fallen out. Helena lost her job.'

'When they asked us a lot of questions,' Pip explains, 'I made notes about all the people they asked us about. Then the police gave up. I didn't. I'm like you. You want to know the truth. Get justice. I do too.'

'You carried on? You talked to the people the police asked you about? The people on Helena's timeline.' I'm impressed, but my heart beats faster. Did the police ever consider it wasn't an accident or a suicide? 'Pip, if you know anything—anything at all—you'd tell me, right? You must tell me. This is important.'

Pip nods, but looks so drowsy, the kind thing would be to let him sleep. Am I making something out of nothing? But I listened to too many people insisting Mrs M's death was just an accident. And then Stacey was murdered.

And Pip's right, there have been *three deaths*.

Three deaths in a tiny village. And Helena worked for Minty and lost her job. Maybe it isn't all just small-village coincidence. Maybe it's a big coincidence that shouldn't be overlooked.

That note, it always looked like it might have been a scribbled reminder to meet someone. It sounds like Minty spoke with Helena the day she died.

But how would Helena's death fit into the picture?

'Pip, I have to ask—was it you who broke into Mrs M's? Were you looking for evidence? Something about your mum?'

'What! Me break in?' He's suddenly more alert. 'No! Why would you think I'd do something like that?'

'Forgive me. Just a theory.' Was it Mrs M being kind and talking to Pip? Or was it Pip talking to her? Trying to find out the truth. What's Pip really been up to? 'You spoke to her. Because you had suspicions she knew something?'

'Mrs M was the one who found Mum's body,' says Pip.

Of course. I knew that. I just… didn't pay enough attention. Pip's right. I have been blind – of course it all has to be connected. Mrs M was right there. 'Did Mrs M tell you anything?'

I ask the question urgently, but Pip looks like he'd much rather sleep.

'I saw this therapist when I went back to school.' He yawns. 'She said people find it helps to write things down.'

'I've heard that too. But Pip—'

'I've been writing everything down.'

'You made notes. That was smart. Where are your notes?'

'Don't worry, no one else knows. But I trust you.'

'Thank you for that, Pip.'

He blinks, rouses himself, and unexpectedly takes down a poster of Back to the Future from his wall. He turns it over, and it's covered with hand-written biro scribbles. It takes hardly a beat for me to realise what I am looking at.

'You've done your own timeline.'

There is so much here. From the time Helena left in the morning, a record of where she went, anyone she spoke to. I'm staggered. I want to tell him how impressed I am as I look at all sorts of names I recognise.

'When did you start all of this? You were never simply wandering, were you? You were making notes. You talked to the people the police asked you about.'

All that time I thought Pip was in danger of running away, of hurting himself, it looks like he had quite a different purpose. One I never even suspected.

I'm scouring the meticulous notes admiringly. The detail! So many names, me, Liv, Cady, and Minty is there, and Mrs McFlintock, who was right there at the otherwise deserted riverside. Helena's husband and children in the morning. She dropped into the bookshop, so I am named along with an estimated time. The last time I saw Helena. I've always felt guilty that I never suspected what was about to happen. Afterwards, I remembered her hug and wondered if it was her goodbye.

Looking at this makes me feel uncomfortable. Crossways is so interconnected, it feels claustrophobic. I'm also immediately fearful for Pip. I wonder what Helena and

Minty met to talk about the day Helena died. I wonder if Pip knows.

For once, I keep control of my mouth and keep my reaction appropriate. He needs help with moving on – not with building a timeline of the people Helena spoke to the day she died. Pip needs to put it behind him and move on with his life.

'You kept this a very good secret.'

'Working in your shop was pretty useful for adding to it. Thought you could add in what you know about Mrs M and Stacey and Minty. Cos it's all connected. Has to be.'

'I'm glad you kept it such a good secret. But...' I need to say the right things, play the grown-up. 'This is a really bad idea, Pip.'

He looks crestfallen. 'Thought you'd be the only person who'd understand,' he says sullenly.

The responsible thing to do would be to help him accept his mother's death. Nothing he does will change the fact that she's never coming back, but everyone's been quick to tell him he should move on.

I wish I could tell him life isn't so shit and believe it. His mother died a tragic death, and he has to find a way to deal with it.

But I can understand how this is his way of doing that. I do get it. It's what I've been doing with Mrs McFlintock's death. Digging. Not able to leave it alone. How would I know the right thing to say to get him to stop?

He's found out so much. Helena even called in to make a hair appointment with Joely, so that should have put paid to the suicide theory. Who makes a hair appointment if they're about to kill themselves?

'Thank you for showing me. But I can take over now. You really have to give this up. This is seriously unhealthy for you.'

Pip slides me a sly smile as I take a couple of photos of his timeline, making sure they are in focus and I'll be able to read them. Now I have all Pip's notes. Now I have to get Pip to leave this alone.

'Knew you'd be interested.' He yawns again. 'I got all my inspiration from a kick-ass bookseller. It helps to be underestimated and the last person people might think is good at solving crimes.'

'Well, it's nice to be an inspiration. I'm nowhere near as kick-ass as I'd like to be.'

'Look at the way you fought for me last year when school thought they knew best. You never gave up.'

'Yes, well,' I replace the poster on the wall. 'Just think, if you'd have put this much work into your GCSEs.'

'Mrs M did tell me something she never told the police.'

I bite my lip to stop myself from leaping in all enthusiastically. Of course, I'm desperate to know what Mrs M told him.

'That therapist was part of the deal when I got time off and helped you in the bookshop, remember? She said write things down, and she asked me every time if I had—it was easier just to do it. Sorry, I feel so sleepy, I want to talk, but you—'

'I send you to sleep, I get it.' I scour the notes on my phone, seeing if he's written it down. Is it here? 'So, all right, what did Mrs M tell you that she never told the police?'

I'm doing the opposite of the right thing as usual. I cannot help it. I'm encouraging him.

'Tell me what she said. Then you are stopping this, just to be clear.'

'Yeah, you say that, but—'

He fumbles to open a drawer in his bedside table.

'I need help. You always say you want to help. This is how you help me.' From underneath the drawer, he unpeels something he's sticky-taped to the underside. Teenagers.

He hands over a slim book, like a school exercise book.

'You want me to read The Secret Diary of Pip Craven, aged seventeen and a quarter? I doubt I can help with the investigation or your homework.'

'Don't worry,' he mutters sleepily. 'Just read it. I thought I'd worked it all out. I'm not in love with a girl called Pandora.'

'There's no kissing, is there? I guess I can skip any parts that make me feel truly squeamish.' He's trusting me with his innermost thoughts. I take the diary.

'I mostly wrote it to keep the therapist happy. I wrote it like it was happening to someone else.'

'Yes, I can see why you might find that easier. I'm no expert, but pretending it happened to someone else doesn't sound great either. Maybe I'll try to track down that therapist.' And what exactly did he mean by thinking he'd worked it all out?

'It would be so much better,' he murmurs, 'if it was all Minty.'

At least, I think that's what Pip said. Unfortunately, the last bit was lost in a yawn and mumbling as he actually falls asleep in a way I can only envy, the sleep of the young.

I am left wondering what Mrs M told him. And what he meant by those last comments. I guess it will all be in his journal.

'Pip,' I lean over and whisper. 'This is also—bloody amazingly brilliant! Just never tell anyone I said that.' Luckily, I'm pretty sure he's asleep and didn't hear me.

I take the diary and leave.

34.

Broken Pieces, Day 275

Daily challenge – Remember it's just an empty house

It was quite fun to see Alys's mouth open, then shut like a trap when Cady asked her that question: What would Alys do with the money if their house was sold?

Alys's role was usually being the one to say stuff that shocked people.

It was pretty easy to see that Alys hadn't been able to stop her attention being snagged.

Money.

A magic word.

How much? Pip couldn't stop the thought, and Alys would have thought it too. But she wouldn't want to let on.

'The money would be ours?' Pip asked, for him and Alys. 'What about—mortgages and things?'

He'd never considered what their tired, cramped old home, full of half-hearted repairs, but with a beautiful, if tiny, garden, might be worth.

'So did Mum leave it to us, like in a will or something?' Alys addressed Rick.

She'd abandoned any pretence of eating the shepherd slop. The adults seemed to have moved on exclusively to wine. Cady went to fetch another bottle.

'Neither of us ever made a will,' Dad said. 'Cady, what about you?'

Cady shook her head.

'But if it's sold, we'd carry on living here?' Pip asked, looking at Dad, then Cady.

Cady nodded with one of her smiles. 'I hope you'd like to. I've got used to you. One day, I might even say I like having you around.'

'And what happens if something happens to you?'

Pip found himself asking the question before he'd properly thought about how it would sound.

'Well, because, well—we lost Mum, didn't we?' He tried to explain, thinking he'd said it badly. 'If we sold our house, what would happen to us if something happens to Cady?'

'I understand,' said Dad, with a glance as he poured Cady more wine. 'You don't feel secure. I guess... Would you be happier if we did things formally? If you don't have a will, Cady. I mean, it's not a bad idea. Maybe the answer is you should make one?'

'Never thought about it before,' said Cady. 'Guess it is a sensible idea.'

'Would there be enough so I could buy a flat?' said Alys.

Could this be happening? Alys was being sold on this idea?

'You needn't rush into anything,' said Cady. 'I thought you might all want to do something first, you know, take off somewhere. Family road trip. Australia or something?'

Have Dad and Cady planned how to drop this? Because Alys's big dream had always been to travel.

Pip felt twisted by the idea. A big, exciting family adventure. But Mum would miss out. Would Cady come?

'Or don't sell it and we can live in it,' said Alys, ignoring the temptations of Australia.

We? Did she mean him too?

But they couldn't, could they? The idea was ridiculous because they were at school.

Especially not with Pip stuck going round the same year again, who knew when he'd finally get off the roundabout. They'd need to buy food and stuff. Alys was still in sixth form. She only worked part-time at Halfway.

'Would be a long way to commute when you go to university.' Dad smiled. 'You don't want to be stuck living in Harcourt forever.'

'I don't need to go to university. I've got a job,' said Alys.

'A part-time job in a little cafe,' pointed out Dad.

Perhaps it was better when he didn't try to join in.

Because Alys swung around to look at him, and lifted her chin. 'And Jaxx makes more money with that cafe than Mum ever made with her hundred-mile-an-hour new business schemes. Or her lottery tickets. Or any of the jobs she did for five minutes and got bored. Cady got this house and doesn't have to work. I don't need university, not if I've got a whole house.'

'It's because my parents died, Alys,' says Cady, crumbling the remains of a bread roll. 'Why I've got this lovely house. It's why I understand more than you think I do.'

'You understand us all brilliantly,' said Dad. 'Thank you for looking after us all.'

Pip saw a look pass between Dad and Cady. It was too much for Alys, who was away from the table and thundering up the stairs. Then the familiar sound of a door slamming.

Pip followed, but caught a drift of the conversation continuing.

'Those kids are more grown-up than they should be. But they have a point. If we sell our house, they lose their security of ever going back. Sadly, they both know the unexpected, the worst, happens. I wish it wasn't true. But it would be devastating if they lost everything all over again.'

'Yes, of course, I understand,' Cady murmured. 'It might make them feel their future's more uncertain.'

'Why didn't I think about us making wills?' Dad said. 'Trust those kids to think of it.'

'You're right. It's a good idea. They come first. Let's do it. We'll both make wills.'

'Thank you, Cady. We'll do it as soon as possible.'

Despite a whole load of new thoughts going around Pip's brain, he slept well that night, not even dreaming of Mum. And in the morning, his first thought was that Cady really did want them. Cady was going to take care of them.

35.

I started reading Pip's diary last night. As it turned out, not the best day to arrive at the shop bleary-eyed, anticipating another quiet day of slow sales. But of course, I'd got things totally wrong.

There's an unexpected steady stream of people. All asking how I am after the shock of finding a dead body. Some even pretend they're here to buy a book.

Caroline Birkman from the posh boutique where Cady buys her clothes surprises me with her first-visit-ever and a not-very-convincing interest in my incredible range of two Middle-Eastern cookery titles.

'Terrible what you went through yesterday,' she says as she picks up a much cheaper air-fryer cookbook. Her eyes widen. 'Was that really not your first dead body? Everyone's saying it's not the first time you've been at a crime scene.'

I'm saved from answering by the arrival of Maggie Crump, gossipy front-of-house at Kasia's – the posh bakery where Cady buys delicious pastries.

Maggie doesn't even pretend she wants to buy a book, just rushes up to the counter. 'What was it like, walking in on a murder scene? I heard you didn't even realise, and you stepped in blood?' Maggie actually looks over the counter to peer at my shoes as she hands over a white bakery bag.

'This is such an obvious bribe, Maggie,' I say, prodding the white bag containing my favourite vegan blueberry croissant. 'I'm refusing to spend my morning discussing how grisly it was—I'm spending it, as usual, not selling many books.'

'Isn't this enough? Would a loaf of seeded wholemeal sourdough be better? I don't really read. I guess I could get a couple of books for my grandchildren.'

'Maggie, this is fine.' I take the bribe. I will need it to fortify myself for what I now suspect will be a day of my being on the wrong end of intrusive questions.

Elegant Caroline drops any pretence of being interested in books and asks if it's true that Minty was standing over Stacey with a gun in her hand (still smoking presumably) and admits she watches a lot of true-crime television, just as Joely arrives.

At least Joely wants to buy a book, but she and Caroline quickly get into discussing some multi-part serial killer drama-doc they've both been bingeing.

'And Stacey's death coming right after Mrs McFlintock,' says Caroline. 'And Minty arrested! What's it all about?'

'What's Crossways coming to?' says Maggie.

'Stacey was no accident. Bet they'll be looking into her mother's death. I bet you're not sorry to see the back of Mrs M,' Caroline says to Joely. 'She put out a lot of lies about you.'

'Not just me,' says Joely.

Grant Michaels arrives from his estate agency and looks surprised to see four people in the shop. As it's so small, it's now officially full.

Maggie turns to him eagerly. 'Well, here's one person who won't be sorry to see the back of Minty.'

'What are you—'

'Oh, Grant. What's that saying about ill winds? You won't be slow soaking up all Minty's business,' says Maggie. 'Bet it's difficult not to be super hyped about all those clients coming your way. Even in terrible circumstances, of course.'

'Who wants to be a landlord with Key Keepers when they go around murdering their customers?' says Caroline.

'Killed in the estate agent's office,' says Joely. 'Only in Crossways.'

'I'm sure it was nothing to do with property,' says Grant.

Everyone's here gossiping and not buying anything. It can't do any harm to do a little digging myself. 'So, er, talking of estate agent business, has anyone heard why Minty sacked Helena Craven?'

Cady arrives and has to weave her way past everyone to reach me at the counter.

'I know what you are all here for!' announces Cady loudly. 'What did Liv call it, Keera—malice and tea?' She gives me a wink. 'Keera's quite the celebrity! Well, we all value Keera, and January's a grim time for bookshops. Keera had a terrible shock yesterday. So, do her a favour, buy a book. Make it an expensive one. I'm on the till, so I will be watching.' She actually makes a snake-eyes gesture with her fingers. 'If any of you try to leave without buying, I'll know who you are.'

She reties her messy bun and plants herself behind the till. People, amazingly, shuffle to the counter rather than the door, even if it's only to buy a greeting card. I do have a very good selection of cards. Cady shoos me out.

Before I know it, I'm outside, but my vegan blueberry croissant is still inside.

I think this gives me the perfect excuse to scuttle along to Halfway. Can't hurt to see how Alys is while I pick up something to eat.

'Today's special is curried coconut quinoa with roasted cauliflower and pumpkin seeds,' Alys is explaining to a teenager with platform trainers and heavy eyeliner and, I'm guessing, his grandmother.

'That's a special?' enquires the grandmother. 'Do you mean special as in, experimental, and wouldn't risk putting it on your main menu? What's your most popular dish?'

'Vegan stir-fry. It has egg-free noodles.'

'No burgers? Just a wild guess.'

'Butternut and black bean burgers. Very popular.'

'It's all surprising, isn't it?' says Gran. 'I'm going to need serious time to think about this. I may have to adjust my whole lifestyle before I feel qualified to order.'

They take a menu and find an empty table. I smile at Alys. Chatting to Pip has made me ask myself questions, like: How seriously did the police talk to Helena's children when they investigated her death? Or possibly: How seriously did they listen?

'Jaxx must be pleased,' I say. 'You seem to be becoming a full-time member of staff.'

'Is this you checking up on me? Are you asking if I'm doing enough A-level study?'

'Very probably. So are you?'

'Going to pass my exams? Guess we'll see, won't we?'

'And how are you?'

Alys gives no answer, just gestures to a blackboard and an array of drink choices and cakes. She might think question time is at an end, but I'm not that much of a pushover.

'I do kind of feel that maybe you don't have enough people looking out for you, Alys. It makes me want to do that job.'

'Lucky for you then, that the position isn't open. I don't need anyone.'

'Everyone needs someone, whether they know it or not. If I was in a good mood, I'd avoid saying anything cheesy like I think it would be good for you to talk. But actually, I'm in a really foul mood, so I can't quite be bothered to skirt around.'

'This about me going easier on Cady, right?'

'I was going to tiptoe around how to bring up you and Cady, so thanks for saving me the trouble. I think I'm just saying no one's getting an easy ride here. We can all use a little kindness and understanding. My nerves couldn't take living in your house.'

'And that's all my fault?'

'There's a chance Cady will listen if I try to smooth over whatever the issues are here. I will try very hard not to take her side, promise. But I do want to talk. Not here when you're at work, obviously. After work? Tomorrow?'

From Pip's diary, I have so many questions, assuming Pip's diary isn't just stories.

Rick doesn't exactly appear to do a lot to smooth things over. Or anything. Alys has thrown in the unexpected idea of not going to university.

Could her or Cady's nerves stand her staying? What's happening with their old house?

Did Alys ever suspect that Helena's death might not have been an accident or a suicide?

'All I ever hear is about how wonderful Cady is, how lucky we are. Cady always makes me look bad, even when it's not me who's in the wrong. She does it all deliberately, you know.' Alys's glance over my shoulder tells me more customers are arriving.

'Does what deliberately?' I say quietly.

'The whole scatty, "*I can't cook; I forgot you're vegan* crap,"' Alys waves her hands theatrically, making air quotes. 'That.'

'I think she's—'

'Nope! Forget I spoke. I knew you'd swoop in with some conciliatory shit.'

From the dark rings around her eyes and the jumpy way she starts to tidy a counter that doesn't need tidying, I can tell that Alys really does need someone to talk to.

'I'm sorry you feel no one listens to you or believes you,' I say. 'I've done my best to help Pip. He cares about you. Helping you helps him.'

'How can I talk to you when you'll take Cady's side? When everything she does is planned to make me look bad,' snaps Alys. 'She really lays it on when anyone's over. Makes me look like I'm being super-awkward when I won't eat her food. She is so not what you think. She can put a perfectly good meal together if she wants to.'

'It's true.' I nod. 'Sometimes Cady can be organised.'

'Exactly, totally manipulative. All that endearing scattiness is a tactic. It's just amazing how she gets her own way. Have you *seen* how Dad has changed?'

For now, I think I need to just let Alys let it all out. But I also feel it's up to me to put this right, because who else will? It's going to take time. A lot of time.

'Dad's just as bad. He has this super-charming act everyone falls for. But he doesn't give a crap about anyone other than himself. He's never once stood up for me, takes Cady's side Every Single Time.'

'I couldn't possibly understand what you've been through,' I say gently. 'But if we can meet and talk, I will do my best to listen. I won't just take Cady's side and dismiss everything you are feeling. Promise.'

'It's not just feelings! It's all to drive me out. She wants me out. I'm the only thing stopping her and Dad getting together.'

I refrain from reminding her Cady was the one who insisted the Cravens move in.

Behind me, more customers are queuing.

'Can we talk properly? Please. A coffee? Somewhere else? Just try me. Just talk. I do think I've helped your brother. You're not alone, Alys. I really want you to believe that. And what you say won't get back to Cady, I promise. I want to… no, I *will* help. Just give me a chance.'

She's actually considering. Then Alys finally nods. I finally breathe properly.

'I'm working tonight—Jaxx is experimenting with opening later now we've got a licence. I'm off tomorrow.'

'Tomorrow's great! Thank you, Alys. I live in Harcourt, above a takeaway that's best known for its permanent low-hygiene rating rather than its food.'

'Well, let's not go there.'

'Agreed. Strictly for people who like the smell of slightly off cooking fat.'

'Whatever.'

'Quite. Thanks, Alys.'

Alys suggests a coffee shop in Harcourt and a time that means I'll need to close early.

'Perfect.'

I don't know it. I spend little time in Harcourt. It's a prosperous town, but somehow manages to be a great example of how town centres can go horribly wrong.

I had been going to order the stir-fry and call it brunch. But Cady will be valiantly fending off the gossips. So I leave with a coffee and pause to drink in the smell of the artisan bakery.

'Still not feeding yourself?' says a voice behind me.

I turn and it's my favourite hot customer, Sully Blake, wrapped up in his luxury dark wool coat, breath steaming gently in the cold January air as he sidles up next to me, close enough so I get that alluring aura of woodsmoke again, which mixes really well with the warm and buttery bakery smells.

'Just busy noticing a new bakery addition—a cruffin. A cross between a croissant and a muffin, apparently. That, and torturing myself with bakery smells. There's actually a children's story about how bakery smells cost nothing. *Sanji and the Baker.*' Why am I gabbling like this? 'How's your mum?'

'Perked up with those great books to read. You have impeccable taste.'

'Actually, I really do. But too few people appreciate that.'

I'm pretty sure this is flirting. Luckily, a small, grey-haired customer puts a stop to it by coming right up to us.

'You're a dark horse, Keera, finding the only tall, dark, and handsome stranger in town to talk to. I don't think we've been introduced.'

I would say Dahlia Figgis is one of the worst gossips in Crossways, but honestly, competition is so high we could set up an annual award. Get people to vote. Maybe a trophy and an awards ceremony in the village hall.

'I'm sorry, Dahlia, but I'm due back at the shop.'

I dive back into the safety of Between the Lines, and the last person I expect to see is Pip Craven tidying some of my shelves. 'Hello. After your old job?'

'We've talked about this.' Liv appears behind him. '*Job* usually hints at some element of payment. Where would you be without us *volunteers*?'

'Actually, I got a lift over with Dad. I wanted to ask you a favour,' says Pip.

'Ok?'

'Dad's insisting we go to see this band in this pub this evening. And it'll be completely cringe with Dad. He said I could bring a friend.'

I'm pleased the offer of bringing a friend made Pip think of me, even though I'm sure Rick meant a school friend. And me tagging along with Rick Craven for an evening out is not exactly smooth, as I am already the centre of too much gossip.

'Cady unfortunately suggested Pip and Rick go as a father and son bonding exercise, so of course Pip doesn't want to go. Dear Cady,' says Liv.

'She thinks it'll encourage me to play the guitar again,' adds Pip.

'I didn't know you played the guitar,' I say.

'I don't. I mean, I did. Will you come? It'll be a really bad evening, but it'll be slightly better with you there.'

'How can you resist an offer like that?' says Liv.

'Where is Cady?'

'I took over,' says Liv. 'She was doing a valiant job, but I think she needed some retail therapy that didn't involve being on the wrong side of the counter.'

'Please?' says Pip.

'Of course I'll come.'

The door opens, and Sully Blake walks in. 'You give the impression you never have customers, but your shop is always busy,' he says.

'These are not customers.'

'They never are,' says Liv.

'So, it's my last night tonight, leaving tomorrow.' Sully fidgets, eyeing Liv and Pip awkwardly. 'I've got no one to eat with, so I thought, rather than you just taking in the smell of baking, we could help each other out.'

That sounded less like flirting. That sounds like a proper date. I was not expecting that.

'Actually, I am unexpectedly busy,' I say.

'What Keera means,' says Liv, 'is that it's a kind offer. And if you are interested in seeing an iffy band at a grotty pub...' Liv turns to Pip. 'Does the Waggon and Horses stretch to food?'

'I think it does burgers. And it's not grotty.'

'Then what Keera means to say is that if your idea of dinner could stretch to a burger and an iffy band at the local pub, then you are very welcome to get in on what passes for action in Crossways. The more the merrier, eh, Pip?'

Cheers, Liv, taking over my life again.

Of course, I fully expect Sully to say no.

But he gives me that irresistible twinkle. 'Can't think of anything nicer. What time shall I pick you up?'

36.

Broken Pieces, Day 268

Daily challenge – Have a normal conversation instead of an argument

'What are these doing here?' Alys demanded the second she saw one of Cady's expensive flower arrangements on something called the dresser in the hall.

Cady looked genuinely puzzled. 'I thought they looked pretty?'

Listening to arguments about flowers wasn't new. His mum and dad had them all the time.

'We hate cut flowers in this family, don't we, Dad?' said Alys.

Dad did his usual when asked to get involved in anything unpleasant. He was suddenly utterly absorbed in reading some plant catalogue.

Cady turned to Keera, who looked like she wished she knew the right thing to say.

'Where were they grown? Usually in very poor parts of the world. Do you even think about that?' said Alys.

Alys had arrived just as they were about to eat, and amazingly, it was pizza, which Pip considered the best food.

Keera called in sometimes with a suggestion of a family movie night, which everyone thought was a terrible idea. But she also brought pizza, so they all went along with it.

Keera said the deal was they sit around together, pretending to watch the most terrible film they could find, one they can all rip to shreds.

So Keera brought pizza along with a list of suggested films, ones she guarantees all of them will agree are terrible, so they would all agree on something.

The best evenings were when Keera was over.

But it didn't stop the family arguments.

Cady felt family film night and Keera being over meant Alys should not go out and meet friends. But Keera had a gentle word that Alys was studying for exams and should relax in a way best for her.

But after seeing the fresh flowers, Alys was far from relaxed. She was steaming.

'Working conditions are terrible. The flowers are smothered with every known fungicide and pesticide—banned in all sensible countries.'

'Well, I—'

'I don't think Cady knew that. Most people don't think—' Keera had begun.

'And there you have it!' Alys made a sweeping gesture, and Pip thought that would be her exit line, but Alys could never leave anything alone.

'They contaminate the local water, poisoning everything. Then they are *flown in* and we look at them and chuck them in the bin after two days. But at least your house looks *pretty*.'

'I'm sure—' Keera had begun.

'If Cady had *thought*,' Alys went on, 'she might have done something useful, like insisting she'll only buy locally grown flowers from her florist. Or at least organic flowers.'

'I love locally grown flowers. Your mum loved sweet peas,' said Cady gently. 'Maybe your dad can grow them here.'

It was meant as a peace-making solution, but Cady seldom got it right.

'You suggest having Mum's favourite flower here!' said Alys. 'It's like you think of everything possible to trigger me, so I end up looking bad—particularly in front of other people.'

Her glance took in Keera, who looked lost for a response.

Pip noticed Alys teared up and knew she would hate showing this sign of weakness. He braced himself for what would come next.

Alys swirled to face Dad. 'Do you remember?'

'Remember that her favourite flowers were sweet peas? Of course I do,' said Dad, unable to ignore the argument any longer. 'But there was nothing she loved more than you two.'

'Then why do you let *her* get away with everything Mum was never allowed to do?' Alys was yelling now. 'You always used to give Mum a lecture if she *bought* flowers. It's like you're a different person.'

Pip often felt a rage building inside of him too, and if he didn't let it out, he might explode. That was the great thing about having a sister like Alys, she was never afraid of speaking out.

Then Dad made a big mistake. He grinned. He was limbering up to come in with a joke, Pip knew it, Alys knew it. Keera must have known it and saved him by lifting the lid on a pizza box.

'Let's not let this pizza get cold. Cady's turn to choose the film tonight.'

Pip really wanted to get stuck in to the pizza, even if it meant watching some awful, soppy film Cady would choose, where bits would be embarrassing to watch with his family. Alys simply melted away into her room, which was better than the usual door slamming.

Cady turned to appeal to Dad. Muttering under her breath, 'Rick, this has to stop. You should say something to her. You shouldn't let her talk to me like that.' She turned to Keera. 'God knows I try.'

'She really couldn't have more on her plate than she's got right now,' said Keera. 'Exams on top of everything else.'

'How long do I have to be patient and understanding before we can have a normal conversation instead of an argument?' said Cady.

Keera gestured to Pip to have pizza, and Pip heaped a plate with a good amount of slices. Keera went after Alys. He didn't want to watch the film, so he drifted off to go and listen.

He had to put his ear right to the door as they were speaking in low voices.

'I think maybe you should apologise,' said Keera.

'And I think I was restrained. I should have just dumped those flowers right in the bin. You and I both know Dad should have said something.'

'Your dad's got a lot on his plate too. He's so grateful for everything Cady's done.'

'None of us asked her to do it.'

'If you're going to change someone's mind about something, especially something big and political that makes people feel uncomfortable, it's kind of a good idea to do it calmly, away from where arguments are going to flare,' Keera soothes reasonably. 'Confrontations seldom work.'

'So my approach is wrong as well? Every time! She always makes me look like the criminal here.'

'Don't forget Cady's still grieving too. We all lost her, you know. Kindness doesn't cost anything.'

'Believe me, kindness costs a lot. It's a shame Dad wasn't kinder to Mum when he had the chance.'

Pip didn't think anyone would notice he'd broken the deal and didn't go back to watch the film.

He had his food. He went to his room and switched on the computer and tried to get lost in General Oblivion, a game that always worked. It was just about the only strategy that did – to stop thinking, stop going over everything. Endlessly.

But that night it failed for the first time, and it was clear not a single thing about his life was working anymore.

37.

It's no surprise that Sully arrives in a proper expensive car. I arranged to meet him down the road a bit because I wanted to save him from being exposed to the full horror of the horrible part of town I live in. I don't want to be embarrassed, but I am.

I have no intention of explaining the life choices and bad decisions that led to me living in quite such a crummy flat. Although, seeing it through someone else's eyes should maybe force me to face up to just how badly my life is going. Maybe force me to fully admit how poor some of my decisions and life choices have actually been. Even start doing things differently. Maybe.

Sully turns up on time, which is good as I've put on my favourite jacket, because: vanity. I know I look good in it. But it's totally January-inappropriate. If I had to stand around for long I'd be a shivering mass of chattering teeth.

'Nice car,' I say as I slide into the warmth. Sully's car is even clean inside and out. Who has a clean car in January? 'I hope I'm not contaminating the clean smell by bringing a lingering aroma of takeaway.'

'No, you smell nice, and nice hair,' Sully says.

'Thank you. I brushed it specially.'

I did want to look nice, but I wanted more to go over the pictures I'd taken of Pip's timeline from his Back to the Future poster. I've read some of Pip's therapy journaling. I am desperate to ask what he meant when he mumbled something about, '*It would be so much better if it was all Minty.*'

Because we do all think it was all Minty. I'm left with an uncomfortable dread of what Pip concluded from all his talking to people. Minty makes sense.

Although Liv had questions, like what Minty and Stacey argued about if Stacey brought cash to do a deal.

'Why do you think you smell of takeaway?' asks Sully. 'You promised me a burger. Have you already eaten? And we're meeting your young friend?'

'Pip. And quite possibly his dad, Rick, yes.'

'Want to tell me more?'

'Are you asking if this is how I normally spend my time? The truth is it's complicated.'

'But the kind of thing you do often?' Sully asks.

'Things that are too complicated to explain? Yes. Going out for the evening, rather than staying in reading, not so much. Going to hear local bands? Never. Spending an evening with teenagers and their dads? More often than I should. Are you hinting I might be doing things wrong?'

'I'm hinting I find you very intriguing and unusual.'

'That sounds bad.' But we grin at each other in the dark car.

Here I am, heading out for an evening with Sully, when I am totally sworn off letting anyone get close to me. But he's one of the few people who reacted to my whole 'so I opened a bookshop' story by saying he thinks my following my dream is brilliant. He even likes the name, Between the Lines. But also it's Liv, it's always Liv. She's bulldozed me into another situation I'm not ready for.

Does he think this is a date? Do I think it's a date?

At least spending an evening with Sully is going to be pretty risk-free since he's not local, so no chance of a second date, let alone any involvement.

It's probably lucky we're being joined by Pip and Rick. I'm probably panicking. But maybe I've made a good choice. Maybe it's the start of many.

'Is it too complicated to tell me more about this band we are going to see?' says Sully.

'Afraid we are both taking a plunge into the dark on the band front.'

In the time it takes to drive to the Waggon and Horses, I do explain a little about Pip. The troubled teenager who has got under my skin. The death of his mother, my friend.

How nothing about my life has turned out as I expected. How two of my customers have died. How this was supposed to be a simple life.

'You said the other day about what you should have called your bookshop,' says Sully. 'You're making it sound like you should call it the Little Bookshop of Murders.'

'That would make it sound like me and trouble are friends, when we are not even on speaking terms.'

Sully turns and grins at me as we pull into the car park. 'Yeah, but I can tell that you do attract trouble, whether you want to or not.'

232

I hope at least this evening nothing will go wrong. It's time to leave trouble behind; time to concentrate on my business. But I wasn't expecting Pip to have made that timeline. I certainly wasn't expecting one so meticulous. Pip may take more convincing than me to give it all up.

What did Pip say? That Mrs M said there was something she didn't tell the police?

I can imagine Mrs M sitting in her chair with a view, doing her crossword.

I wish Mrs M had chosen to get worried a little sooner. But in that raging water, Helena wouldn't have stood a chance; just going in was a death sentence. Nothing anyone could have done.

Minty's been arrested. And when do we ever get all the answers we'd like? I guess I could talk to Elliott again. Even thinking about that makes me stressed.

All thoughts of Helena are shoved from my mind when the Waggon and Horses is way busier than I expected. People are loading up with drinks, and the whole place is clamouring with anticipatory noise.

'Clearly the place to be,' says Sully. 'Never thought Crossways would be—'

'Me neither. I'm not sure I even rate our chances of getting any drinks.'

I spot Pip slouching against the wall near where I can see Rick has sandwiched himself at a table with a group of women who have bunched up to make room for him. Rick is the sort of person women bunch up to make room for.

'Hey Pip! This is popular!' I call out to him.

The corner Pip is in is a little quieter, and I get near enough to overhear a little of Rick's conversation.

He's looking not only relaxed, but in his element, chatting affably, while Pip lurks nearby nursing a lemonade.

'Surprised ourselves coming to see jazz,' giggles the girl with the reddest painted lips – a big, glossy pout.

'We don't even like jazz,' says another.

'You'll like these guys,' says Rick. 'They just got back together and really making a go of it. I can introduce you afterwards…' Rick talks knowledgeably about the band.

In the background are sounds of tuning up.

'Any of you play?' Rick asks.

'I played the recorder at school, but dropped it when I realised it didn't help getting boyfriends in the slightest,' giggles the dark-haired one.

'Pip, playing the guitar, does that help to get you girlfriends?' Rick finally looks to where Pip is standing.

'I'm going outside,' Pip says. I doubt Rick even hears.

'Maybe we should go outside,' I say to Sully.

'Maybe it's up to Rick to go outside?'

'Yes of course, you're right.' But it takes a lot of effort not to follow.

The music starts up in a back room, and I shout an apology in Sully's ear. 'Sorry. I know this wasn't what you signed up for.'

'I didn't have a clue what I'd signed up for, just guessed any time spent with you would be complicated. We can see the band, eat later?' Sully says.

I nod distractedly, wishing Rick wasn't having such an obviously good time.

The minute Rick goes after Pip, I tell myself, we can leave, go somewhere else, find food, not get involved, well, any more involved with the Cravens than I am already. But still Rick doesn't go, and I stand there, biting my lip.

I cannot leave it any longer. I tap Rick on the shoulder. He turns, looks surprised. I tell him I think he needs to go and check if Pip is all right.

'I think we both know he's not all right,' Rick says tetchily.

'I'm sure you'd have had a better evening if you hadn't brought him along, but seeing as he's here, why don't you at least talk to him?'

Rick's face loses its affable charm for a moment. He gives me a look that's more resigned than angry. With an exaggerated sigh and slumping of his shoulders, he does at least go after Pip.

I turn to Sully. 'I know, I know, what's with the parenting advice. I shouldn't be interfering—and now, I'm going to make things worse by eavesdropping.'

'It's ok, I get it. You're not the sort who stays on the sidelines,' says Sully. 'I will try my luck at the bar. If I manage to get anywhere near, what would you like?'

I ask for a pint of the local ale and head outside into the dark and cold to lurk and listen because I can't help myself. I absolutely cannot stop sticking my nose in.

38.

I hear Rick's voice clearly in the darkness. Always so affable, today it definitely has the tinge of fed-up about it, maybe with a hint of angry.

'I don't think I should apologise for enjoying myself—I think *you* need to lighten up.'

There's a paved area that leads to grass covered in a sea of wooden seats edged with frost. Patio furniture is stacked in a corner. It smells of things stored in the damp for a long time. I'm in the shadows just outside the doorway. Pip's leaning against a wall just beyond where light from the windows falls.

'Sure. I'll walk home,' says Pip. 'As you say—enjoy yourself, why don't you?'

'Thought that's what we came here for.' Rick sighs. 'The band is great! This place is buzzing.'

'Yeah, you look so interested in the band.'

'Can't you try to stop blaming me for wanting to have a little fun?'

'I kinda wish you didn't look quite so happy about it.'

'You want a burger? Have a burger.' Rick finds his wallet, waves a note.

'Do you think this is about a burger?'

'I don't know what it's about. What does it take for you to stop being weird and make some effort? Doesn't cost anything to be friendly. Enjoy yourself. Is school ok?'

Pip laughs. 'You are comically bad at this.'

'Don't be like this, Pip.'

'Like what?'

'You know what I mean—like her. Some people just aren't good at being happy.'

'Always the expert on what made her happy.'

'How is this going to help?'

'Help you, you mean? Why does it always have to be about you?'

'I thought this *was* about me. All right, d'you think I've been happy? Do you know what, ok, I'll admit it. It definitely feels good to know I'll never hear those dreaded words from your mum ever again. "*I've got a great new job idea.*" Come back inside. It's bloody freezing.'

'Why was Mum so unhappy?'

'Think I know? Nothing's ever perfect. You gotta learn, Pip, to grab your happiness where you can. It's been a year. A year! Why can't both of you just move on? Alys is bothered by too many things. At least she's managing to do her studies, have a job, is heading to uni. Moving on.'

'So, Alys is ok?' Pip runs a finger around the top of his glass musically. 'The fact that she never eats? Or that she spends every moment she can at the cafe? Do you ever think she feels like she doesn't really have a home anymore? And she's got questions.'

'Questions?'

'Like when did you start getting so into Cady? More than a year?'

'I do not think that is any of your business,' Rick answers, definitely angry.

'Maybe that's the trouble,' says Pip. 'I feel it is very much my business. Are you going to pretend Mum didn't know? That it might've made her unhappy.'

'I've had enough of this; I'm going back inside.'

I should move before he sees me, but I've lost all feeling in my feet. Rick might have finished, but Pip hasn't.

'Is that why you lied to the police?'

That makes Rick stop. It gives me a chance to dart back just inside the door, but I can still hear.

'Look. I don't know why she did what she did. I don't know what you've got into your head. Christ! I've nothing to hide, but I don't have to explain myself to you.'

'Nothing to hide, eh? I can't quite get it straight. When the police asked, you'd shrug and smile and make out things were ok. Guess I understand how you might not want to admit she was miserable.'

'You are too young to get it. All couples are miserable part of the time.'

'And now here you are, feet under Cady's table.'

'I don't get what's wrong with—'

'Got yourself the easy number. But like you say, all couples are miserable some of the time. I was close to thinking... Then, suddenly, we've got Minty, who's possibly killed two people. Two more deaths.'

'That's all about money and some property row.'

'Is it?'

'You're asking me? Honestly, I don't know. I don't get why you're asking me.'

'Because suddenly there's you with this new contract 'n all. That never happened before. And Minty again. Feet under the table again?'

'That's not... I do not have to explain myself to you.'

'But you got yourself an easy deal there too. Life's suddenly looking pretty good. Not miserable any more.'

'I do not know what you are on about.'

'I only hope that's true.'

'Where is this all coming from? Pip, I—' Rick sighs. 'Mum, she...'

'Someone was with her.'

'What?'

'Mum wasn't alone when she died.'

'No, you've got that wrong,' Rick now sounds icily patient. 'The police looked into it. They talked to me, I don't know how many times.'

'Mrs McFlintock told me.'

'Is that where all this is coming from? Mrs McFlintock was a nasty liar.'

'What about that note in Mum's car? Why have a note with a time and a place if you're just going for a walk? Why, if you're going to kill yourself? She was meeting someone.'

'Take no notice of what that old bat said. The police clearly didn't.'

'She didn't tell the police. But she wouldn't tell me either,' he admits.

'Don't you think that's because she didn't know anything?'

'And I remembered one evening when Mum was going out. She was really happy about something. Triumphant even. She told me she had a little secret.'

'Again, Pip, you've lost me. And I think you are really losing it.'

'You probably see why I hope it's all Minty and that's the end of it. But why did Minty and Mum meet earlier that day? They weren't exactly friends. Why'd she lose her job? Why are you suddenly working for her? I thought I was getting close to understanding what it was all really about. Now we've got three deaths and I don't actually think I've got a clue.'

'This,' splutters Rick, 'is nonsense!'

Pip's not satisfied. But Rick's got a point that Mrs M might have told him a pack of lies.

Maybe she liked Pip visiting and kept stringing him along. Pip's determined to keep digging, keep stirring. But if you ask too many questions, some of the answers you're not going to like.

'I don't have to listen to this!' splutters Rick.

This time, Rick storms past me. I'm squeezed into a corner, but Rick's in too much of a hurry and filled with too much fury to see me, so he doesn't know I've listened to every word. But what am I going to do about it?

Sully is standing there holding two drinks. I don't know for how long or what he heard. Or what he can possibly think. 'Still want this?' He hands me a pint of

Abingdon Bridge that he went to the bar for ages ago, and I gratefully accept.

'More than you know.' I take a big gulp. 'Sorry, this is probably your worst evening ever.'

'It's an evening I won't forget. I should have said that I have a really early start in the morning.'

'Time to leave me to deal with my own shit. Good decision.'

'That's not what I said,' Sully says gently. 'But it's time to go. Shall we take Pip home? Then I'll take you home. I really do have an early start.'

'I'm so sorry. I didn't mean… This evening really wasn't anything I hoped.'

'It was a little bit what I hoped.'

'You hoped it would be an utter disaster?'

Sully twinkles at me. 'I expect many evenings with you don't turn out to be what anyone expects.'

'Huge drama and everyone deciding they need to leave early?'

'Perhaps that's your unique quality—I suspect nothing you do ever turns out how anyone expects.'

39.

Alys doesn't show for our meeting.

I've been in the cafe for over half an hour, wondering how long I should give it before admitting I've blown my chance of getting Alys to trust me. I thought – I hoped, I'd made a little dent in her back-off aura. I've spent the time thinking about what I think Pip was accusing his dad of last night, of his being involved somehow. Is Rick right, and it's all in Pip's head? Everything Pip said, about Rick being in a much better place a year on, could all be coincidence. Even the job with Minty.

How much of a fan of coincidence am I? Even in Crossways.

Every time the door opens, I look up. Its never Alys. I would call, but I don't have her number. I try Pip, but Pip never seems to look at his phone. I refuse to involve Cady. If Alys found out, it'd send her ballistic, I'm sure. Would Jaxx give me her number?

Pip didn't say a word in the car when Sully and I gave him a lift home, just sat there brooding, while I silently speculated.

Rick's won that big contract from Key Keepers. What's the truth of Helena leaving Key Keepers? Helena

worked for Minty. She spoke to Minty the day she died…
And Pip hinted something might have happened between
Rick and Cady before Helena died. How does any of it add
up to anything?

Luckily the cafe staff are a bit shoddy with their
clearing up and don't remove my empty cup so I will wait
a bit longer, still thinking through everything.

Was there anything between Rick and Minty? That
might explain why Rick won that contract and even why
Minty no longer wanted to work with Helena. Where
would that leave Minty now? Out in the cold? Actually, in
jail. Because in all of this, maybe what no one could have
expected was Cady doing what she did, swooping in,
moving the Craven family to her more suitable home.
Forging that close bond with Rick.

But Rick had only a tenuous relationship with Stacey.
Then I loop back to my very first thought when I
discovered Stacey's body – was Stacey killed because she
was mistaken for Minty?

You could say people around Rick do have a habit of
dying. And something else from Pip's therapy journal
makes a tremor of unease go through me – how Rick used
the kids to put pressure on Cady to make a will.

My phone rings. It's Liv. 'Hi! Are you busy doing
anything?'

'Being stood up, I think.'

'Things not go well with the adorable Sully last night?'

'On a scale of one to appalling, it was pretty much off
the scale. Why does everything I touch go wrong? I have

to face up to being cursed. Do you think Rick was having an affair when he was with Helena? And if so, who do you think is more likely—Cady or Minty?'

'How deliciously intriguing! How much more interesting your life is than mine. You can give me all the details of what that marvellous brain of yours is inventing when I see you. You closed the shop early. Where exactly are you currently being stood up?'

'I'm waiting in a Harcourt cafe for Alys Craven. I guess you're phoning with some urgent and exciting news that's going to make my life immeasurably better?'

'Elliott wants to talk to you.'

'Not entirely the answer I wanted.'

'And it's not even because he's cross with you. There will be no lecture about not sticking your nose in, I have a promise.'

'I've had a couple of surprises in the last few days, but I think that has to be the biggest twist of them all.'

'Have you had enough of being stood up?' Liv asks.

'You think I should abandon sitting alone in a coffee shop wondering where it all went wrong?'

'You could spend all day doing that. Or admit she's not going to show and come and have coffee with me instead.'

Liv is right. I've given it nearly an hour. Alys most likely got cold feet because she isn't convinced I won't side with Cady. I have more work to do there. Plus, a couple of things are kicking off my instincts, and Liv does keep telling me I need to trust those. Pip's instincts are telling him this isn't over yet. He told me he hoped it was all Minty, because that would make things easier. He's been thinking about this for months. Pip has put together a meticulous timeline and has written about their family life leading up to Helena's death. He suspects there's more to it.

So what's Pip thinking exactly? That there's still a murderer out there? One who thinks they're getting away with it.

40.

I may have ruffled Elliott's feathers once or twice. I suspect it's possible.

Even so, I expect he wants to see me to congratulate me that I suspected from the outset there was something rotten in the heart of Crossways. No doubt he's eager to give me crucial inside dirt, grovel and ask for my help. Is Minty talking?

But first, when I get back in my car, on the familiar journey from Harcourt to Crossways, I make a detour.

At Halfway, I ask Jaxx if she's seen Alys (no), but Jaxx does give me her number when I explain I'm worried about her. Alys's phone rings out. I can't see exactly how things went so badly wrong from where I thought I'd started to build a bridge yesterday to her ghosting me today. I message her and can't help staring at my phone, hoping to see she's read it.

As I arrive at Liv's I send another *Hope you are OK. Love to talk soon. Hope I can still help*. Now I need to face Elliott. Why am I thinking of this as facing him? Liv takes me through to her so-amazing-it-belongs-on-a-film-set kitchen, to where Elliott's fidgeting with a coffee cup next to a plate of posh biscuits. I help myself to three.

'Sorry, I seem to keep missing out on opportunities to eat. Plus, these are my favourites.'

'Keera went on a hot date last night,' says Liv, as I take a third seat at a central counter on a tall, vibrant scarlet chair that stands out in the monochrome kitchen. Liv offers a choice of coffee or wine, which makes me realise how late it is already.

I'm tempted to answer wine, but I'm refusing to lose hope Alys will contact me, and I want to be on it and ready. So I take another biscuit and ask for coffee.

The kitchen is all glass and hidden lighting and feels comforting even on a dark evening, especially with the smell of decadently expensive coffee and the aroma of a rapidly diminishing pile of expensive biscuits.

'Hot date?' says Elliott, arching one eyebrow.

'It does happen. I don't think it quite deserves the smirk.'

He gives me a shifty look, like a sullen teenager, which goes well with his baggy jeans and worn hoodie, as if making a point this isn't work. When Mrs M's had been broken into he'd had a different look and a recent close shave and, despite the terrible jumper, I suspected he might have been going on a date and I interrupted him.

'Knowing Keera, the evening went badly, ended with a row, everyone deciding to leave early and no chance for dinner.' Liv's smirking, waiting to be entertained by another of my disasters.

'You paint such a terrible picture of my life.'

'Tell me if it's not accurate?'

'We didn't get to the eating part.' I take two more of the very gingery and heavy on the dark-chocolate biscuits. 'If I had to live the rest of my life on only one food, I think it would be these biscuits,' I sigh, checking my phone again. 'It was never going to be a hot date as I was mostly there to keep an eye on Pip.'

'I'm sure Sully thought you were very entertaining.'

'That's not quite the compliment I want it to be, is it?'

The coffee is followed by a sandwich. Liv's remembered to make it vegan. 'You've certainly made my life more interesting. What's happened with Alys?'

'She's so many issues, it makes her a thorn in the side of the Cravens, and Cady. I feel she's stopping them moving on. Thought she was going to talk to me. But I've screwed up and not making the great progress I imagined.'

'Alys is standing in the way of Rick and Cady getting together properly?' says Liv. 'I wondered what was taking them so long. But you're worried about her.'

I devour my sandwich in about three enormous bites. Liv offers more of those expensive biscuits.

I haven't had chance to fill Liv in with everything Pip's been up to. Alys probably simply changed her mind today. But *three deaths*. And Pip's *I hope it's all Minty*. Pip thinks there's still more. How worried should I be about Alys?

I turn to Elliott. In this lighting, I notice his eyes are very blue. 'I'm not a great one for asking favours. But could you trace her phone? Even if it's switched off?'

'Might it be a little too soon to press the panic button and call the police just because a teenager forgot to turn up for coffee?' says Liv sensibly. 'I could find a reason to call Cady and drop in a question, see if anyone knows where Alys is?'

'Would you Liv? Thank you. Be super subtle. Alys has got a real thing about Cady and I'm trying to smooth feathers, not make things worse between them.'

Liv makes the call. Alys is not at home, but Cady isn't worried.

'Alys might be taking some time to herself,' says Elliott. He's been nursing the same cup of coffee. He's the sort who doesn't always have to be the one speaking – definitely a listener. Taking it all in. 'How old is she?'

'Eighteen.'

'Why are you so worried?' asks Liv.

'Because I hate how I feel in a fog, not seeing a clear picture. I'm worried I'm trying to see the wrong picture. And there have been three deaths in Crossways—one of them her mother.'

'You're bringing Helena's death into this?' Liv shares a look with Elliott.

'I don't know. Pip's been... connecting it all, thinks there are more answers. No, you're right. I am panicking. Elliott, you wanted to see me? I'm hoping it's good news, like Minty confessed already, we do have all the answers and I don't need to worry there's something we're missing.'

'Minty's sticking to her story that she was called away and came back and found you standing over the body.'

'Do you believe her? Not about the *finding me standing over the body* bit—that is true. Unfortunate, but true.'

'It's not about what I believe, it's what we can prove. As you know.'

'But? I can tell there's a but,' I say.

'But it's a great cover story as it'll be difficult to establish exact timings. So far, we've so little on her we don't even have enough to keep Minty in for questioning for much longer.' Elliott drains his coffee.

I wonder at Elliott suddenly sharing things about an ongoing investigation as Liv has been clear that Elliott never discusses his cases with her.

But is there really nothing that proves beyond doubt that Minty killed Stacey?

'You were there, on the scene, right about the time Stacey was killed,' says Elliott. He puts me on the spot now with his forensic gaze.

'I'm the alternative? You think it was me!'

'That's not what I… No. You hinted you think there was something we missed, something was wrong about Stacey's mother's death, and now Stacey's been killed and we cannot absolutely put Minty there when it happened,' says Elliott. 'So we need more. You told me we didn't look into the first death properly. I know you've been sticking your nose in—'

'Investigating.'

'Investigating, of course.' Elliott gives me a small smile. 'My guess is if you'd had evidence, you'd have come straight out with it. That means you have suspicions. I want to hear what you think we missed. There might not be much chance of tying the two together, but if we've any chance of nailing this, we need something. And this is all unofficial. Say what you like. Mum says you talk to a lot of people and you've picked up on things. However stupid or unlikely or outrageous, I'm ready for it,' Elliott says with a sudden grin.

'Keera is not stupid,' says Liv. 'Although, she is quite unlikely. You need to be ready for her. She kept telling me something was going on in Crossways. I accused Keera of bringing big-city ideas and morals to our quiet part of the world and looking for something to clean up.' She sets about making more coffee and opens a second pack of the very expensive chocolate biscuits. 'Sorry for not taking your ideas seriously sooner.'

'I've been slow too,' I admit. 'It's the Crossways effect. I moved here wanting a different version of what life can be. I wanted to live somewhere people don't keep letting you down. Among nice, civilised people. But people are just people. And I thought the coincidences were because it's a small place.' I shrug.

'Mum said you already suspected Minty,' says Elliott. 'Have you got anything for me?'

'Just a muddle of questions and contradictions that catch my attention, which I find difficult to ignore.' Elliott and Liv are both so smart and organised. Anything I say is going to make me sound overimaginative and dramatic. I don't want to sound like that person in front of Elliott.

'But connections that other people might miss. Connections that have made you worried about Alys,' says Elliott.

'If it's really shocking, say it quickly, like ripping off a plaster,' says Liv. 'Besides, I'll take the biscuits away if you don't share.'

I take a deep breath. 'It's mostly dull, small things. Like Mrs M having a super-fancy car when she didn't really drive. Stacey telling me the rent was low even though Minty wanted to get her mother out.'

I look at Elliott, wondering what he's making of this, but he just gives me a nod to continue. 'People don't always act rationally or make sense. We know Mrs M lied. She might have been forgetful.'

'She had a notebook in the sugar caddy,' says Elliott.

I should have guessed he'd always been paying close attention, even when I thought he was being dismissive.

'Keera thinks Mrs M had *serious* shit on a lot of people.' Liv surprises me as she isn't someone I've heard swear very much. 'Two things matter in a place like Crossways—reputations and money. Mrs M knew that. You're asking yourself how she paid for her fancy car?'

'I have no evidence of anything at all.'

'Elliott asked for leads and outrageous ideas,' says Liv. 'Evidence is up to him. Carry on.'

Another deep breath.

'So I guessed Mrs M had something on Minty. The rumour about Minty and the backhanders—was that a secret? Was it even true? Helena got a job with Minty, but that ended really quickly. Did Helena find out something about Minty? Should we bring Helena's death into this? Because I just found out Helena spoke to Minty the day

252

she died. I found out because Pip's been talking to everyone, busy doing an impressive timeline of his mother's death.'

'That's not great to hear,' says Elliott.

'I know. But it's done. Pip's convinced his mother's death wasn't simply an accident, or even suicide. Pip asked his dad about this new contract with Minty—yet another connection. Pip had talked to Mrs M.'

'That's not great to hear either,' says Elliott.

'I know. But she dropped hints, not that she ever did more than drop hints. But she did find Helena's body. My guess is she saw Helena arrive at Harcourt Pools. Something got her worried.'

'Your guesses are very good,' says Liv. 'You asked me if Rick was involved with someone before Helena died, and who was more likely—Cady or Minty? What's your guess? Because I didn't know Helena, but from what I know of Rick, it sounds possible he was involved with someone. I hope Cady would have sent the Cravens home by now if she didn't think there was a future there. But is that how you're thinking? Rick was with Minty? And now he's switched to Cady?'

'Could anyone have predicted that Cady would scoop up the family and move them into her lovely home? Pip pointed out how much better off his dad is now than a year ago. It has got me asking myself more stupid questions. Not just about Helena's death and if it's connected, but about Minty's alibi. The call Minty's alibi hinges on, the one she claims took her off to a fake meeting? That call certainly took her out of the way. Was there a call and where did it come from?' I ask Elliott.

'There was a call, from an untraceable number. A burner, if you like. We haven't got anywhere near locating where the call was made from, let alone who made it,' says Elliott. 'And finding out will take time.'

'Now I'm asking questions too,' says Liv. 'What if Minty's not working alone? Have Rick and Minty been involved for a while? Are they still involved? What did Mrs M know? Would Rick give Minty an alibi? Will that alibi be enough to get her off? Does Minty know it's possible Rick is going to ditch her for his cushy number with Cady? I cannot see him giving that up.'

'I've been asking myself those exact same questions. But there's one more thing I can't stop thinking about. Rick's been putting pressure on Cady to make a will leaving everything to him and the kids. And she's finally agreed.'

41.

So here I am, putting up a notice in the window saying that due to unavoidable circumstances, the shop will be closing early today. The unavoidable circumstance is that neither Cady nor Liv was free to help.

And I have an appointment to visit a police station, even though I definitely decided that was part of my past, and I'd walked away from all that.

Last night I had no choice but to go home when all I really wanted to do was to be out looking for Alys. I sat in my horrible flat and spent hours pretending to read, staring at the damp on the walls, unable to sleep, worrying about everything I wanted to do today. Now it begins.

We cooked it up, me, Liv, and Elliott. Minty's alibi rests on a phone call. Who made that call? Could it hint she's working with someone?

I can come up with all the imaginative theories I like, but we're running out of time to make anything stick. And rather surprisingly, Minty has agreed to talk to me.

She must know she's walking a knife-edge of whether they'll get enough evidence to prove that she killed Stacey. But Stacey was found dead in Minty's office with a bundle of cash. Not a great place to start if you're facing a jury.

I wouldn't want to be in Minty's shoes. What might I be able to get her to share?

I have to push aside worries about Alys. I feel that the best way to be sure the people I've grown close to really are safe, is to get proper answers. And Minty is right at the centre of everything.

I arrive outside Harcourt nick and it all floods back. Everything I hated about my old life, everything I've tried so hard to walk away from.

Elliott is here to meet me, and I'm grateful for his friendly, if serious, face. 'Sure you want to do this?' he asks.

My doubts and how queasy I feel must be written on my face.

'Don't give me a get-out,' I say. 'Being outside a police station, about to go in and talk to a witness, brings back memories that make me want to run—but I already did that when I ran to Crossways.'

'I guess if it's bringing *back* bad memories, then you are making a success of moving away from it. Maybe it's time to stop running?' says Elliott.

He is too wise. 'I would. I mean, who wouldn't want to run away from a life that felt full of trouble, lies, and deception? Trouble is, my lovely chance at a new life looks like I've walked into another one full of trouble, lies, and deception. Do you think it's me—that trouble really does follow me around?'

Elliott looks like he'd rather avoid the question and is probably pretty happy when my phone rings. It's Cady, and I answer quickly, hoping for good news. She became worried about Alys when she never arrived home last night. But we disagreed about involving the police.

'I'm at my wits' end,' Cady says breathlessly. 'I phoned her friends again and this time, I pleaded. But nothing. Are they holding out on me? Do *they* think it's my fault?' she wails, losing it completely. 'I tried, but I know she resents me for not being her mother and now... Is it the vegan thing?' I can hear her holding back tears. 'I do struggle with how to make vegetables interesting. I just don't think vegetables are interesting.'

'Vegetables are interesting; you just have to give them a chance. I'll up my range of vegan cookery books in the shop. The Happy Pear is my favourite and will steer you towards the delights of stir-fries and chickpeas for when she comes home.'

This is a bizarre conversation to be having outside a police station. 'But there's a lot more going on with Alys. None of it's your fault. But maybe it's time for the police?'

'She's not a missing person!' Cady responds with horror.

'She'll very likely show up soon enough. But I do think the more people looking for her, the better,' I say, doing my best to be reassuring.

Now's not the time to mention that with three deaths in Crossways, how much I really want to call it in officially. But as Liv, Elliott, and I agreed last night, it's probable she's just with a friend who is covering for her.

Alys might even be enjoying causing Rick and Cady a bit of anguish.

After more reassurances, I hang up and focus on my immediate task.

I'd rather be out looking for Alys, but I press on, and my unease at being back in a police station gets worse as we pass offices buzzing with people who may be solving serious crimes or catching up on last night's viewing binges and disappointments.

Blood is rushing in my ears as we descend into the bowels of the station, down to the interview rooms, beyond where natural daylight reaches, where everything is functional metal and easy-wipe plastic and a chemical smell takes over. But it's the smell of desperation that's really strong. The sweat of people who know they've reached the lowest ebb and may never again bob up to the surface.

Minty's brought in, and classy, confident Minty has somehow vanished. Her hair no longer maintains its confident, gravity-defying vanilla ice-cream quiff. She's swapped business fashion for prison sweats, and although I'm pretty sure Minty's in this up to her neck (and the pussy-cat bow on the blouses she usually wears), I feel sorry for her.

She looks diminished, and I guess that's the whole idea of keeping her here.

A couple of days in jail on suspicion of murder might dent anyone's brittle confidence. It can make the most hardened people start talking. That's what I'm hoping for. Her even agreeing to talk to me is a better start than I'd hoped.

Now I just need to make it count.

42.

'Keera, this is desperate. I've done nothing!' Minty bursts out before I even get a chance to speak. 'I'm so glad to talk to someone who knows me, who knows I wouldn't do this thing they are accusing me of!'

We both say that we want to be left alone to talk.

'You have to help me!' Minty pleads. 'My solicitor is useless! So glad I've got a friend with a criminal law background; everyone says how helpful you are.'

And there's me thinking when people talk about me, they say how easily I get cross if things don't go my way.

'Your lawyer will help you build a defence,' I say, hating myself for being so bland. But I'm hard-wired to be careful, not make promises I absolutely cannot guarantee to deliver on.

Minty bites her already well-chewed fingernails. 'Yeah, but you'll help me—you'll tell them. Someone needs to fight my corner. It's not my fault someone killed Stacey in my office.'

'You need to stay strong, Minty. There's only one way through this. Just take it one day at a time.' Bland again.

Minty must know things look bad for her. Stacey was killed in her office. But there's that phone call that took her away, and the fact that Minty was not there when I found Stacey's body.

'Do you mind if I ask you a few questions?'

'Anything if you think it'll help me. My lawyer says I've got a chance of challenging the evidence at a trial, like that's a good thing! I don't think I can stand a trial. I don't think I can even stay here another day. I'm desperate.'

My instincts tell me Minty is genuinely scared. I need to tap into that.

'I'm here for the truth,' I tell her.

'The truth is, I'm in the middle of a nightmare.'

If she's keeping up a pretence she's doing a good job. I guess she has hope there won't be enough evidence to prove she killed Stacey. The biggest piece of evidence, however circumstantial, is Stacey being killed in Minty's office. But that phone call. It's a case where they need to build a very precise timeline, and that's always tricky.

When did Stacey arrive? When did Minty leave? That phone call is crucial in setting up her alibi. Someone made the phone call that took her away. Who?

'What would Stacey be doing in your office if not to meet you?' I begin.

'I've no idea why she was in my office, let alone got killed there. You got in, didn't you, Keera? That was how I ended up finding you standing over Stacey's dead body.'

I need to shift this from being about me.

'But Stacey did want a meeting with you. She wanted to discuss Mrs McFlintock's lease.'

'Then you'd think she'd have called when I was there.'

'Tell me more about how you got called away.'

Her eyes narrow. 'I can only think someone set me up deliberately. Took me a while to realise it was a fake call. It looks like someone wanted to get me out of the way. But who would do such a thing? Why me? What's it about?'

'Any ideas?' I ask carefully. 'Who might want to get you out of the office just at the time Stacey got in?'

The obvious answer is often the one that's true. Someone luring Minty out of the way is not the obvious answer. I am not swallowing what she's trying to sell me.

'Well, you put it like that, it makes me think maybe it was Stacey,' says Minty.

To be honest, that was something I hadn't thought of.

'That, or someone who really does not like me very much,' adds Minty.

'Anyone who really doesn't like you?'

Minty spreads her hands, showing her once-perfect nails. 'I'm not perfect, but someone killed Stacey and they put me in the frame for it. I have no idea who would want to do something as vile as that.'

'I know you and Stacey rowed about her mother's lease,' I say.

'Yeah, Stacey did get worked up about that,' Minty agrees easily. 'And I have had one or two rows about leases. But this cannot be about that! What is this about?'

'I guess you're in the best position to be able to find an answer to that one. Tell me more about Mrs McFlintock's lease. Why did Stacey get so worked up about that?'

'Well I can't tell you, can I? If you want something else that's odd about this whole business, it's that. You brought up that lease, so I went to check it. Mrs McFlintock was a bit old-school. She would only sign a hard copy. She didn't even sign it every year. The whole lease was very old-school.' Puzzlement crosses Minty's face. 'I couldn't even find when she last signed.'

I think of that tatty file on the desk alongside Stacey's body. 'What do you mean? Is when she signed important?'

'Important? I don't know. I mean I couldn't check it because her paperwork was gone, all of it.'

It takes a second for me to understand. 'You've lost the paperwork?'

'Lost? I'm not sure. The folder was empty when I checked a few days ago. And I am *very* organised.'

I'm not sure what that means, so I think it's time to move on and see what else I can persuade Minty to tell me.

'Talking of contracts, you recently gave Rick Craven a big contract.'

'I did. How is that relevant?'

I don't offer an answer. I wait for her to say more.

'I cannot even imagine why you're asking about that, but yes, all right, he seemed the right person for the job.'

She moves her hands in front of her. It can be a defensive sign. Is this a topic she's not comfortable with?

'Right person? Sure about that? Not something else?'

'What are you saying?'

'I'm here for the truth, Minty. I don't think I've heard anyone question Rick's gardening talents. His reliability, less so. I was surprised. Then I heard about you sacking Helena Craven. Is there some connection here I'm missing?'

'Whoa, Keera—what's this about? That was ages ago.' Minty's chewing the skin around her nails enough to draw blood. 'And what can that possibly have to do with Stacey? Or anything?'

'I'm just looking at alternative scenarios.'

'I can't see what you're getting at. How can it possibly be connected?' Minty looks at me, her eyes huge, her skin grey and paper-thin around her eyes. 'I can't even think in here. You'll have to tell me what you're getting at.'

Minty is doing a really good job of denying everything. And of course, if she keeps doing that, plausible deniability is a gamble that could pay off.

Is there any evidence that puts her in the room when Stacey was killed? But if it comes to a trial, Minty's the one who'd have to go through all that. That's a pretty big gamble.

'You know what Crossways is like. People talk,' I say carefully. 'There are rumours. It's just something I heard. Like, people saying that there was more to it than arguing about a lease. That maybe Stacey had something on you and that's the reason you argued with her. You needed to keep her quiet.'

'Keep her quiet? Something on me? Like what?' Minty grabs at her hair; there are tears in her eyes, and she brushes them away. 'You said that before, that there are rumours I was taking bribes or whatever.'

'Stacey's body *was* found with an envelope of cash.'

'These rumours! That phone call that lured me away from my office! That envelope of money! The police keep questioning me about that. Did Stacey bring that? You have to help me, Keera, if this is what they're saying. Someone's setting me up.'

'The police will look at your accounts. Will they find large cash deposits?'

'It's all lies.'

She spreads her hands wide, then tears at her hair again. 'Please tell me you believe me, Keera. I need someone to believe me. I can see now, it's clear, someone is doing this. Someone must hate me. What have I done to them? I don't even have a clue who it can be. It's just rumours. But who's behind them? Someone's really out to get me. You see this is deliberate, don't you? Someone got me away from the office and killed Stacey there. Someone who's out to get me. I'm being well and truly stitched up.'

'Or, some people might say that phone call gave you an alibi.'

'Some alibi!' Minty gestures around her. 'I'm in here, no one believes me. I don't even have the first clue who would do such a monstrous thing. Kill Stacey. Implicate me. What have I done to deserve this? Any of it?'

She's sticking to her story. I pride myself on being able to tell when someone's lying. Mostly. Right now I'm not sure what I believe.

'What did you speak to Helena Craven about the day she died?'

She gives me a wide-eyed, startled response. 'Where's that come from? What's that got to do with anything? Why bring Helena into this?'

'Do you remember what you spoke to her about?'

'Actually, yes, because the police asked me. I guess someone saw us together—someone always does, right? I asked after her, how she was doing. I guess it felt a bit awkward. It was not a long chat. We didn't really talk about anything.'

She leans across the table, looking right into my eyes.

'What are people trying to imply? What else are people saying? Anything else you want to warn me about?'

I sit across this table with its legs screwed to the floor, looking at Minty, trying to work out if she's wide-eyed and innocent. Or incredibly clever and manipulative.

'You visited Mrs McFlintock on the day she died,' I try.

'You asked me about that before.'

'Were you there?'

'No.'

'You sent a letter about a rent increase.'

'I did that. I sent everyone a letter about a rent increase. Whoever said I saw her is lying. Again! Who's doing this? Making me look like I'm somehow in the centre of loads of bad shit happening in Crossways. What a horrible place.'

'Everything is going to come under scrutiny. If you're covering for someone…'

'Covering? Who would I be covering for?'

'You asked for my advice, Minty, if you're in any kind of relationship, or ever have been, with anyone who's persuaded you to do anything—anything at all that's led to the situation you're in—now is a good time to start talking.'

Minty looks at me for a long time. 'I am really, really not hanging around in here on some mission to save anyone. Who do you think…? Believe me, if I were covering for anyone, anyone who'd left me to fester in here, you think I wouldn't say something? I'm not stupid. Where's this coming from? Are these more stories you've heard? You know there are loads of rumours running around Crossways—you should know better than to believe them. I told you there's one about you.'

And the conversation has come around to Rick Craven.

'So, one last stupid question: *you've* never been involved with Rick Craven?'

'Me? I told you, I heard you were making moves on him. You told me that's not true either. That's Crossways for you. Horrible little place. These rumours are just plain out of control.'

'If you thought this would all end up with you and Rick disappearing off into the sunset—you should know it looks like Rick will be doing that with someone else. Rick's moved on to newer opportunities. Just thought you should know.'

She thinks for a moment. 'Cady, you mean? You realise that might not be any more true than any of the other rumours?'

Is that what Minty's banking on?

How convinced am I now that Rick and Minty are in this together? In Rick's new relationship, he's sitting very pretty. If it goes the same way as his wife, he'll be sitting even prettier.

Will he be sitting very pretty with Minty? I just do not know.

'Minty, last chance to deliver me something, anything I can work with. So far you've given me nothing I can see that will help you. Who do you think killed Stacey?'

Minty drags her hands through her limp hair.

'You think I haven't had anything else to do other than go over and over it? The only reason I can come up with was is that she was killed to set me up. But that's crazy, right? Unless someone can find out what the actual truth is, why I'm being thrown under the bus… it looks not just bad, it looks way more than really bad. If someone doesn't find out the truth, there's nothing I can say, is there? It's over for me. I'm going to jail, aren't I?'

43.

I don't have the luxury to think whether I believe Minty, because there's still no sign of Alys.

I called Cady the second I stepped outside the police station and Cady's now barely keeping it together

'Rick says to wait before we panic. But you can't just *decide* when to panic. Panic is not something you decide. I'm already panicking,' says Cady.

No surprise that Rick is being his usual carefree self. I want to give in to this growing fear that Rick's carefree attitude is a clever front. Does Rick know what's happened to Alys? Is that why he doesn't want the police involved?

I tell Cady there are lots of places Alys can be, and she can still be perfectly safe. I try to be reassured by my own words.

'Cady, for Alys's sake, you do need to stay calm. She's eighteen. If she's at a friend's, even their parents can't insist she talks to you. Just give it a bit longer.'

I say reassuring words, but I don't believe them. Cady's right that you cannot decide when to panic.

'But a friend would find a way to let me know she's safe, surely?' wails Cady. 'I wish I'd listened to you and called the police yesterday, but Rick's dead against it.'

We don't know anything for sure – not if any of my suspicions are right, not if Rick Craven was ever involved with Minty, definitely not whether he was involved in the death of his own wife. I need to start separating facts from imagination.

Elliott's hovering. I'm not telling Cady the police are listening to every word. But maybe Elliott can help?

I try to find more reassuring words, but Cady's buying none of it. Where is Alys? If she's not at home, not with a friend? Where can she be?

The instant the call ends, Elliott asks how he can help.

'They don't want police involved—not yet. I shouldn't really involve you.'

'You should involve me. And I can help more if you make it official.'

I shake my head. 'What can we do under the radar?'

'With three dead in Crossways, including Alys's mum, is this the time for under the radar? I'm guessing Minty didn't give us any new leads?'

'I did my best. She didn't bite. She's sticking to a story that she's being set up. But I can't think about Minty now.'

'It can't be easy to think straight because you believe Alys is in danger. But you are great at spotting what no one else does. We need you to think.'

'Exactly. I can't think. I'm too busy panicking.'

'You don't trust your own instincts because they've let you down in the past. But you need to trust them now. You are good at this, very good. I do have instincts occasionally. Want an outrageous theory?'

'Now you've surprised me! You have a theory? Not based on fact?'

'I think you know where we should be looking. You need to trust yourself. And you might need my help.'

'I do not need anyone's help.'

'Except that you do, you just don't like to admit it. I want you to talk me through it. You've talked to Alys, you tried to get her to meet you. In fact, you've done something more important than talking to her. You listened to her. Alys hinted she doesn't exactly feel safe at home.'

I sigh. I kind of hate that Elliott is right.

'You think that's why I started to question Rick's role in all of this?'

'Where should we be looking?' Elliott presses me.

'Well, I thought Jaxx at Halfway might cover for her. If Alys told her about not feeling wanted at home. Alys feels she's the only thing standing between Rick and Cady getting together.'

'So we talk to Jaxx?'

I shake my head. We're still standing right outside the police station. I do so want to move. 'Jaxx might have given Alys a place to stay, but I doubt she'd leave everyone panicking. She'd have found a way to let us know Alys was safe.'

'Ok, we keep working on the assumption Alys has gone somewhere she feels safe. Where else would Alys feel safe? We are still under the pact,' he reminds me. 'The one where I don't laugh at anything you tell me, however outrageous. Hit me with your best theories.'

I try to remember if I've heard of any friends who don't live locally that Alys might have gone to. And then it comes to me. 'Do you know, you might actually have helped.' I start heading to my car, but Elliott is suddenly my shadow.

'You're going to have to tell me your outrageous theory or I will follow you,' he says. 'I know you think going to recover Alys with police in tow might be the wrong move. But it is exactly the right move.'

'You are annoyingly perceptive. But I don't need backup.'

'And you are annoyingly stubborn. And I will make sure no one sees me unless it's necessary.'

Elliott's not going anywhere. I think I can trust him to keep his word. I don't want to waste time arguing.

'Is there anywhere I can buy fresh fruit? Preferably organic.'

'You need fresh fruit right now?'

'I do.'

'And then we go to where you think Alys might be?'

I get in the car. Elliott gets in the passenger seat.

'The deal is I tell you the nearest place you get fresh fruit from and you tell me where you suspect a missing teenager is?' he says.

'I suppose that is the deal, yes.'

'Then, for fresh fruit, go left at the crossroads.'

It doesn't take long to get armed with supplies. I have only one idea of where Alys might be. But when we pull up outside, the place looks disappointingly empty. It's been another of those horrible days where the sun never penetrated the thick cloud. It felt like morning never arrived, and now evening's here early, and in some of the other houses, lights have already been switched on.

But this one looks as empty as when I arrived at Mrs M's and discovered the break-in.

I park up a little way down the road. I need to consider my next move.

'This probably isn't going to turn out to be the brilliant idea I am hoping,' I say, unable to squash this horrible fear that Alys made enough of a nuisance of herself that getting her out of the way became crucial.

'It doesn't look like anyone's in.' Elliott stares at the house I've pointed to.

My one idea.

'But I need to check. And Alys cannot see you, because I'm still working on the assumption she's just decided to come here herself.' My voice sounds hollow. 'And the very last thing I want to do is spook her and lose any trust I've built up. You know now where I thought she might be. You'll have to make your own way back.'

'Leaving you to go into a dark house alone? I'm not doing that.'

'And you can't ask me to go in with police. I do this bit alone. I did it last time and it turned out all right.'

'But Mum told you no one goes in without backup, and she called me. What I'm saying is that I'm your backup. Because what if Alys is being held against her will? What if you find—?'

'I'm not going to find her dead body,' I say, getting out of the car. 'I'm simply not. All right, you can wait for a bit—but not in the car where someone may see you.'

'You haven't told me. What is this place? Why do you think she might be here?'

It's been a while since I stood outside this house in Primrose Side. It's not a great part of town. We've parked a few doors down from the one with the For Sale notice outside. I'm trying not to get my hopes up. It's not the part of town that inspires an awful lot of hope. Even so, the house I'm headed for is notable for having a small, yet beautiful front garden in a part of town where a parked car is more common than plants. Even an old fridge dumped out front seems more popular than growing anything, apart from resilient weeds.

'This is the Cravens' old house,' I say, grabbing my bag of fresh fruit. 'It's being sold. I think it's going through in the next day or so.'

It's been empty for months, yet colourful winter wallflowers tell me Rick's been here, and recently. The plants climbing up the outside of the house seem to be saying that there was always love, optimism, and yes, hope, growing in this home. At least, I hope that's what they're saying. There always has to be hope.

Elliott's doing a terrible job of leaving.

'All right, here's the deal,' I tell him as I stand and glare at him. 'The deal is, you can wait ten minutes. If I don't come out in ten, you have to leave.'

'That is not the deal. That is the opposite of the deal.'

'Ten minutes will mean she's here and she's talking to me.'

'If you don't come out in ten minutes, it could mean something quite the opposite of Alys being there and happily talking to you. You know I can't let you go in there alone. So, no. When someone goes into the spooky empty building, the correct thing to say is—if I'm not out in ten minutes, get backup. Because this is a potential—'

'When you know me better, you'll find out I'm not exactly the best at following the rules.' I slam the door and I'm off.

44.

I walk up the short path to the front door before Elliott can start to argue, particularly as he might be right.

I slammed the car door and strode off as he was saying something that might have been about hoping he would have the chance to get to know me better – at least, I think that's what it was. But I'm hurrying, wishing I thought of this place sooner.

At least I haven't got Cady's hopes up with my idea, as it's a long shot. The sign outside no longer even says For Sale; it's been changed to Sold. This house might not even belong to the Cravens anymore. Someone else may be living here already. But it looks empty. Do I knock on the door? Do I want to alert anyone inside that I'm here? What am I going to find?

I crouch and open the letterbox and call through. 'Alys? Are you there? It's Keera. I just want to check you're all right. I've brought some apples in case you're hungry.'

Silence. I knock in what I hope is a gentle, non-threatening way. Almost unbelievably, the door opens. And there she is, her face obscured not only by shadows but by the corkscrew hair she got directly from Helena. It could be Helena standing there.

'Alys!' I breathe. 'You look so like your mum. Are you all right? Everyone's worried sick about you. You are ok?' I breathe easier since she's opened the door herself. My worst fear was that she was in danger; that we'd find her too late.

I cannot believe that, for once, I seem to have got things right. The worst thing about her appearance is that she's in a bulky coat that disguises how thin I know she's become. I can feel how cold it is inside.

'Are they though? Worrying about me?' Alys says.

'Of course they are!'

I hate the way her voice sounds so hopeless, but she's opened the door and is stepping aside to let me in. I hand her the carrier of food choices as I enter.

'This makes the memories flood back, doesn't it?' I say. 'I had a lot of fun evenings in this house. I loved your mum. I miss her so much.'

I glance along the short corridor to the familiar kitchen. Everything's in darkness. The lounge has been cleared. Nothing much more than dirty grey rectangles, ghostly signs on the carpet and walls where furniture once was, where pictures once hung.

'Already doesn't feel like the house I remember. It doesn't even smell familiar,' I say.

Alys's hand brushes away a tear. 'Can a place smell sad?'

'Absolutely. I guess there's no chance of a cup of tea?'

'Everything's switched off. Even the water. Cheapskates.'

She reaches into the bag and takes out an apple. She bites into it so enthusiastically it makes me feel this has been another of my better decisions.

If she planned this, and I guess she did, did she bring food? How much? How long was she planning on staying?

How can I get her to go home? Her other home. But for now, Alys eating is a massive deal, and it gives me hope that I can get her out of this.

I touch one of the walls. 'I think this house wants to be happy again. Does that sound stupid? I guess there will be a new family to bring back the happy memories buried in the walls.'

Alys shrugs.

There are happy memories. Of course there are.

I'm focusing too much on what I've been thinking about Helena lately.

I let myself be convinced it was possible she ended her own life deliberately, and it's coloured my memories and made me doubt that I ever really saw the true picture of her life.

'She didn't even ask if we wanted to keep anything,' says Alys, leading me upstairs to her old bedroom. 'I know nothing Mum had was worth anything—actual money, I mean. There was this horrible still-life painting of roses that most people would dump straight in a skip. They got it in a car boot because Mum complained she was married to a gardener but never got brought any flowers. It was beyond ghastly. But I'd have had it.'

I shiver. 'This is icy.'

The back bedroom is almost empty, except for a sleeping bag on the floor, a rucksack, torches. A cardboard box for a table. A thick candle already half burned down. This is her old bedroom. She lights the candle. It barely gives out any light. Alys digs around in my bag for more food.

'I didn't think to bring spare batteries.'

'You brought food. And you came. How come it's you who's come to find me?' Alys asks.

'Because I have a nose for trouble. And probably a habit of causing it too. Maybe you have one too!'

'What trouble am I causing?'

'Alys, they're worried sick about you.'

'I don't believe you.'

I need her to leave with me. She cannot stay here, not in the dark, no heating, no electrics, no water. 'How long before the new family takes over and you have to go home?'

'Home. Interesting word.'

Alys sits on the floor and slides the sleeping bag across her legs. We sit for a while as I sift for a way to get Alys talking. Everything feels too big, too loaded. Moving towards her leaving with me tonight feels like a mountain climb away. I'll take it one step at a time.

'How are you managing with no running water, just out of interest? Not pooing outside? Not in your dad's lovely garden?'

Luckily, Alys smiles. 'Not yet, no.'

'I'm trying to think of a way to improve your situation.'

'No one can.'

'I'm not talking about this room, I think we could improve on this pretty easily, as your current situation is bunking down on an old carpet in a sleeping bag, with no heating and not enough candles. It can't be beyond us to improve your home situation either, not if we work together. Did I bring water?'

Alys rustles in the bag. 'You did. And bourbons.'

'Bourbons are both everyone's favourite and vegan. And improves both our situations. Pass me one. We can talk about how to improve your situation between now and when you head off to uni. Which uni are you planning on heading for?'

'I'm not going back to Cady's. Never.'

'OK, we start there—that's an easy one for me to agree to. You don't have to go back.'

I have no plan, no alternative, but I'll just have to conjure one from somewhere. When I saw Pip out walking, I thought one day he might just carry on, never look back. But I've been worrying about the wrong Craven. Alys is at greater risk of becoming a statistic. So if she refuses to go home, where else is there?

'You can't live here. I think the new family would notice. You don't want to live at Cady's. Maybe you're learning what you don't want?'

'Maybe.'

'That's a start. What else *don't* you want to do?'

'I don't want to do A-levels. I've no interest in university. I don't exactly love working in the cafe—seeing people making bad food choices, you know, I find it hard not to point it out.'

'Yes, I saw that.'

'I feel squeezed out, like there's not enough left of me. I feel I don't own my own life, I don't know what I want anymore. I don't want any of it.'

'I think that's despair. At one time you wanted to travel. As a change of scene goes, it might be better than here.'

'You really do listen, you know.'

'Well, one thing everyone knows is that places to live don't come cheap around here, but there's always a way. Any thoughts at all on how we can make his work?'

'Jaxx and Maya are building these rooms at Halfway,' says Alys quietly, 'for guests, you know? I thought if I got a permanent job there, they might make it live in.'

Didn't she just say she didn't really want to work in the cafe?

'I'd offer for you to come and stay at mine. I wouldn't have thought you'd consider it, but actually, here is the first place that makes mine look base-level attractive. It beats this by having interesting black mould that I see as drawings. There's quite a convincing seagull if you'd be interested in seeing that.'

'I might be.'

'Of course, what I really want to do is sort out your future a little more permanently. But we might need to do something before that, or police helicopters will be swooping overhead.'

'Is that true?' Alys picks at her sleeping bag. 'I cannot believe Dad was worried enough to call the police. No one can fix me. It's not your problem. I just want to be on my own for a bit, you know? Just want to think. Thought I might find some answers if everything didn't crowd in. This was the only place I could think of that felt like me.'

'Not easy to think when you're shivering and hungry,' I say. 'Did you reach any conclusions?'

'Dunno. Maybe. Have you ever thought Dad is a little bit of a psychopath?'

'Interesting. Perhaps not entirely fair?'

'You should study A-level psychology. There are a lot more psychopaths around than you might think. Psychopaths aren't really what people think.' She takes a bite out of another apple. 'Dad's classic in the way people only see his charm. People miss how self-obsessed and single-minded he is. Imagine Mum being married to someone like that for years. He never does a single thing he doesn't want to, but he has this way about him... He manipulates people into getting what he wants without you really noticing. Just smiles and jokes his way through it, you know, but is completely implacable.'

'Or maybe he just has an amazing ability to go with the flow,' I counter. 'Maybe he convinces himself that whatever happens is what he wanted. Avoids conflict. Makes life quite simple.'

'Huh. So how come everything always goes his way?'
'Everything?'
'Don't you think life has turned out amazing for him?'

'His wife died. He's dealing with that in his own way. He is bad at showing he cares. Wanting to think, wanting to find a way out—those are good, Alys. You are dealing with it all in your own way.'

'Because Pip is still mostly just trying to shut it out?'

'He's dealing with things in his own way, too. He's doing better than he thinks.'

Pip wasn't thinking about running away. He was doggedly talking to people and building his timeline. Pip says he hopes it will all turn out to be Minty, because that would make things much easier. I wonder what Alys thinks? But my focus right now is making Alys safe. Everything else can wait.

'Pip says he can talk to you.'

'He can. You can too.'

'Be honest with me then.'

'If you're honest with me.'

'I think I'm already doing that if you noticed.' Alys smooths the silkiness of the sleeping bag. She chews her lower lip and reaches into the bag for more food. 'I do... I want to talk to you, but at the same time, you're the last person I can tell. It'll sound like I'm being vindictive, or... mad. You won't believe it.'

'You said you're the only thing standing between your dad and Cady officially making a go of it as a couple. It doesn't feel like home. You feel in the way.' My heart clenches that despite everything Cady's done, Alys won't accept her.

'You think I'm trying to stop Dad moving on.'

'Very little surprises me, you know,' I say. 'Although I am surprised you've gone for the bourbons in quite such a big way. But life often sounds mad. You've heard the expression truth is stranger than fiction? I currently have a pact with someone that he'll listen to all my ideas, however outrageous, and he won't laugh. It's a good starting point. Wanna try it?'

'Sounds like a really good relationship.'

'I don't know, but actually, I think you are very wise, Alys Craven.'

'Wise, or delusional, or very stupid. You might think differently when you've heard what I'm going to say. If I tell you.'

'You can't hold out on me now. I am interested now, so if you don't tell me, I'll have to kill you.'

'Cady says you have a shady, mysterious past,' says Alys.

'That's just Crossways trying to make drama out of poor material.'

'Is it drama if I say that you have to get not just me, but Pip out of that house?'

What do I say?

'The truth is, they are worrying about you more than you know, whether you like it or even believe it. Please can I call them, tell them you're safe? If I promise I will find you a better, or at least, alternative, place to stay, I call them? Even if, at a pinch, the offer is my flat, which is hardly habitable for one. The offer is there if you don't object to noise and light pollution, bad smells, and damp.'

Alys considers. 'Why do you have such a shit life?'

'Ouch, do I? I thought that was a good offer. No, you're right, the flat is shit. And you're right, my life's not great. Bits of it are terrible. But I'm making a go of it.'

'But weren't you earning like, loads of money? Were you really a lawyer? Why don't you tell me about that?'

'As in, if I tell you what went spectacularly wrong, and made me want to leave behind my old life, I can let everyone know you're safe?'

'All right. Yes. That.'

'I wasn't planning on talking about me. I've never told anyone here what happened. This is a bigger deal than you know.'

'Don't worry, I'm not expecting it to be pretty. And you'll find me somewhere to stay—don't forget that part of the deal. And I know you're making out your flat is worse than it is to convince me to go back to Cady's.'

'I'd reserve judgement until you've seen the flat.'

I am definitely breathing easier now. Me and Alys, we have a deal.

45.

'Thank you Alys. Thank you for letting me do the right thing. We'll talk, I'll call them. And you leave with me today? Say your goodbyes and leave this house behind tonight. Could that be part of the deal?'

'I'd say that depends on how good your secrets are.'

'I'm revealing my secrets, ones I haven't told anyone. I'm not promising how good they are.'

'Not even Cady?'

'Not Cady, nor Liv. I'd appreciate it if you kept it to yourself.'

Alys weighs this for a moment. 'Might be too hot for me to promise.'

'Fair enough. That's honest. Worth a try. My life isn't completely shit. It's a bump in the road. Everyone has those.'

'Moving to Crossways is the bump in the road—or what made you move here in the first place?'

'Haven't entirely decided. When I moved to Crossways I was yearning for a simple life. My only aims were to sell enough books to pay the bills and to steer clear of trouble. I had a clear plan: stay on the outside; stay cool and aloof; not get involved. But you try resisting the Crossways cult of everyone thinking they've a right to know everyone else's business.'

'How's it going for you?'

'I guess it quickly got complicated. How's it going, honestly? I've been here just over a year and I seem to have spectacularly failed at every single one of my aims.'

'Is that because you'd hate a simpler life really?'

'This is what my well-meaning family and friends—new and old—keep trying to tell me. I keep trying to prove them wrong.'

'Cool and aloof? Is that you? You're more: see trouble, throw yourself in. Maybe it's possible to be a kickass bookseller and be a kickass righter of wrongs and seeker of truth and justice? Pip reckons so, anyway.'

'A superhero in bookseller disguise? Do I need a cape?'

'You're avoiding spilling all on your sordid history, but I reckon I can guess most of it—stressful job, but believing you were making a difference. The reality of too many hours spent in unwholesome places, like police stations. Too many guilty clients. Nah, don't think I could do that job either.'

'You paint a pretty, but not completely accurate, picture. I felt I *was* making a difference. I coped, or thought I did. The part you left out was the bit about the guy.'

'The guy?'

'Yeah, there's always a guy, isn't there.'

'Is there?'

'Well yes, or a gal. For me, I thought this guy was, you know, *the* guy. Thought I'd been pretty lucky. It's possible

I'm not easy to live with. I thought I was sailing through life, despite the time spent in police cells and courtrooms. I really wasn't expecting what he did.'

'And you just said nothing surprises you.'

'Guess I lied about that.'

'What did he do? Apart from the obvious bit about he broke your heart and sucked out your spirit and left you fit only for dull Crossways and bookselling.'

'He took a lot more than my spirit. He took quite a lot of my money and savings. Vanished. Left me with debts, including owing six months' rent. So I know about feeling hollowed out. Turns out, I'd never even known his real name. It was all a lie.'

'Wow! That is seriously shit. No wonder even Crossways seems better. Why'd he do it?'

'Seriously shit. But the answer is, I don't know. Doubt I'll ever know.'

'That must really bug you—you wanting answers all the time and all.'

'Only if I let myself think about it. But I have moved on.'

'Have you really, though? And there was me hoping your deep, dark secret would be you had to get out and hide yourself somewhere anonymous cos you'd murdered someone.'

I hear myself swallow. 'You think I'm the type?'

'Is there a type? You do get a little angry. Do you argue with everyone?

'Me? Of course not.'

'I guess you really do know about getting kicked out of your old life. Or tricked out of it. No wonder you needed to restore your faith in humanity. You made a pretty poor decision choosing to move to Crossways.'

'When you get to know me, you'll discover bad decisions are my speciality. Anyway, got to meet you, didn't I? How else would I end up sitting on what I feel sure is a slightly damp carpet, running low on candles, thinking of a way to explain what I'm doing here when the new family moves in?'

'You should have called the bookshop that.'

'What: Bad Decisions Are My Speciality? Think that would bring people in?'

'Better than Between the Lines.'

'Another of my regrets. Everyone seems to have a better suggestion, although yours possibly would not solve the problem of my having to explain it rather too often. Should have called it Crossways Books and have done with it. No one could question that decision.'

'Dull though? So how far does your tendency for poor decisions extend? Further than choosing the wrong guys, moving to Crossways, bookselling, wrong name for your business…?'

'Arguing with my customers. Yes, possibly my whole of my life, now you mention it. I have been accused of having many more unfortunate traits by my all-too-observant Mum. Apparently, I fall for a sob story.'

'Ah. Did the cute guy tell you about his tragic childhood? I guess he was cute?'

'He might have done and he might have been. My mum reckons it's me who attracts trouble, so wherever I go, there will always be trouble. I can never have a quiet life. But everyone needs a bit of trouble, don't they? Maybe I have too much. The trouble right now might be that I wish I'd thought to bring gloves, and my butt is beginning to freeze. How much longer are you going to need before I can persuade you to get out of here, because I'm ready about now?'

She watches me blow on my hands. 'Do you want to snuggle in my sleeping bag?'

'Kind though that is, if I'm being honest, I was hoping I was going to cut to the chase and successfully and triumphantly persuade you to leave. I'm still hoping the only reason you haven't rushed to leave yet is because you don't want to look like you agreed too easily.'

Alys still looks like she's weighing things up. 'We haven't solved the problem of where I can go.'

'Then I guess it's my terrible flat for now. I've just told you my deepest, darkest secret, and we have a no-laughing-at-outrageously-ridiculous-theories pact that may last until the end of time. So it's over to you. What are you going to tell me? Like, exactly why you reckon I need to get you and Pip out of your home? I think that was the deal.'

'Was that the deal?'

'The deal definitely involved me being able to let people who care know that you are safe.' I wave my phone. 'So I'm calling Cady. Cady was frantic. I'm telling her first.' I call before Alys can object.

Cady picks up immediately. I hear her choked sob, her gasping out of thanks.

'And Pip's with you?' Cady says.

There's a beat before I answer. 'Pip? No. Why?' My heart goes cold.

'He never came home from school. Rick's out driving around, looking for him, looking for them both.'

My heart freezes over. It's difficult to breathe. I was worried about Alys. But now Pip's missing too. Pip's the one who's spent the last year putting together a dangerous timeline by digging out secrets. A lot of people might have a problem with Pip doing that.

Alys overhears. 'Pip's missing?' She looks as distraught as I feel.

'He could be out looking for you,' I tell Alys. 'Or just walking.'

Cady overhears. 'But it's dark. He's not picked up his phone or any messages, and I've sent some frantic ones.' There's a catch in Cady's voice. 'Any ideas—anything at all? It's so hard to just stay here, waiting.'

'You're doing the right thing. You stay home, Cady. I'm sure he'll come home soon. He'll be ready for his usual hot chocolate. I'm bringing Alys home.'

Alys gives me a look that tells me that is definitely not happening.

But one minute I'm wondering how exactly I get Alys to leave; now she's already stuffing the sleeping bag into its cover, blowing out the stump of the candle and gathering her few possessions into her rucksack.

'We need to find him. Guess I'll just say a final goodbye.'

I know it's more than saying goodbye to a house that already doesn't feel like her home. She's saying goodbye to her mother, her childhood even. In the end, she takes hardly any time over it. We are out. The front door is shut. It will be someone else's soon. Alys is going to have to move on. She doesn't even look back, just heads for my car. Elliott must have made his own way back, even though I half expect to see him lurking. I guess he's someone who sticks to his promises.

'I'm glad it was you who found me, Keera,' says Alys, yanking open the car door. 'Now let's go find Pip before anything bad happens to him.'

46.

Alys is moving as if she knows this isn't over. As if she instinctively knows a murderer who thinks they've got away with their crime is one of the most dangerous people there is. We get in the car and are away. Just how much trouble is Pip in?

'Harcourt Pools, first place we check, right?' Alys says. 'He's got a thing about going back to that place.'

'I can't say it's his happy place. But he finds some sort of peace there. Probably because it's so loud and intense, it's impossible to think. But would Pip go there looking for you? The only time I've seen him there after dark was that time Mrs M's place got broken into. No, we should check, because would your Dad think to go there?'

'I'm not sure Pip *is* out looking for me. And Dad never really thinks about anything. No, it'll be Harcourt Pools because it'll need to look like another accident.'

'Accident?'

'Now is not the time to be obeying the speed limit.'

I put my foot down.

'Come on! Can't believe you're still not getting it. Anniversary of Mum's death. My disappearing. Too convenient to waste an opportunity like this.'

'I'm sure your dad didn't—'

Alys gives a hollow laugh. 'You think any of this is Dad? Dad never did anything. That is the entire point of Dad. He just floats along, smiling charmingly, avoiding looking at anything uncomfortable. Thought you were famous for your intuition.'

'I'm also famous for getting things wrong and being a bit dumb.'

'Well, that's true. Can't believe you were thinking he planned all this? Dad!' Alys scoffs. 'Dad couldn't plan anything.'

I can't see Alys's face, it's too dark.

'I knew you were the last person I should talk to, despite people saying you look anything uncomfortable right in the eye. Even you can't see it. That's my trouble. No one else sees it. Does this piece of crap go any faster?'

We've a few residential roads to navigate before we reach open countryside.

'You were a lawyer, right? Pip says you're a good listener, that what you really want is truth and justice. So I thought if I could find evidence, you'd believe me. So I started looking for proof. And I found some. Kind of.'

'Evidence is trickier than you might think,' I say, carefully. 'There are many different ways of interpreting evidence. What kind of proof do you mean?' I can't work it out. *What is Alys talking about?*

'I knew no one would believe me,' Alys says quietly. 'No one sees her as she is. She drugs Pip's hot chocolate when you come over.'

'What?' I cannot help it, but I dart Alys a disbelieving glance before I can stop myself.

'Don't forget all your promises about our blood pact and that I could tell you anything,' Alys reminds me quickly.

Does she mean Scatty-Cady? Alys thinks I've got Rick so wrong, but she has Cady so wrong. She's ended up with such a distorted view of Cady. She doesn't want to see Rick for who he truly is. But my heart squeezes. All Cady has done is be kind. And this is what she gets. How am I ever going to sort this out?

'Yes. Sorry,' I say. 'It's…'

'A lot. I get it. You're asking yourself, why have I got this twisted view of Cady? How could I have got this so wrong, believe such a monstrous thing? It's because she's a planner, that's why. She works it all out. It's why no one gets her, except me.'

It takes all my willpower not to leap in and defend Cady. I bite my lip so hard I draw blood. *Now is not the time.* The important thing is getting Alys to trust me. We can build from there.

'It took me a while,' Alys goes on. 'I think Pip was moving towards a hunch it was Dad who was responsible for Mum's death—not shoving her, not literally that, but pushed her over the edge.'

I try to sift this version of Alys's truth and how it's come to this. Cady tried to take the place of Alys's mum, and there's a lot of hurt here, hatred even. But drugging Pip's hot chocolate? Alys's thoughts are not sound.

Although, I remember how very sleepy Pip gets.

Why would Cady do that?

Ok, I can imagine Cady putting something in Pip's drink – Scatty-Cady might think she was helping, by helping him sleep.

'Alys, I—'

'You promised! You said you'd listen to anything, no matter how outrageous, until the end of time. I get that you moved here because you think Crossways is all lovely. You thought Mrs M was a sweet old lady. But there was me thinking you came from some tough environment where you'd see the truth. Cady takes everyone in the same way. So easy when people don't want to see it. Thought you would be, like, not naïve. If people don't want to face reality, it means you can get away with murder.'

We've left the town behind and are in the darkness of the country road between Harcourt and the pools. I can't see her face. Not too far now.

Is Rick manipulative enough to make it seem like Cady's at fault? Alys says her dad goes with the flow, isn't capable of planning anything. That I've got it all wrong.

Both of us can't be right.

'I said about evidence being tricky,' I say. 'What if Cady gives Pip something to help him sleep in a misguided idea she's doing the right thing?'

'Well then, why does she only do it when you're over?'

'What?'

'Because she's a planner, that's why. I think I've worked it out. I reckon she's covering her tracks.'

Alys told me if she shared, I'd end up thinking she was crazy. I say nothing. I just keep my eyes on the road.

'I cannot believe she didn't panic even a little bit when the police wouldn't let it go after Mum's death,' Alys goes on. 'But, have to say, she played it cool throughout, played a blinder. So kind, moving us to her house. I didn't start to suspect until much, much later.'

'Suspect what exactly?'

'Everything. Anything. How much of a planner she is.'

I wait for more. It isn't easy. My mind is spinning, but I stop myself asking questions; let Alys talk it all out.

'Pip thinks he's been so secretive and clever. But he's my brother, I was onto what he was doing and he started as soon as it was obvious the police were clueless. I guess we've my annoying brother to thank for the fact it never quite went away.'

'So you know Pip's been asking a lot of questions?'

'Course I do. But even he hasn't seen it.'

'Seen what exactly?'

'Everything. I haven't worked it all out yet. I can't explain why she had to kill Stacey. Why didn't that look like an accident? I guess because she managed to get Minty to take the fall? Like I say, clever! Haven't yet worked out why she picked Minty, but there'd have been a reason. And now everyone thinks it's all tidied away. She must think she's finally in the clear, and that'll give her the confidence to deal with Pip. So put your bloody foot down.'

We are racing, but this speed is nothing compared with my racing thoughts.

'You think she's your friend,' Alys goes on. 'But a nosy lawyer who cannot stop diving in where they see trouble, is the very last friend she'd want Pip to have. Not when he wouldn't stop talking to people about Mum's death after the police filed it as not-really-sure-what-happened. You might be slow, but she'll have worried you'd work it all out eventually, cos you're not the sort to give up. Why d'you think she suddenly was so keen to help you in the shop? Didn't that start when Pip started working for you? Now Cady's got all friendly with you, and I bet you've been telling her all about things you've been finding out, because you've been even less subtle than Pip.'

I want to say she's got this so wrong. I really want to.

We're nearly at the turning.

'Can't believe I end up here so often as I hate it so much.' My voice sounds cracked and unnatural, giving away how hard I'm fighting to keep this normal.

'I knew no one would ever believe me, so I looked for evidence. I found out the hot chocolate was drugged when she sent a sample to a lab,' says Alys. 'I was lucky to find that. But I just didn't get why—Why send a sample to a lab if she was the one drugging him? I couldn't see her plan.'

'Cady sent a sample of Pip's hot chocolate?' I echo. 'To a lab?'

'Exactly. Expect it cost a fortune too—private forensics. But she's got money, you know that, right? She likes to keep that all hidden. And she has this whole scatty thing perfected. It's all an act. Took me a while to get it.'

Alys keeps right on talking.

'I opened the letter from the forensic lab. Opened it very carefully. But I always wondered if she guessed. I took a picture, but I never leave my phone around and change the password all the time. She'd dated and timed this sample she sent off. Then I realised it was when you were round.'

I promised she could say anything outrageous and I wouldn't laugh. I'm keeping my promise, just listening, saying nothing. But I'm a long way from laughing.

'But why?' I didn't mean to say anything. I particularly didn't meant to have so much disbelief in my voice.

'I can't quite get inside her twisted mind.'

Alys deals with my disbelief calmly.

'But you spent a lot of time with Pip and I reckon the hot chocolate means you must be her new backup plan. If you were feeding him some sort of drugs it makes you look bad—even just some sleeping stuff with a long name, you suddenly look pretty dodgy. I reckon she's cranking it up to say your relationship with Pip was not what it seemed. She'll say she suspected something else was going on there.'

That was the monstrous accusation Mrs McFlintock threw at me that made me lose my shit with her the day before she died. Alys is saying that *Cady* was at the root of that nasty rumour? That Cady planned for that rumour to get around and even planted evidence?

'She'll be planning Pip's death to look like another accident or suicide. But just in case the police don't leave it alone, she needs a fall-guy. You are just too perfect.'

When I agreed Alys could tell me anything, however outrageous, I wasn't expecting this. My mind is slow to take it in, but I find myself going over a lot of things.

Pip wouldn't leave his mum's death alone. He kept coming back to talk to Mrs M, who'd dropped hints she knew things, something she'd never passed to the police. She saw Helena with someone, isn't that what she said?

But I'd begun to assume she was playing with him, stringing him along. Probably liked his visits, made her isolated life a bit less lonely.

But Mrs M had found Helena's body.

'I last saw Pip here when I suspected he might have broken into Mrs McFlintock's house,' I say as we're finally at the turning.

'Why would Pip do that?' Alys asks.

'She told him she saw someone with Helena the day she died. But she liked playing games, even with her own daughter, Stacey. She threw out hints she knew things. Gave her some power. I think some people paid Mrs M to keep quiet about things and not spread her nasty rumours.'

'Stacey? The one who got murdered?'

I take the turning too fast and the car skids as we hit the gravel road and, for a second, I think I'm going to lose it and we'll skid right off the road. But I keep it together.

'Yes,' I say. 'My guess is Mrs M wrote down things she found out about people. She had a notebook that went missing. I think Pip was after it, but I interrupted.'

'So Mrs M had some serious shit on people and passed it on to her daughter. That explains why Stacey had to die.'

Alys reached this conclusion in seconds.

'The police tried to work out your mum's last movements as accurately as they could and would have interviewed Mrs McFlintock,' I point out calmly, hating how official I sound. 'I'm sure she'd have told them if she knew something important.'

'Yeah, right. Didn't you just say she used her secrets? So yeah, she'd never tell the police when she could use it herself. Doubt either of them knew how dangerous it was if they had something on Cady.'

Alys is right in so many ways.

Mrs M was manipulative enough so that people were more than a little scared of her. If she had known something, she'd have tried to use it. She wouldn't have told Pip. No value in sharing with a teenage boy.

She's even right that moving to Crossways has made me naïve and slow. I want to kick myself hard.

'Mrs M was the one who found Mum's body, right?' says Alys. 'Mrs M was the sort who'd never think Cady was dangerous, but to be fair, no one does. I bet Cady's been paying her. I bet Cady got all soulful and told her mum's death was all an accident. Bet she offered her a shedload of money to keep her secret. Because she's got plenty. I bet Mrs M properly underestimated what she's capable of. Underestimating Cady. That was her big mistake. It's everyone's big mistake.'

47.

It hasn't taken long to reach this place I hate so much. But I feel the world has shifted during the short journey. We are in complete darkness, the headlights barely penetrate the mist.

'It's going to be difficult to see if anyone's here,' I say, having doubts that this was even the right place to start looking for Pip.

We're on the last stretch. I fly across the potholes. The place is utterly wretched, freezing and dark. Will Pip really be here?

'I never thought he came here looking for me,' says Alys. 'Cady planted that idea. Cady will have brought him here. Probably told him they were out looking for me.'

But Cady's frantic, waiting at home. I just spoke to her on the phone. I still want to believe that.

I don't want to believe Alys's version of events. Certain things might want to fall into place. But there's still room for Alys to have this all wrong.

It's impossible to see almost anything, even with headlights, because of the dark and the continuous mist rolling in from the river. But I know what we're hurtling towards. The horrible, raging river that killed Helena. And maybe because I cannot see much, I get a clear picture in my mind's eye. I see Mrs M sitting in her isolated cottage in her chair with a view of the river, watching. Two people arriving in separate cars to meet and go for a walk on a bleak January afternoon. It would have been almost dark. Did she see only one coming back? One lonely car still in the car park? Started to wonder?

'Think I might have an idea why Cady picked Minty to take the fall when she decided she had to get rid of Stacey,' says Alys. 'Her big mistake was taking Mum on as her assistant. Cady would have hated Mum finding out her business.'

'How would Helena have found out Cady's business?'

'You do know how come she's got so much money?'

'Cady lost both her parents?' I say. 'Isn't that the sad reason she has a lovely home and no job? Her mum and dad died?'

'You don't even know, do you? Thought you were one for the endless curiosity. Cady's got properties.' I can't see the pitying look Alys shoots me, but I can feel it. 'Jeez. She doesn't like people to know. She rakes it in as a landlord. Minty does all the front of house, leaving Cady comfortable in the background, particularly if she wants to put the squeeze on. And Dad got the contract doing all the groundwork for Key Keepers! Poor guy doesn't even know Cady puts all her business through them.'

Alys almost takes my breath away, and not just for shining a spotlight on just how stupid and naïve I have been.

The Crossways effect. It's the sort of place where you think bad things can't happen, but they happen just the same as they do anywhere. I thought it was that trouble follows me, but trouble is everywhere. And it has made me stupid.

I wanted to believe I'd chosen a lovely community, that I live among lovely people, have made a new start. New friends. This was my new beginning. But there's been something dark right in the heart of Crossways, and I've been guilty of looking away, of not wanting to see the truth.

'After I saw that letter from the lab, I took a lot more interest in what was in Cady's mail,' says Alys, holding on as the potholed road throws us both around. 'Cady did lose her mum and dad, did come into some money. Guess she started investing it in properties. Cady and Mum were cousins—you knew that, right? Mum might've had nothing, but she had love, and Dad. Cady was always into Dad. But Dad, despite his faults, was actually pretty loyal to Mum. Cady had the money, but she was still jealous of Mum. Working at Key Keepers, Mum must've twigged how loaded Cady was. Might even have thought having a little secret about Cady meant she was on to a good thing. Might even have done the dumb thing and asked Cady for money.'

We screech to a halt. I switch off the lights. We're plunged into utter blackness. Nothing but silence.

'Bad move, crossing Cady. Now you'll start to see it— the nastiness of what she does,' says Alys, climbing out of the car almost before we've stopped. 'Now it'll be like you've woken up. You'll see it isn't just me being crazy, or vindictive, or resenting Cady for trying to take Mum's place. Now let's find Pip.'

'There's a big torch in the boot,' I say.

Alys sees me reach for my phone.

'Who're you calling?'

'Someone who can help.'

'To get Cady, you mean? You don't believe me?'

I still want to believe there's room for Alys to be wrong. But as well as listening, I've been thinking. I've thought of something else, that detailed timeline Pip scribbled on the back of a poster in his bedroom. I didn't know what Pip was doing, secretly talking to everyone, finding out things even the police didn't know. But Cady took everything from Pip's old room and moved it to her house. She told me she'd taken down every poster from his walls and put them back up in the exact same position.

I'm cured of thinking this all comes from Alys having a warped view of Cady because she's tried to step into Helena's shoes and move in on her dad.

Alys has the torch and she's already speeding into a run. I'm close behind, but I'm making my phone call.

My senses might be kicking in late. But there's the final proof, if I still need it.

Cady's car is in the car park.

48.

Alys is already too far ahead with the torch and I stumble in the dark as I try to keep up. I feel I've been stumbling in the dark for a while now.

Cady was supposed to be waiting at home. She told me she was waiting at home when we spoke on the phone.

But she's here, ahead of us.

I hear the roar of the water, slide in slippery mud, my legs getting tangled in long grass, but I manage to keep up.

'Pip!' I yell. 'I'm here! I'm coming.'

He's never going to hear. The water feels even louder than usual, and there's no chance of finding Pip with a single torch. I'll cling to there being a small chance we've got this bit wrong and Pip isn't here at all. Then I hear a voice in the darkness. A light coming towards us.

'Thank goodness, thank goodness you've come.'

The light of our torch picks out Cady coming towards us out of the mist.

'Where's Pip?' I demand.

Cady points urgently. 'He's gone into the water.'

What I can see of the water is just inky black. Even when Alys does a sweep with the torch beam, we can see nothing. The water rushes, there are so many twists, inlets, sluices and places designed to slow the water. Mrs M found Helena's body in the water.

'I've been trying to reach him,' says Cady.

'Then you know where he is?' A small hope wants to rise in my chest.

'Thank goodness you've come.' Cady's voice is all breathy and anxious. 'I should have known this is what he's been thinking when he kept coming here. I wish I'd got here sooner. We're too late.'

'It's never too late. Just show me.' I push past Cady, going closer to the water. 'Where?' I demand.

I gesture to Alys, who shines the beam of my powerful torch across water that churns so fiercely it makes me feel sick. If he's gone in already, he won't stand a chance.

Alys does not waver. She stands on the bank, calling and calling his name, and I join in.

Cady shouts in my ear above the roar: 'He's gone. We're too late!'

It's never too late, I tell myself, wanting to believe it.

'Where did he go in?' I grab Cady's shoulders, suddenly fearful that she could be lying and we're searching in the completely wrong place and we'll be missing even the smallest chance of saving him.

'Pip!' I scream again, trying to be heard over the sound of the roar, straining to hear any reply.

He can't have gone. I refuse to accept that. Helena's body got caught up in one of the inlets, the water doesn't run in a straight line. My one hope is he's tangled up somewhere. I have to believe he's clinging on, in the same way I'm clinging onto the hope that we're not too late. We can't be too late.

'I'm not leaving here until I find him, alive or dead,' I say.

Alys and I keep on calling.

Even the strong beam of my torch barely pierces the dark, but Alys keeps on shining it. The light barely falls beyond the bank, and there is nothing there but dark, treacherous water. We carry on, shining our one beam methodically along the edge and sweeping further into the water.

Cady chatters inanely, wringing her hands, but I tell her to shush, we need to listen, to hear if Pip manages to call back.

The longer this goes on, the less chance we have that we can do this. We cannot do this, not without a hundred people, a boat, a helicopter. There's no time to raise a search party. We are too late.

And then finally, just when I think his body must already have been swept away downstream, there comes a sound, faint above the fierce rush of the water.

Alys hears it too and trains the beam in that direction. It alights on something that is more than just a mass of gathered leaves and twigs. Or is it just that my mind is ready to see it as something?

But the beam lands on Pip's face, and he's there, right there, not even that far from the edge, clinging onto something. But he's there. And he's alive.

My heart nearly explodes in my chest.

'I can see you!' cries Alys. The beam picks out his white face, a mixture of hopelessness and horror. 'Pip, we're here! Just hold on!'

I have to stop myself from following my instincts and just throwing myself in. I need to be rational.

He's not far out. But he is far down.

I lie flat on the bank and extend my arm as far as I can, but I can't reach him. But I have to. He's clinging onto a branch, mostly in the water, and he's fighting not to be swept away. The current is pulling at him, wanting to drag him in. I don't know how long he's been there. His fingers must be ice, but he's not letting go.

'It's ok Pip,' I say. But it is so far from ok. I cannot afford to panic, because this is no rescue, and I need a miracle to turn it into one.

My fingers almost touch him. I need a way to not only reach him, but to haul him out. I don't think I can do it. But he must be freezing, and I have to get to him, and quickly. He won't be able to hold on much longer.

I try to say reassuring words to Pip, even though inside I cannot imagine how we are possibly all going to get out of here alive.

Cady crouches low alongside me, stretches forward. One hand grabs scrubby grass at the edge, and she stretches further. Her fingers actually touch him. 'Grab my hand, Pip. You need to grab my hand. You're going to have to let go with one hand.'

'No, Pip, don't let go!' I cry. 'Just hold on. I'm coming for you.'

I've no idea how we're going to do this. How is he holding on? In the light of the torch I see he's wrapped one arm around a branch.

Finally, my brain does something useful.

'Alys, there's a rope in the car. Go back and get it. Take the torch. It's all right, Pip!' I call. 'Not much longer.'

Alys has disappeared before I've said the words, plunging us into darkness. I lie flat on the soaking ground and try to reach further, one dodgy handhold on some grass that doesn't feel strong. Now I have only the weak light from the moon and stars, so I'm mostly feeling my way forward.

'Cady, if you grab my legs, I can reach a bit further.' Will she do it?

And I've touched him. I just about reach his arm, I grab his jacket. It's thick, wet, and it's difficult to get a grip, even so I tell him I've got him. 'You won't be going anywhere,' I call reassuringly over the thunder of the water. I need to believe it. I need a firmer grip. 'Just hold on a little bit longer.'

I carry on talking to Pip in a low murmur, inching forward as far as I dare, but I can't go further without tumbling in. If I go in, we'll both be swept away.

I hold onto his jacket, a weak grip, and I don't have the strength to pull him. I can feel the violent tug of the current, the monster wanting to drag him away from me and claim him. I cannot let go of him now, but already my fingers are numb.

'Cady, please! I'll never pull him back alone.'

I no longer trust her. But what's she going to do?

I inch further forward very, very slowly. I can't lose my balance. I need to keep a firm grip on the bank. I feel someone grabbing my legs. Cady's going to help.

'I've got Pip. If you just pull me, we'll come up together.'

I can feel her hands. She's trying to get a firmer grip on me. I'm stretching so far, I hardly have any grip on the ground. There is hardly anything stopping me from going headfirst into the swirling water, but I feel hands on my legs and wait for her to start pulling. But nothing happens. I hold on, my hand around Pip's arm and brace myself, ready to pull, to not let go. I can barely feel my fingers.

But it feels like she's trying to push me forward, to lever me off the ground. Cady's not going to pull me back. But I hardly have any contact with the ground. I'm going to go in.

Then there's a crack behind me. There's a thud, someone falling. I half turn, but I can't see what's going on. 'Alys?' I can't save everybody. I just can't.

'Should have done that a long time ago,' Alys says.

Then I feel a rope being tied around me. Then I feel a warm presence, and Alys is leaning into me and speaking, and holding onto me.

It gives me strength to do more than hold onto Pip, but to pull on him. I hope the rope is firm around me. I'm too far forward to do much. I still might go in, but Alys is there. I feel myself inch backwards. I renew my grip on Pip's arm. We pull. We pull together.

Pip's clothes are making him heavy. The current is so strong. Alys grabs my legs, and I lose any ability to tell what's happening. All I can do is focus on holding on. I inch backwards, and suddenly I feel Pip's weight increase. He's let go. He's holding onto me, and I'm the only thing stopping him from being swept away.

With Alys's help, I edge backwards and Pip comes with me, hauled slowly upwards. Then he's near enough, and Alys grabs his jacket. Together, the miracle happens. Suddenly, we are all panting on the bank, lying in a heap alongside the prone figure of Cady. I can see she's got a gash and blood leaking from a wound on her head. I can see because of the flashing blue lights approaching.

I'm out of it. I don't remember much more than silver blankets and a stretcher. And suddenly there is Elliott's face, leaning over me.

'No. Please be all right, Keera.'

I rip away the oxygen mask that's been placed over my face that I don't really need. 'Pip—is Pip ok?'

'He will be,' says Elliott.

'A little bit sooner would help next time.'

'Next time? Shit—tell me you're not planning on doing this again?'

49.

Liv is sipping tea. I am crunching on ginger biscuits. I have no customers.

'How do you feel about Crossways? And bookselling?' Liv asks, out of the blue. She's wearing an elegant coat, even though the heating is turned up to create something approaching a warm browsing ambience. 'Is selling books too dull for you?'

'Well, right at this moment selling a book would excite me very much,' I respond.

'You know that's not what I'm asking.'

I gesture around me. 'You mean the boxes, the poor stock decisions, the lack of customers... Could I bear to give all this up?'

'That can be sorted. It's time for you to write your own new chapter. The thing is, I'm not sure we need someone to clean up Crossways. But we need our bookshop. Is Crossways your new chapter? I can see it hasn't been the best start. But will you stay? And if so, do we have to keep creating a crisis so it doesn't get too dull for you?'

'Crossways wasn't supposed to need clearing up.'

'But you have cleared up. And your landlord problem is no longer... urgent.'

'I don't know. One thing I hate about it is how it's made me dumb about so much. I knew that Minty was just the agent, and you kept telling me I needed to speak to my landlord. Who knew Cady was my landlord. Tea?'

'I don't want more tea. What I do want is to please panic about the very real issue no authors are on that events invite list? I want you to take your business seriously.'

'It has to be serious? There's me thinking you understood I only do this because bookselling's supposed to be fun.'

'It'd be more fun if you had a more reliable income.'

'I miss Cady. Is that wrong?' I say as I make myself another brew.

'You miss the Cady she wanted you to see. And you miss the person who turned up regularly with vegan blueberry croissants.'

'I know.'

Liv understands I can't talk about me pulling Pip out of the water yet; or Alys cracking Cady over the head with a heavy torch. Both will live. But I know Liv wants me to move on.

'Cady's denying everything, but she must see there's no way out,' says Liv. 'You said Pip worried what would happen to them if anything happened to Cady. What is going to happen to them? Are they still living at her house?'

'Guess she does know she won't be needing that house any time soon, because Cady's given it over to them. It can't make up for what she did to that family... I think

Rick's already putting it up for sale, planning a fresh start for all of them.'

'So you came here to save yourself, but ended up saving everyone else. It means you still need to save yourself.'

'I didn't save anyone,' I say quietly.

'You saved Pip.'

'That was mostly Alys.'

'You saved Alys.'

'Alys saved me. If she hadn't dealt with Cady...'

'You listened to Alys,' says Liv gently. 'Never underestimate the power of that—particularly with teenagers who get used to adults giving advice. I think you believed her version of things because deep down, I think you knew it already.'

'I was too late and too slow. I didn't save Mrs M, or Stacey.'

'That is not on you, and you know that. You saved Rick. You even saved Vampire Minty. You also made an unpopular nuisance of yourself with people.'

'You mean Elliott.'

'Not just Elliott. To be fair, I think he needs a bit more trouble. But before you say it again—You did not bring trouble to Crossways. You find trouble because you have a nose for it. You see what other people don't. Your mum is completely wrong about you.'

'Mum knew I could never have a lovely, easy life. Crossways not needing clearing up was supposed to be the whole point. And I am a terrible bookseller.'

'January is a bad time for bookshops. Besides, you have me. And I am going to make sure you spend this quiet time planning your triumphant events schedule. I'm sorry about what happened—with your ex—it happens.'

'Does it, though? Falling in love, moving in with a guy, who then moves on, taking most of everything you have and who is untraceable because he was using a false name from the beginning? That happens a lot? And how do you know about that anyway?'

I look at Liv resignedly. 'Does everyone know? Yes, of course everyone knows.'

'So everyone knows your darkest secret. You may as well stay.'

'How does that follow?'

'You move on somewhere else, everything will just happen all over again.'

'What—rescuing a teenager from the woman who killed his mum, and I have to reveal my deepest secrets in order to get another teenager to trust me? That again?'

'Maybe you do have a teensy point that trouble follows you around. But maybe we've cleared out the trouble round here, at least for a bit. Maybe you're safe for a while. I know you don't want to talk about it, but I have one question. Why did Mrs M's get broken into and was it to steal the notebook?'

'I don't have all the answers, Liv. No one ever does.'

'But you're good at theories. What do you think?'

'I think when Stacey said her mum told her she'd left her something valuable, she thought it was to do with the lease. But I think it was the notebook. I guess Cady was paying Mrs M. I think Stacey found the notebook and thought things could carry on. Did she suspect Cady shoved her mum down the stairs? Or was she another one who underestimated Cady?'

'So Cady broke into Mrs M's?'

'This is more than one question, Liv.'

'I know. But just your best guess.'

'My guess is that Pip broke in, even though he denied it, and I'm happy to leave it at that. Mrs M dropped hints she knew someone was with Helena when she died. Maybe he hoped answers didn't die with her. But I don't think he had time to search the place and my guess is Stacey had already found the notebook. Now you have to answer me a question. Tell me seriously. Do you believe I can make a go of this?'

'Absolutely! But you shouldn't try to do it all alone.'

'Look what happened when I let Cady help.'

'You still have me.'

'But that just makes me notice you are so much better at it than me.'

'So not true. We do need a bookshop. You are an asset to Crossways. We need people like you, which says something, as you have brought your brash city ways into lovely Crossways.'

'You mean I'm rude to the wrong people. I don't play nice with the golf club and the parish council, or join committees. If I'm honest, I'm pretty tired of failing at everything.'

'This time next year, you'll look back and see this was the start of your brilliant rise to starry success. And I do not want to be here every day.'

'You say that, but you almost are.'

'Just until you're on your feet.'

'Although, what else would you do all day? I mean, apart from the long lunches, the volunteering, and the committees. What do you do? I've never asked. I think it's time you tell me.'

'You're worried I'll turn out to be another Cady—a secret source of income you're ashamed of that leads to… Well. You are asking politely how do I live in such a nice home and don't appear to work for a living even though I am clearly far too young to retire? My husband died.'

'Ah. I'm really sorry to hear that, Liv. I wasn't trying to—'

'It was a long time ago. He was in the police. Died in the course of duty, so that meant there was a payout. I'm not thrilled Elliott has been inspired to follow in his footsteps. But one of the ways I dealt with it was writing a thriller about a woman whose husband is in the police and dies in mysterious circumstances, and her son follows him into the police. It did rather well. I published a few more. Under a pseudonym, of course. I don't want Crossways knowing my business.'

'You're an author? That's your deadly secret? Way cooler than mine. And definitely better financially.'

'I have a few author contacts, which is why you should let me help you organise some events. I wasn't sure how much help to offer as I didn't want to look like I was taking over.'

'You were already taking over. What you mean is you didn't want to reveal your deadly secret.'

'If you want access to my author contacts, I do not expect this secret to be all around Crossways by Tuesday.'

'Understood. I can probably manage that.'

Liv raises one eyebrow.

'Honestly. I think I am finally getting how things really work around here. Is this the deal—I know your deadly secret, so blackmail you into helping me get some authors to drag themselves to the wilds of Crossway to give a talk? Thanks to you we might get an audience too big for Halfway. I think we need to reconsider the village hall.'

'Not the village hall. Never the village hall.'

'We can talk about that.'

'We absolutely cannot. But we agree this is a new chapter where you leave behind your exciting life of crime and make a success of this bookshop?'

'Sure. We do things your way. Where do we start?

'Where all my plans start,' says Liv. 'I make a list. All you need to do is pretend you're interested and not sit there secretly hoping something bad happens in Crossways soon.'

These are the favourite books Keera refers to or recommends, if you want to know more about them, or read them! uk.bookshop.org/lists/little-bookshop-of-murders-book-recommends

The Sentence is Death - Anthony Horowitz

The Antique Hunters Guide to Murder – CL Miller

How to Solve Your Own Murder – Kristen Perrin

Everyone in My Family Has Killed Someone – Benjamin Stevenson

None of this is True – Lisa Jewell

Intermezzo – Sally Rooney

Midnight Library – Matt Haig

The Graveyard Book – Neil Gaiman

Ninth House – Leigh Bardugo

Raising Hare – Chloe Dalton

The Final Empire: Mistborn Book One – Brandon Sanderson

Past Lying – Val McDermid

The Secret Diary of Adrian Mole Aged 13¾ – Sue Townsend

Sanji and the Baker – Robin Tzannes (Author), Korky Paul (Illustrator)

Plenty – Yotam Ottolenghi

Persiana: Recipes from the Middle East & Beyond

Hamlyn All Colour Cookery: 200 Air Fryer Recipes

A Court of Thorns and Roses – Sarah J Maas

The Happy Pear: Vegan – David and Stephen Flynn

Nicki Thornton ran her own bookshop for more than ten years, but luckily, none of her customers were ever murdered.

But the bookshop was at the heart of the local community and was certainly a place where gossip was swapped. Nicki thought it would be an ideal place to set a murder mystery series.

Nicki has always adored crime fiction and first turned to writing crime fiction for children as a fun way to introduce young readers to the genre.

Now she works as a mentor for booksellers and also writing stories for readers who like their mysteries in the golden age tradition, but with a modern edge.

She also reads way too much and scours as many new releases as she can to share all her favourites in her newsletter.

You can find out more about her books on her website, or through her reviews pages at Bookshop.org
www.nickithornton.co.uk
uk.bookshop.org/shop/nicki_thornton

Follow Nicki on social media and Substack:
instagram.com/nicki_thornton
facebook.com/nickithorntonauthor
nickithornton.substack.com

The next thrilling instalment in the Little Bookshop of Murders mysteries will be out in Spring 2026.

Who Shot Jackson Brodie?

An unsolved cold-case and a bookgroup that wants to solve a crime

When an ex-police officer-turned-author asks for support for his true-crime memoir, Keera Munroe hopes it will bring much needed sales to her little bookshop business.

But some locals are horrified when they learn Mitch Ravenscroft's biography features an unsolved murder in their own idyllic village.

Keera's crime-fiction bookgroup seizes the chance to solve a real-life crime. But soon it's clear someone will stop at nothing to prevent the truth being exposed.

Why were a couple shot dead on the first night they moved to Crossways?

Once again Keera asks herself if it isn't true that the loveliest places hide the darkest secrets as she's plunged right in the heart of uncovering truths that too many of the locals seem very keen should stay buried.

pre-order here: **nickithornton.co.uk/links**

You can get news from Nicki, share what she's reading and get a sneak of her writing life by joining her VIP Club. It's free to join and is part of the Substack community: **nickithornton.substack.com**

And as an **exclusive offer** to readers of this book, signing up will get you access to a **secret page on Nicki's website** where she shares many of the locations that inspire her books.

Nicki is the bestselling author of six fantasy crime thrillers for children, starting with the award-winning The Last Chance Hotel, which has been translated into 15 different languages.

The Last Chance Hotel

Hard-working Seth is the kitchen boy in the remote Last Chance Hotel, owned by the nasty Bunn family and their toxic daughter, Tiffany; his only friend is Nightshade, the kitchen cat.

Seth dreams of leaving, and of a future beyond the Last Hope Forest, away from Tiffany's schemes to torment him.

He wonders if his chance for change might finally have arrived when a bunch of strange characters come to stay.

But things go terribly wrong when the dessert Seth carefully made to impress kindly Dr Thallomius, instead poisons him.

Seth finds himself at the heart of a murder investigation with a lot more than Tiffany to worry about when he becomes the main suspect and accused of the crime.

The Bad Luck Lighthouse
The Cut-Throat Cafe
The Howling Hag Mystery
The Poisoned Pie Mystery
The Floating Witch Mystery